The
FORGOTTEN
SEAMSTRESS

LIZ TRENOW

 sourcebooks landmark

Published by Sourcebooks Landmark, an imprint of Sourcebooks, Inc.
P.O. Box 4410, Naperville, Illinois 60567-4410
(630) 961-3900
Fax: (630) 961-2168
www.sourcebooks.com

Library of Congress Cataloging-in-Publication data is on file with the publisher.

Printed and bound in the United States of America.
VP 10 9 8 7 6 5 4 3

To David, who has, as ever, been a
constant source of love and support.

Patchwork (noun):

a. Work consisting of pieces of cloth of various
   colors and shapes sewn together.

b. Something composed of miscellaneous
   or incongruous parts.

Quilt (verb):

a. To fill, pad, or line (something) like a quilt.

b. To stitch, sew, or cover (something) with lines
   or patterns resembling those used in quilts.

c. To fasten layers of fabric and/or padding in this way.

From the Medical Superintendent
Helena Hall, April 2, 1970

Dear Dr. Meadows:

Thank you for your letter in reference to your student Patricia Morton. We are always keen to support the work of *bona fide* research projects and will certainly endeavor to provide her with the contacts and other information that she seeks.

However, before giving permission, we would like your personal written confirmation that she will observe the following:

- All interviews must be carried out anonymously, and no information which might identify the patient or staff member must appear in the final publication.
- No patient may be interviewed without their prior informed consent, supported by their psychiatric consultant and, where appropriate, a key family member.
- Any member of staff must seek the prior written consent of their senior manager.

In regard to former staff members and patients, Eastchester Mental Health Service has no jurisdiction, but we would seek your reassurance that Ms. Morton will observe the same conditions of confidentiality as above. I am sure she will appreciate that, in terms of research data, existing and former patients may not be the most reliable of informants. Most, if not all, will have suffered from lifelong illnesses which may lead them to hold beliefs and opinions which have no actuality or validity in real life.

You will understand that while patient confidentiality precludes us from giving information about individuals, I would be grateful for the opportunity to provide Ms. Morton with guidance in relation to specific interviewees. Please ask her to contact my secretary at the number above to arrange an appointment at the earliest possible opportunity.

With kindest regards,
Dr. John Watts, Medical Superintendent,
Helena Hall Hospital, Eastchester

1.

THEY TOLD ME YOU WANT TO KNOW MY STORY, WHY I ended up in this place? Well, there's an odd question, and I've been asking it meself for the past fifty years. I can tell you how I got here and what happened to me. But why? Now that's a mystery.

It's a deep, smoke-filled voice, with a strong East London accent, and you can hear the smile in it, as if she's about to break into an asthmatic chuckle at any moment.

They've probably warned you about me, told you my story is all made up. At least that's what those trick-cyclists would have you believe.

Another voice, with the carefully modulated, well-educated tones of a younger woman: "Trick-cyclist?"

Sorry, dearie, it's what we used to call the psychiatrist, in them old days. Anyway, he used to say that telling tales—he calls them fantasies—is a response to some "ungratified need."

"You're not wrong there," I'd tell him, giving him the old eyelash flutter. "I've been stuck in here most of me life. I've got plenty of ungratified needs." But he'd just smile and say, "You need to concentrate on getting better, my dear, look forward, not backward, all the time. Repeating and reinforcing these fantasies is just regressive behavior, and it really must stop, or we'll never get you out of here."

Well, you can take it or leave it, dearie, but I have to tell it.

"And I would very much like to hear it. That's what I'm here for."

That's very kind of you, my dear. You see, when you've been hidden away from real life for so many years, what else is there to do but remember the times when you were young, when you were meeting new people every day, when you were allowed to have feelings, when you were alive? Nothing. Except for me needlework and other creations, they were the only things that would give me a bit of comfort. So I tell my story to anyone who will listen, and I don't care if they call me a fantasist. Remembering him, and the child I lost, is the only way I could hold onto reality.

So, where do you want me to start?

"At the beginning would be fine. The tape is running now."

You'll have to bear with me, dearie. It'll take some remembering, it was that long ago. I turned seventy-four this year so the old brain cells are not what they used to be. Still, I'll give it a try. You don't mind if I carry on with me sewing while I talk, do you? It helps me concentrate and relax. I'm never happy without a needle in my fingers. It's just a bit of appliqué with a buttonhole stitch—quite straightforward. Stops the fabric fraying, you see?

She is caught by a spasm of coughing, a deep, rattling smoker's cough. Hrrrm. That's better. Okay, here we go then.

My name is Maria Romano, and I believe my mother was originally from Rome, though what she was doing leaving that beautiful sunny place for the dreary old East End of London is a mystery. Do they all grow small, the people who live in Italy? Mum was tiny, so they said, and I've never been more than five foot at the best of times. These days I've probably shrunk to less. If you're that size, you don't have a cat's chance of winning a fight, so you learn to be quick on your feet—that's me. I used to love dancing whenever I had the chance, which wasn't often, and I could run like the wind. But there have been some things in my life even I couldn't run away from—this place being one of them.

The strange thing is that after all those years of longing to get out, once we was allowed to do what we liked, we always wanted to come back—it felt safe and my friends were here. It was my home. When they started talking about sending us all away to live in houses, it made me frightened just to imagine it, and if it was worrying me, what must it have been like for the real crazies? How do they ever cope outside? You're a socio-wotsit, aren't you? What do you think?

"I'm happy to talk about that later, if you like, but we're here to talk about you. So please carry on."

I will if you insist, though I can't for the life of me imagine what you find so interesting in a little old lady. What was I talking about?

"Your mother?"

Ah yes, me poor mum. Another reason to believe she was Italian is my coloring. I'm all gray now, faded to nothing, but my skin used to go so dark in summer, they said I must have a touch of the tar brush, and my shiny black curls were the envy of all the girls at the orphanage. Nora told me the boys thought I was quite a looker, and I learned to flash my big brown eyes at them to make them blush and to watch their glances slip sideways.

"The orphanage?"

Ah yes, Mum died when I was just a babe, only about two years old I was, poor little mite. Not sure what she died of, but there was all kinds of diseases back then in them poor parts of the city, and no doctors to speak of, not for our kind, at least. They hadn't come up with antibiotics or vaccinations, nothing like that—hard to believe now, but I'm talking about the really old days, turn of the century times.

I never heard tell of any grandparents, and after he'd had his fun, my father disappeared off the scene as far as I knew, so when she died, I ended up at The Castle—well, that's what we called it because the place was so huge and gloomy and it had pointy windows and those whatchamacall-ums, them zigzaggy patterns around the top of the walls where the roof should be.

"Castellations?"

It was certainly a fortress, with high iron gates and brick walls all around. To keep dangerous people out, they told us—this was the East End of London after all—but we knew it was really to stop us lot running away. There was no garden as such, no trees or flowers, just a paved yard we could play in when the weather was good.

Inside was all dark wood and stone floors and great wide stairways reaching up three or four stories; to my little legs, it felt like we was climbing up to heaven each time we went to bed. It sounds a bit tragic when I tell it, but I don't remember ever feeling unhappy there. I knew no different. It was warm, the food was good, and I had plenty of company—some of them became true friends.

The nuns was terrifying to us littl'uns at first, in their long black tunics with sleeves that flared out like bat's wings when they ran along the corridors chasing and chastising us. Most of 'em was kindly even though some could get crotchety at times. No surprise really, with no men in their lives, and just a load of naughty children.

It was a better start in life than I'd have had with my poor mum, I'll warrant. Pity it didn't turn out like that in the end.

Anyway, the nuns' sole aim in life was to teach us little monsters good manners and basic reading and writing, as well as skills like cooking, housework, and needlework so we could go into service when we came of an age, which is exactly what happened to me. I 'specially loved needlework. I was good at it, and I loved the attention it give me.

"It's a gift from God," the nuns would say, but I didn't believe that. It was just 'cause I had tiny fingers, and I took more trouble than the others and learned to do it properly. We had all the time in the world, after all.

D'you do any sewing, Miss?

"Not really. I'm more of a words person."

You should give it a try. There's nothing more satisfying than starting with a plain old piece of wool blanket that no one else wants and ending up with a beautiful coat that'll keep a child warm through many a winter. Or to quilt up scraps of cotton patchwork to make a comfy bed cover that ain't scratchy and makes the room look pretty besides.

The needlework room at The Castle had long cutting tables and tall windows set so high you couldn't see out of them, and that was where we spent most of our days. In winter, we'd huddle by the old stove in the corner, and in summer, we'd spread out around the room in gaggles so that we could gossip away from those nuns' ears, which was sharp as pins.

It was all handstitching, mind, no sewing machines in those days, of course. And by the time I was ten, I knew what needle to use with which fabrics and what kind of thread, and I could do a dozen types of stitch, from simple running stitch and back stitching, to fancy embroidery like wheatear and French knots, and I loved to do them as perfect and even as possible so you could hardly tell a human hand had made them. Sister Mary was a good teacher and loved her subject, and I suppose she passed her enthusiasm on to us, so before long, I could name any fabric with my eyes closed just by the feel, tell the difference between crepe and cambric, galatea and gingham, kersey and linsey-woolsey, velvet and velvetine, and which was best for which job.

Not that we saw a lot of fine fabrics, mind. It was mostly plain wool and cotton, much of it secondhand that we had to reclaim from used garments and furnishings. But on occasions, the local haberdashery would bring rolls of new printed cottons and pattern-weave wools they didn't want no more, out of charity, I suppose, for us poor little orphan children and the other little orphans we was making the clothes for.

You look puzzled. Sorry, I get carried away with me memories. The reason we was so busy sewing at The Castle was because the nuns had been asked by the grand ladies of the London Needlework Society to help them with their good works—which was making clothes for poor people. It made us feel special; we had nothing in the world except our skills, and we were using them to help other children like us.

The days when those haberdashers' deliveries arrived was like birthdays and Christmases rolled into one, taking the wrappers off the rolls and discovering new colors and patterns and breathing in that clean, summery smell of new fabric, like clothes drying on a line—there's nothing to match it, even now. When we was growing out of our clothes, the nuns would let us have remnants of patterned cotton to make ourselves new dresses and skirts, and Nora and me would always pick the brightest floral prints. We didn't see too many flowers for real, so it brought a touch of springtime into our lives.

"Nora? You knew each other even then?"

Oh yes, we go way back. She was my best friend. We was around the same age, so far as we knew, and always shared a dormitory, called ourselves sisters—the family kind, not the nun kind—and swore we'd never be parted. Not that we looked like family by any stretch: she was blond, and by the time we was fourteen, she towered above me at five feet six with big feet she was always tripping over and a laugh like a tidal wave which made anyone around her—even the nuns—break out into a smile. She had large hands too, double the size of mine, but that didn't stop her being a good needleworker. We was naughty little minxes, but we got away with it 'cause we worked hard.

Like I say, we was happy because we knew no different, but we was also growing up—even though my chest was flat and my fanny still smooth as a baby's bottom, Nora was getting breasts and hair down there, as well as under her arms, and both of us was starting to give the eye to the gardener's lad and the baker's delivery boy, whenever the nuns weren't watching.

That day, we was doing our needlework when this grand lady with a big hat and feathers on the top of her head comes with a gaggle of her lah-di-dah friends, like a royal visit it was, and she leans over what I am embroidering and says, "What fine stitching, my dear. Where did you learn that?"

And I says back, "It's daisy chain, ma'am. Would you like to see how it works?" And I finish the daisy with three more chain links spaced evenly around the circle like they are supposed to be and quickly give it a stem and a leaf which doesn't turn out too bad, even though my fingers are trembling and sweaty with being watched by such a grand person. She keeps silence till I've finished and then says in her voice full of plums and a bit foreign, "That is very clever, dear, very pretty. Keep up the good work," and as she moves on to talk to another girl, I breathe in the smell of her, like a garden full of roses, what I have never smelled before on a human being.

Afterward I hears her asking Sister Mary about me and Nora,

was we good girls and that sort of thing, but we soon forgot about her and that was it for a few months till my birthday—it was January 1911 when I turned fifteen—and me and Nora, whose birthday was just a few days before, gets a summons from Sister Beatrice, the head nun. This only usually happens when one of us has done something wicked like swearing "God" too many times or falling asleep in prayers, so you can imagine the state that Nora and me are in as we go up the stairs to the long corridor with the red Persian runner and go to stand outside the oak door with those carvings that look like folds of fabric in each panel. I am so panicked that I feel like fainting, and I can tell that Nora is trying to stifle the laugh that always bubbles up when she's nervous.

Sister calls us in and asks us to sit down on leather-seated chairs that are so high that my legs don't reach the ground and I have to concentrate hard on not swinging them 'cause I know that annoys grown-ups more than anything else in the world.

She turns to me first. "Miss Romano? I think it is your birthday today?" she asks, and I am so startled at being called "Miss" that I can't think of anything better to say than, "Yes, ma'am."

"Then God bless you, child, and let me wish you many happy returns of this day," she says, nearly smiling.

"Thank you, ma'am," I say, trying to ignore the way Nora's body is shaking beside me.

"Miss Featherstone?" says Sister, and I know that if Nora opens her mouth, the laugh will just burst out, so she just nods and keeps her head bent down, but this doesn't seem to bother Sister Beatrice, who just says, "I understand that you two are good friends, are you not?" I nod on behalf of us both, and she goes on, "I hear very positive things about the two of you, especially about your needlework skills, and I have some very exciting news."

She goes on to tell us that the grand lady who came a few

months ago is a duchess and is the patron of the Needlework Society and was visiting to inspect the work that the convent was doing for the poor children of the city. She was so impressed by the needlework Nora and me showed her that she is sending her housekeeper to interview us about going into service.

A duchess! Well, you can imagine how excited we was but scared too, as we haven't a clue what to expect, and our imaginations go into overtime. We was going to live in a beautiful mansion with a huge garden and sew clothes for very important people, and Nora is going to fall in love with one of the chauffeurs but I have my sights set a bit higher, a soldier in the Light Brigade in his red uniform perhaps, or a city gent in a bowler hat. Either way, both of us are going to have our own comfortable houses next door to each other with little gardens where we can grow flowers and good things to eat and have lots of children who will play together, and we will live happily ever after.

There's a pause. She clears her throat loudly.

Forgive me, miss, don't mind if I has a smoke?

"Go ahead, that's fine. Let's have a short break."

No, I'll just light up and carry on, please, 'cause if I interrupt meself, I'll lose the thread.

A cigarette packet being opened, the click of a lighter, a long inward breath, and a sigh of exhaled smoke. Then she clears her throat and starts again.

Not that there's much chance of me forgetting that day, mind, when the duchess's housekeeper is coming to visit. We was allowed a special bath and then got dressed in our very best printed cottons, and Sister Mary helped us pin our hair up into the sort of bun that domestic servants wear and a little white lacy cap on top of that.

At eleven o'clock, we got summoned into Sister Beatrice's

room again, and she looked us up and down and gave us a lecture about how we must behave to the visitor, no staring but making sure we look up when she speaks to us, no talking unless we are spoken to, answering clearly and not too long. She gives Nora a 'specially fierce look and says the word slowly in separate chunks so she's sure we understand: and there is to be *ab-so-lute-ly* no giggling.

"How you behave this morning will determine your futures, young ladies," she said. "Do not throw this opportunity away."

She went on some more about if we got chosen we must do our work perfectly and never complain or answer back or we'll be out on the streets because we can't never return to The Castle once we have gone. My fantasies melted on the spot. We was both so nervous even Nora's laugh had vanished.

The housekeeper was a mountain of a woman almost as wide as she was tall and fierce with eyes like ebony buttons, and she spoke to us like she was ordering a regiment into battle.

She wanted to see more examples of our needlework because, she said, we would be sewing for the highest in the land.

"The highest in the land?" Nora whispered as we scuttled off down the corridors to the needlework room to get our work. "What the heck does that mean?"

"No idea," I said. My brain was addled with fear, and I couldn't think straight for all me wild thoughts.

We were told to lay our work out on Sister Beatrice's table, and the mountain boomed questions at us: what is the fabric called, what needles did we use and what thread, why did we use those stitches, what did we think of the final result? We answered as well as we could, being clear but not too smart, just as Sister told us. One of my pieces was the start of a patchwork. I'd only finished a couple of dozen hexagons as yet, but I was pleased with the way it was shaping up, and when I showed her the design drawn in colored crayons on squared paper, she said, "The child has some artistic talent too."

"Indeed," Sister Beatrice said back, "Miss Romano is one of our best seamstresses," and my face went hot and red with pride.

When the housekeeper sat down, the poor old chair fair creaked in torment, and Nora's giggles returned, shaking her shoulders as Sister Beatrice poured the tea. Not for us, mind. We just stood and waited, my heart beating like I'd just run up all four staircases at The Castle, while they sipped their tea, oh so ladylike. She ate four biscuits in the time it took to give us a lecture about how we must, as she called it, *comport* ourselves if we was to be invited to join the duchess's household: no answering back, no being late for anything ever, no asking for seconds at dinner, no smoking, no boyfriends, wearing our uniform neat and proper every day, clean hands, clean face, clean hair, always up, no straggly bits.

When she stopped, there was a pause, and I was just about to say we are good girls, miss, very obedient girls, but she put her cup and saucer down on the table with a clonk and turned to Sister Beatrice and said, "I think these two will do very nicely. Our driver will come to collect them the day after tomorrow."

Oh my, that drive was so exciting. Don't forget, we'd been stuck in The Castle for most of our lives, never been in a coach, never even been out of the East End. Our eyes was on stalks all the way, like we had never seen the wonderful things passing by, watching the people doing their shopping, hanging out their washing, children playing. In one place, we passed a factory at clocking-off time and got stuck in a swarm of men on bicycles—like giant insects, they looked to us—and so many we quickly lost count. They saw us gawping through the coach windows and waved, which made them wobble all over the place, and it was an odd feeling to be noticed, not being invisible for once.

It was just as well we had plenty to distract us, 'cause by the time we'd said our good-byes at The Castle, both of us were blubbing. Strange, isn't it, you can spend so many years wishing yourself out of somewhere, and once you get out, all you want to do is go back? Not that I ever felt that about this place. It's a funny old feeling, coming here today, I can tell you.

"It was very good of you to take the trouble to see me."

Don't mention it, dearie. Makes a good day out, Nora said. Now, where was I?

"You were sad to leave The Castle."

Ah yes, them nuns was a kindly lot, as I think I've said before—forgive my leaky old brain, dearie—but they never showed it, not till the last minute when both Sister Mary and Sister Beatrice gave each of us a hug and pressed little parcels into our hands. I nearly suffocated in all those black folds, but this was what set me off on the weeping—it showed they really did care about us after all. We waved at all the other children peering through the windows and climbed up into the coach with the lay sister Emily, who was to be what Sister Beatrice called a *chaperone*.

After a while, the dirty old streets of the East End turned into clean, wide roads with pavements for people to walk and tall beautiful houses either side.

"I didn't know we was going to the countryside," Nora whispered to me, pointing out her side of the coach, and sure enough it was shrubs and trees stretching away as far as our eyes could see.

"That's Hyde Park, silly," sharp ears Emily said, "where the

grand ladies and gentlemen go to take the air, to walk or ride."
Well, that silenced us both—the very idea of having the time
to wander freely in a beautiful place like that—and it wasn't
long after that the coach passed beside a long, high wall and
slowed down to enter a gate with guardsmen on either side,
went around the back of a house so tall I had to bend down
beside the window to catch a glimpse of the roof, and then we
came to a stop.

We had arrived.

*The voice stops and the tape winds squeakily for a moment or two
then reaches the end, and the machine makes a loud clunk as it switches
itself off.*

2.

PANIC STATIONS, DARLING. THE COZY HOMES PEOPLE are coming next week, and they say I have to clear the lofts before they get here, and Peter down the road was going to help me, you know, the man who suggested it all in the first place, but he's gone and hurt his back so he can't come anymore, and I don't know what I'm going to do…"

My mother Eleanor was seventy-three, and her memory was starting to fail, so it didn't take much to upset her. Plus she tended to be nervous on the telephone.

"Slow down, Mum," I whispered, wishing she wouldn't call me at work. The office was unusually quiet—it was that depressing post-Christmas period when everyone is gloomily slumped at their desks pretending to be busy while surreptitiously job hunting. "You're going to have to tell me what all this is about. For a start, who are Cozy Homes?"

"The insulation people. It's completely free for the over-seventies, imagine that, and they say it will cut my heating bills by a quarter, and you know what a worry the price of oil is these days so I could hardly refuse, could I? I'm sure I told you about this."

I racked my brain. Perhaps she had, but with everything that had been going on in the past few days, I'd clearly forgotten. On our first day back after the break, we'd received an email announcing yet another round of layoffs. Happy New Year, one and all! Morale was at an all-time low, and the rumor mill working overtime. And, joy of joys, next week we were all to be interviewed by some of those smug, overpaid management consultants the company had called in.

I didn't really want to be here anyway—it was only meant to be an "interim job" to raise enough cash to realize my dream of starting my own interior design business. But the macho, target-driven environment, the daily bust-a-gut expectations and ridiculous deadlines had become surprisingly tolerable when I saw the zeros on my monthly paycheck and annual bonus-time letter. The financial rewards were just too sweet to relinquish. Especially now that I was newly single, with a massive mortgage to cover.

"It's okay, Mum," I said, distractedly scrolling down the recruitment agency website on my screen. "I was planning to come on the weekend anyway. I'm sure we can get it sorted together in a few hours."

I heard her relieved sigh. "Oh could you, dearest girl? It would be such a weight off my mind."

My Mini could virtually drive itself to Rowan Cottage, home for the first eighteen years of my life. My parents moved there in the sixties, after they married and my father was recruited by the new university that had recently opened on the out-skirts of Eastchester. He was already in his fifties, and there was a twenty-year age difference between them—they met at University College London, where he had been her doctorate professor—but it was a very loving marriage. I was born five years later, to the great joy of both.

When I was three years old, he and my grandfather were killed in a terrible head-on collision on the A12 in heavy fog. All I can recall of that dreadful night is two large policemen at the door and the woman officer who held me when my mother collapsed. She took my hand and walked me down the lane in my pajamas and slippers, clutching my favorite teddy, to be looked after by our neighbors.

My grandfather was fairly senior in the local police, and my father by then a noted academic, so the accident was widely reported, but no cause ever explained. When I turned seventeen and began to take driving lessons, I asked Mum who'd been at the wheel that night, whether anyone else had been involved or whose fault it had been, but her eyes had clouded over.

"We'll never know, dear. It was a long time ago. Best let sleeping dogs lie," was all she would say.

Thanks to my father's life insurance policy, she managed to hang on to the house and kept his spirit alive by displaying photographs in every room and talking about him frequently. He looked like a typical sixties academic, with his gold-rimmed glasses and baggy olive green corduroy jacket, leather-patched at the elbows, often with his head in a book or a journal. Mum always says that she fell for his eyes, a kingfisher blue so brilliant that they seemed to hold her in a magic beam every time he looked at her.

There he was, frozen in time, lighting his pipe, playing cricket at a family picnic, sitting in the car with our small dog, Scottie, on his knee. In the photographs, he seemed to wear a perpetual smile, although apparently he could also be impatient and bossy—traits which, alas, he's passed on to me. I have also inherited his slight stature, blond hair, blue eyes, and fair skin, although the genes that gave him a brilliant academic brain seem to have passed me by. I'm more like my mother in that, always daydreaming and with a tendency to become distracted.

Money must have been tight. We had few luxuries, but I always felt happy and loved and never overly troubled by the lack of a father in my life. Mum never had any other relationships, not that she let me know about at least. "You should join a dating agency," I suggested once—such things appearing to my teenage self as exotic and daring.

She brushed away the suggestion. "What a stupid idea," she said. "Why would I want a new beau? I've got my house and my health, my friends and my singing. And I've got you, my lovely girl. I don't need to go out dating at my age."

I took the exit off the A12 and into the peace of the lanes. After the urban sprawl and unlovely highways of outer London, North Essex is surprisingly rural and beautiful. At this time of year, furrows in the bare fields collect rainwater and reflect silver stripes of sky against the brown soil; giant elms and oaks stand leafless and black against the wide sky, and rooks gather in their branches each evening, their fierce cawing echoing across the countryside.

Every village is dominated by an outsized flint church, each with its tower reaching robustly toward heaven, built in medieval times by a landed gentry grown fat on wool farming who sought to secure their seats in paradise. These days the villages still attract fat cats: sleek city types drawn here by the newly electrified line to Liverpool Street, who worship the great god of annual bonuses and whose vision of paradise is a new Aga stove in the kitchen, a hot tub on the patio, and a sports car in the double garage.

At the end of the lane, in a shallow dip between two gentle hills, is a small green clustered around with a dozen cottages and farm buildings now converted into the price-inflated dream homes of weary commuters. At the edge of the green is Rowan Cottage, once a pair of farm laborers' houses, with a pan-tiled roof and dormer windows. It's the scruffiest property around but, unlike most of the others, seems to be fully at ease with the landscape, as if it has always been there.

As a teenager, I hated the isolation and the fact that the last bus left our local town at the ridiculously early hour of nine o'clock. But Mum still loved it here. After her shockingly early widowhood, she gave up her own academic ambitions and took a job as a school secretary so that she could be at home for me. Then, when I was about ten, she took a part-time job as a lecturer at the local polytechnic, and on those days, my grandmother would pick me up from school, take me back to her house, and indulge me with chocolate biscuits.

Granny Jean, my father's mother, was a feisty old woman with strong views who read the *Times* from cover to cover, finished the crossword in a few hours, and always had a book or a notebook and pen at her side and sometimes a needle, darning, sewing up a hem, or taking in a seam.

I loved going to stay with her, even though she refused to have a television. After tea, she would read to me all the children's classics: *Wind in the Willows*, the *Just So Stories*, and, my favorite, *Alice in Wonderland*. Of course, I was too young to get Carroll's surreal humor, but I loved the illustrations, especially the ones of Alice with long hair held back with that trademark hair band, her white apron, puffed sleeves, and blue stockings. Oh, how I wanted long hair and a pair of bright blue stockings!

When I grew old enough, Granny taught me how to sew: embroidery stitches and some very basic dressmaking. One

memorable weekend, when I was about twelve and desperate
for the latest fashions, we made a Lurex miniskirt—I cringe to
recall it, but this *was* the eighties, after all—which I adored but
never had the courage to wear. I'm sure it was Granny's influence which led me, in the end, to study fashion.

But after she died and there were just the two of us left, it
became "Mum and Caroline against the world," a close, almost
hermetic relationship which has left me with an overdeveloped
sense of duty and a fear of letting her down. Her job was demanding, dealing with unruly students, and I sometimes wondered
whether the stress of being a single parent, on top of the grief
of losing her husband and father-in-law on a single day, caused
changes in her brain that, many years later, resulted in the tragic
and insidious onset of her dementia.

Mum's face lit up when, after a second's hesitation, she recognized me.

"Caroline, dearest girl, how lovely to see you," she said,
reaching out with skeletal arms. She used to be tall, with dark
curly hair and high color to her cheekbones, but she was
shrinking now, and her hair had become almost pure white, her
skin pale gray. She seemed, literally, to be fading away.

"Come in, come in, I'll get the coffee on," she said, leading
the way to the kitchen, all stripped pine and seventies brown
and orange decor. Little had changed at Rowan Cottage since
I left home, and my interest in interior design must surely have
been triggered by my parents' lack of it. Their minds were
focused on higher matters; what did anyone care what the
inside of their house looked like, or how ragged the furnishings,
so long as they were still serviceable and comfortable?

As a teenager, I was so embarrassed by what I perceived as my parents' lack of style that I refused to invite friends home. But now I'd come to accept that Mum felt comfortable there and would never change it. Colors and patterns clashed with joyous abandon, chintz loose covers fought with geometric cushions, Persian carpets lay alongside rugs in swirly sixties designs—quite retro cool these days. Books were jumbled higgledy-piggledy on cheap pine bookshelves sagging under their weight of words. Some of the furniture, such as the Parker Knoll chairs and G-Plan coffee table, was so old-fashioned that it had become desirable again.

The two bedrooms, built into the roof of the cottage, each had a dormer window, and hardly any proper "attic" above them. But the space between the walls and the angle of the roof was converted into long cupboards, triangular in section and too low to stand up in, accessed through sliding doors in each bedroom. Despite their awkward shape, these cupboards were spacious and, I knew, contained the junk of a lifetime. Clearing them was going to be a mammoth task.

My initial plan was to help Mum do a kind of "life laundry," sorting out what she wanted to keep and giving the rest away. But the idea was stupidly ambitious and, it soon became clear, was going to take far too long. We ended up hauling everything out of the cupboards and piling it up in my old bedroom, now a spare room.

Before long, we had constructed a small pyramid: boxes of books and papers, old toys, trunks of clothes too good to give away but too outdated ever to be worn again, loose remnants of carpet, broken chairs, ancient empty suitcases, stray rolls of wallpaper, and even several pairs of old-fashioned leather ice-skates, kept in case the pond should freeze over as it did in the seventies. We could sort it all out later, I reassured Mum, once Cozy Homes had done their work.

It was backbreaking, stooping inside the low spaces and lifting heavy cases, and after a couple of hours, the pyramid had become a mountain almost filling the room. My hands were black with dust and my hair full of cobwebs.

"However did you manage to accumulate so much stuff?"

Mum gave me a stern look. "It's not *all* mine. Some of it belongs to you, all those toys and children's books you wouldn't let me give away. If only you'd move into a proper house, you'd have room for it."

I hadn't told her yet, but the prospect of living in a "proper house" and having any need for toys and children's books was looking extremely remote. A few weeks ago, just before Christmas, my boyfriend Russell and I had, by mutual consent, decided that our five-year relationship was really going nowhere, and he'd moved out. Of course I was sad, but relieved that we'd finally made the decision, and I told friends that I was out to enjoy my newly single status. At least, that's what I told myself, although, to be totally honest, what I mostly wanted was to find the right man, whoever that was. At thirty-eight, I was only too aware of the biological clock ticking ever more loudly as each year passed.

"Not just the baby things," Mum was saying. "There's Granny's stuff that I'm keeping for you."

"I've already got the books, the clock, and the dining chairs she wanted me to have. Was there something else?"

"There's that quilt." She looked around vaguely. "It'll be in one of these bags, somewhere."

"The patchwork thing that used to be on her spare bed? She used to tell me stories about it."

"I wonder where it's got to?" She gazed, bewildered, at the mountain.

"Let's not get distracted. Just a couple more things to clear."

I bent into the cupboard once again, crawling to its furthest, darkest corner. Almost the last item was an old brown leather suitcase. I hauled it out, and as I dusted it off, three letters embossed into the lid became clear.

"Who's A.M.M., Mum?"

She frowned a moment. "That'll be your grandfather, Arthur Meredith Meadows. I wonder what...?" She struggled to release the clasps, but they seemed to be rusted closed.

"Why not give yourself a break, Mum? I'll have a go at opening that later. Go downstairs and make yourself a cuppa. I can manage the last few boxes on my own, and then we're done."

When all of the loft spaces were cleared, I lugged the old suitcase downstairs into the living room, and with the help of a screwdriver and a little force, the locks quickly came free. Inside, on top of a pile of fabrics, was a faded yellow striped sheet.

"It's only old bed linen," I called through to the kitchen. "Shall I take it to a charity shop?"

Mum set down the tea tray. "That's *it*," she said, her face lighting up, "the quilt we were talking about."

She was right: the sheet was just a lining. As I lifted the quilt out and unfolded it right side out across the dining table, light from the window illuminated its beautiful, shimmering patterns and dazzling colors. True, it was faded in places, but some of the patches still glittered, almost like jewels. Textiles, plain and patterned, shiny satins, dense velvets, and simple matte cottons, were arranged in subtle conjunctions so that groups of triangles took on the shape of a fan, semicircles looked like waves on the sea, squares of light and dark became three-dimensional stairways climbing to infinity.

The central panel was an elegantly embroidered lover's knot surrounded by a panel of elongated hexagons and a frame of appliqué figures so finely executed that the stitches were almost invisible. And yet, for all the delicate needlework, the design of the quilt seemed to be quite random, the fabrics so various and contrasted it could have been made by several people over a long period of time.

"Did Granny make this?"

"I don't think so," Mum said, pouring the tea. "She liked to sew, but I never saw her doing patchwork or embroidery."

"Why's it been hidden away for so long?"

"Not really sure. You wouldn't have it on your bed—said it was too old-fashioned or something."

"Can I take it home with me now?"

"Of course, dear. She always wanted you to have it."

It was only when I went to fold the quilt back into the suitcase that something on its reverse side caught my eye. In one corner of the striped sheet backing, cross-stitched inside an embroidered frame like a sampler, were two lines set out like a verse. Some of the stitching was frayed and becoming unraveled, but I could just about make out the words.

I stitched my love into this quilt,
sewn it neatly, proud and true.
Though you have gone, I must live on,
and this will hold me close to you.

"It's a poem. Did Granny dedicate it to Grandpa? Or was it for Dad?"

"Just a mo...I'm just trying to remember something." Mum rubbed her temple. "I don't think it *was* Jean who sewed it. It was something she said once..."

I waited a moment, trying to be patient with my mother's failing memory.

"Something about the hospital…"

"Eastchester General?"

"No, the other place, you know? It might have been someone she met there. Oh, it's all so long ago now." She sighed wearily. "When your father was a boy. Had a bit of a breakdown, poor old thing."

"Granny had a breakdown? I never knew about that. She had to go into the hospital?"

"Not for long. Just till she'd got better. It wasn't far from here…"

"And you said she met someone there who might be connected with the quilt?" I prompted, but it was no good. I could see she was exhausted now. I started my usual routine before leaving her: cleaning up the kitchen, sorting out the fridge, taking out the garbage, and making a sandwich for her supper.

When I returned to the living room, she was still fast asleep. I wrapped a rug around her and kissed her tenderly on the forehead. It tore at my heartstrings to see how vulnerable and old she looked these days, and I wondered how long it would be before she was unable to manage on her own.

Back at my flat in London, I unfolded the quilt across the spare bed, scanning both sides to make sure I hadn't missed any clues, and reread the cross-stitched lines of that sentimental little verse several times, as if by studying them long enough, they might yield their secret. One thing was clear: it certainly wasn't the sort of thing my feisty grandmother would ever have written.

3.

—

THAT WAS A NICE CUPPA, THANK YOU, DEARIE. MUCH needed. So where was I?

"You and Nora were going into service. You had just arrived at the big house."

Oh my lord, yes. What a day! We was terrified, of course. Nora, me, and Emily got bundled out and straight down some steps like into the basement; the servants' entrance, you see, away from the eyes of upstairs. We stood in a dark, echoey hallway for what seemed like an hour while they called someone to call someone else, and finally a maid came and said she was to take us to our room.

We said good-bye to Emily and dragged our bags up hundreds of stairs to our room, which had four beds in it, and the two closest to the fire was already taken, so Nora and me put our things on the other two cots and waited for someone to come and tell us what to do. The room was bare and the beds narrow and hard, but we weren't much bothered by that 'cause we didn't know any different. While we waited, we opened the little parcels Sister Beatrice gave us and ate the biscuits she had wrapped inside—oatcakes with a sprinkle of brown sugar—and the taste reminded me so much of The Castle that I started sniveling all over again.

The maid came back and told us we must hurry now, as we must never keep Mrs. Hardy waiting. It turned out that Mrs. Hardy was the mountain of a housekeeper, the one who came to interview us. Her office under the stairs was not a large room and felt even smaller with her filling up most of the space.

"Ah, you two, wherever have you been? Come and get your uniforms. Now!" she bellowed. I started to say we haven't been anywhere, ma'am, but Nora dug me in the ribs and put a finger to her lips to remind me that we was not allowed to answer back or do anything except be clean, neat, hardworking, and obedient. Them nuns was so quiet-spoken that we was petrified of the woman's shouting, but we soon learned that was how she usually talked to anyone beneath her station.

We grew used to life at the new place pretty quickly, Nora and me, and it wasn't a bad one. It was nothing near as friendly as at The Castle, mind, but we just had to get on with it, and we had hardly any free time at all to dwell on anything. Our uniforms was plain pale blue with black stockings and we got new black shoes too, and it was a relief to get out of the clothes we was growing out of anyway.

There was hundreds of servants, not to mention the upstairs lot. The two maids who shared our bedroom had to get up early every morning to make fires, so we barely had any time to speak with them. They was nice enough, but kept themselves to themselves, at least till we had been there a few weeks.

We spent our days in the needlework room doing mending for the household and for the rest of the servants too, and there was only the three of us, the chief needlewoman, Nora, and me. It was a small white-painted room with no furniture save for the three cutting tables and hard chairs, with high wide windows and the floor painted white too, what we had to sweep and wipe clean every day. There was no fire, on account of the coal dust would soil our work. Instead there was hot water pipes which we put our feet on when we was working, it were that cold sometimes.

The chief needlewoman, Miss Garthwaite, was surely the ugliest woman we'd ever seen. Not as large as Mrs. Hardy, mind, but she made up for it with several double chins and warts on her eyelids and on her hands too. Though she tried very hard to hide them, if she ever touched us, we'd shiver and have to make an excuse and run to the toilet to wash ourselves, just in case. Her voice was right posh, and we wondered where she'd got that way of talking and how she'd ended up in service. We reckoned she must have been born to a good family but they couldn't find anyone ugly enough to marry her and take her off their hands.

At first, she treated us like we was something blown in off the street, but after a few days, she softened up, especially when she saw we was quite good at needlework. That didn't stop us having a laugh at her expense: Nora would go on about finding a toad in the pond at the park and bringing it back to cure her. "My prince has come," she (that is, Nora) would say, all hoity-toity, "when shall we be married?" And she'd give the toad (which was a rolled-up sock or a pincushion) a great smacker on its slimy lips, and the toad (that was me in a deep growly voice) would say, "I may be able to cure you, missus, but I ain't marrying you, warts or no warts." We laughed a lot, Nora and me, when we was just the two of us against the rest of the world, or so it seemed.

They gave us three meals a day in the second servants' hall and cocoa at night. The food was good, better than at The Castle, and in the evenings, the people who weren't cooking or serving used to sit by the fire and read and smoke and gossip, which is how we learned about who we were working for and where we were living.

Well, you may not believe me, and the psychiatrist fella says I'm making it up, but it turns out that the grand lady of the house wasn't a duchess after all, but had become a princess because, canny soul that she was, she'd married a prince, Prince George, who was about to be king because his old dad had died. King of England! And more than that, this place we was living in was Buckingham Palace! We nearly fell off our chairs when we first heard it.

She erupts into a chesty laugh, which turns into a cough.

Sorry about me cough. Don't mind if I stop for a gasper, do you? Always helps to calm it.

"Please go ahead, Maria." The sounds of cigarette packet, lighter, an inward breath, and a sigh that seems to clear the cough.

Of course, I don't expect you to believe me either, dearie; not many do. It sounds a bit unlikely, don't it, little old me working at Buckingham Palace? But you can ask Nora—she was there. We didn't even believe it ourselves at first, thinking we must have understood it wrong, but later we found out it was the truth. Fancy, Nora and me was working for the future queen of England? Her name was May, which seemed to us the most beautiful name in the world, and after that, on the warm spring days when we was allowed out for walks in St. James's Park, we'd make ourselves daisy-chain crowns and dance under the hawthorn bushes, pretending that we were both queens of the May.

Well, the household was all in disarray because so many important occasions was about to take place, a coronation in June when May would become Queen Mary. And after that, the oldest son, whose name is David, was to be what they call *invested* as Edward, Prince of Wales. Why those people had to keep changing their names was a mystery to us. What would be wrong with Queen May, or Prince David for that matter?

Of course, we never met any of them because our lives was

lived downstairs, and we weren't involved in the planning because all the robes and gowns were made by official costumers and designers and all the fittings took place in the royal rooms, where me and Nora had never been and never expected to go. But there was such an air of excitement and tension everywhere, and because of so much coming and going, so many visitors and suchlike staying at the palace, we got more and more repairs to do: darning socks and stockings, mending torn seams, taking up hems, letting out or taking in darts.

We never knew whose clothes we was working on—Miss Garthwaite kept all that close to her chest—but we could tell they was just servants' clothes. Not the housemaids or outside servants, of course, but the housekeeper, the butler, the valets, and the ladies' maids, we did their mending because they were too busy to do their own and because they had to be dressed perfect every time they went upstairs.

After a while, Miss G came to trust us and started to give us more complicated work on interesting pieces which, we guessed, might belong to the lords and ladies, as some of them fabrics was so soft and beautiful and the designs like paintings you would want to hang on your wall. Their names were strange to our ears—brocade and black bombazine, chiffon and crepe de chine, cashmere and organzine—and this made sense when Miss G told us that most silks were called by French words, on account of the weavers who came across the Channel in the olden days.

Every now and again, she was summoned upstairs to make a last-minute mend or adjust a hem or a dart which the ladies' maids or valets didn't have time for, and this turned her into a right flap. When she got back, she would be flustered and huffy, snapping at anyone who dared to talk. It would take her a good hour or so to recover her nerves.

As Coronation Day came closer, there was more and more work for us, and Miss G got called more often, to the point that one day, we thought she might just go pop with the stress of it all. She never said what she had been doing or who she had been helping, and we wasn't allowed to ask her, but my curiosity was so keen I felt like a kettle boiling with its lid clamped on tight. When she went out and left us on our own, we had a good laugh, Nora and me, and sometimes got up and jumped about a bit just to let off steam.

On the big day, even the underlings like us was allowed to look out of a window on the fourth floor, which overlooked the palace gates and The Mall. Well, I've never seen so many people in one place, not before nor since. There must have been millions, like when you stir up an ants' nest by mistake and they all come swarming about, only this lot were so packed in, there was no room for them to move, so they were just standing and waving.

There was a long procession of red and gold uniforms on horseback, and eventually there was the top of the coach which looked like a crown itself, and though of course we couldn't see inside 'cause we were looking from so high up, they told us it was Prince George and Princess May, who would come back as King George and Queen Mary. When the crowd saw the coach, we could hear a cheer like a roar of thunder which went on for the whole time till everyone had passed, and then we had to go back to work.

In the evening, we was told there'd be a ten-course banquet for a hundred guests, and the chefs and kitchen staff were frantic so we kept well out of their way, and after our supper, we were sent back to work because Miss G kept getting summoned upstairs to help the ladies' maids and valets with emergency repairs to ball gowns and penguin suits.

The following day, the fuss and bother continued, what with all the visiting royalty, and our meals were weird and wonderful leftovers from the banquets. I had never eaten venison before, and I was enjoying it till they told me it was deer, them pretty little animals we used to spy in the parks in the early mornings, and then I lost my appetite for it.

That day, we overheard conversations in the staff quarters about the prince's birthday celebrations, and about how he was next in line to the throne and would become king when his father died. There was a deal of discussion about who he would marry—German royalty or Russian? I remember feeling sorry for him, thinking how strange it must be to have your life all mapped out for you. Of course, I never understood that I had precious little control over what happened to me neither. Like all young girls, I believed I would fall in love and marry who I liked, and if they had enough money, we could have our own little place and not live in servants' quarters for the rest of my life. If only I'd known what life had in store—what a joke fate would play on me.

A couple of days later after the coronation, Mrs. Hardy calls us together after breakfast and tells us that all the servants were to make sure we're dressed extra-smart, polished shoes and the rest, because we had been summoned. We hadn't a clue what this meant, but there was such an air of excitement, it felt a bit like a holiday. We were gathered in the main hall at eleven o'clock sharp, and it took a while for all two hundred of us to traipse up the stairs. At the top, we went through a door into another world, a world of thick carpets and high ceilings, tall windows and larger-than-life paintings of grand people from history. Imagine two hundred people all walking in silence and no footsteps to be heard because the carpets are that deep they swallow all the sound. I got ticked off for gawping with my mouth open at the mountains of glittering glass hung in the ceiling, what I later found out were called chandeliers, not to mention the dazzling redness of the wallpaper and the glowing gold of flowery carvings where the ceilings met the walls. It was like what I imagined heaven to look like, not just someone's home—hard to get your head around for an orphan girl like me.

Then we arrived in a room the size of a football field and got ourselves arranged in rows. I was at the front because I was so short, and Nora was right behind me. After a bit, in came Mrs. Hardy the head housekeeper, followed by the new king and queen and their children herded by a nanny. I couldn't stop goggling at the lot of them, but it was the eldest boy who really caught my eye. He would have been about sixteen then, not tall but fair like a Greek god and with a mischievous look on him.

They stopped in front of us, and we all bowed or curtseyed like we was taught, only I put the wrong foot behind and realized too late and stumbled a bit as I tried to change it, and Nora caught me from behind to stop me falling over. When I dared to look up again, my cheeks were burning, but the golden-haired boy was smiling at me with a face like an angel giving me a blessing, and I couldn't help but smile back till I caught the nanny glaring at me and had to study my shoes again.

The king made a speech with that prune-in-his-mouth voice, thanking us lot for the hard work that we had all put in to make their Coronation Day run smooth as clockwork, and the queen (our very own May) said something of the same, and then they went to leave, except that just as she turned, May looked directly at Nora and me and said quietly, "You two are my little needlework orphans, are you not?" We both blushed fit to match the carpet, but Nora was the first one to find her voice. "That's right, Your Majesty," she said, nipping in an extra little bob curtsey.

May said, "I hope you are settling in well?" and this time I managed to reply, "We are very happy, thank you, ma'am." She smiled and said, "Very good, very good," and walked out with the rest of them.

Well, you can imagine that Nora and me was on cloud nine for days afterward, she because the queen had talked to us, and me because I was head-over-heels in love with the boy. Of course, I knew this was stupid, but if others could idol-worship their music-hall heroes, I reckoned that surely I'm allowed my own?

Over the next few days, by sneaky questions, I managed to find out that this was the same boy whose birthday they celebrated the day after the Coronation Day, the boy who will marry some German or Russian princess and eventually become king. Apparently he attended naval college and now was going to become Prince of Wales, which I thought rather curious. Wales is part of Great Britain, so why should it have its own prince? And why not Scotland or Ireland? It was very confusing.

After the fuss and bother of the coronation, it went quiet for a few weeks, which was just as well because there was a summer heat wave, and we sweltered in the sewing room with its high windows barely catching the breeze. Miss G felt it the worst and had to have a cloth nearby to wipe her hands on every couple of minutes to save staining her sewing with sweat. Then one day, she didn't turn up for work, and Nora and me just got on with the mending pile, only it was more fun because we could chatter all we liked and play our favorite game of "happily ever after."

Nora's changed each time we played it, but usually involved marrying someone she had read about in the newspapers which got left lying around the servants' hall, a music-hall star or perhaps an explorer, like Shackleton or Scott, having six children, and living in a large, comfortable house in the country with servants who never gave her any lip like we did.

My happily-ever-after dreams came from the newspapers: I wanted to be a suffragette like Emmeline Pankhurst, and I would win the respect of women all over the country by persuading the prime minister to allow votes for women, and after that, having become famous, I would marry Prince Edward and become queen. Or perhaps it would be better to become queen first, and then I could change the rules however I liked.

Miss Garthwaite didn't return the next day nor the next, and we were told she had been taken poorly with her nerves and might not be back for a few days. The days stretched into a week and then two, and we were working all hours to keep up, but we didn't complain because we had no one to interfere or bother with us, a kind of freedom we hadn't never enjoyed before.

That night, I had just climbed into bed, weary as a sack of potatoes, when there was a knock on our door, and there was Mrs. Hardy the chief housekeeper with a gentleman in valet's uniform beside her, whose face I vaguely remembered from the servants' hall.

"Miss Romano, Mr. Finch needs your help," she said. "Get dressed at once, smart as you can. We'll wait here for you."

If she hadn't such a serious face on, I'd have thought it was a joke, but since it wasn't, I nearly fainted out of sheer terror. I shut the door and started trying to get dressed, and Nora didn't help by teasing me about going for a midnight rendezvous with my lover.

When I was ready, Mrs. H said, "You're to get your sewing kit, then go with Mr. Finch and do exactly as he tells you. Remember to curtsey when you are introduced. You must not speak unless you are spoken to nor look him directly in the eye, and you must do whatever you are told without saying

anything at all, except if you have to ask Mr. Finch something."
I nodded to show I'd understood, but I hadn't a clue who we
was going to see—surely not the king himself?—and my heart
was pounding so hard I was sure I'd not remember a thing.

Mr. Finch strode off with me trotting to keep up, down the
stairs of the servants' wing to the sewing room to collect what
Miss G calls her "basket of necessaries," then we was off again,
up the stairs to the door which leads into the palace proper and
along those deep carpeted corridors and up more stairs, great
wide ones with shiny brass handrails and massive paintings all
over the walls, and then along another corridor with so many
doors I lost count of them. No one else seemed to be around, no
footmen or other servants, nor any other members of the family.

All the while, Mr. Finch was talking to me. "Urgent alterations
are required, Miss Romano, to an item of clothing for his inves-
titure," he said, and I tried to recall where I'd heard the word
before to give me a clue about where we was headed. Mr. Finch
was rabbiting on, "The costume has been made for him by the
royal costumers, but His Royal Highness is not happy with it. I
have made a number of adjustments, but I have been unable to
please him. Specifically, the breeches are too wide and he would
like them taken in. The fabric is so fine that it puckers with every
stitch, so I hope that your small hands will be more successful
than my own efforts. Are you listening, Miss Romano?"

As it slowly dawned on me where we was heading, I felt sure
I would faint clear away before I got there.

"Yes, sir," I puffed. "I will do my best to please the prince."

"Not 'the prince,'" he snapped in a fearsome whisper. "'His
Royal Highness' it should be, at all times, and you are not to
address him directly, ever."

"Understood, Mr. Finch," I said, praying I would remember
all the instructions flying my way.

"We are going to his private chambers, and afterward you are not to breathe a word to anyone about where we have been, is that understood?"

"Yes, sir," I managed to gasp again, just as we arrived. Mr. Finch smoothed down his hair and pulled his jacket straight, and I checked that my dress and apron were in order and my hair still neatly tied back. Then he opened the door.

The tape comes to an end.

PATSY MORTON RESEARCH DIARY
JUNE 2, 1970

Meeting with Dr. Watts at lunchtime today, as Prof insists, to get the benefit of his "guidance" about my potential ex-patient interviewees. In other words, he wants to make sure I'm only talking to people who will tell it as he wants it told.

To be honest, I didn't take to the man at all. He talked down to me as if I was a child, calling me "dear." I'm not his "dear." We've only just met. Perhaps that's how he treats all women, but by the end, I felt like slapping him.

He didn't seem to have any objections to the other three patients on the list, but when it came to Maria Romano, he's definitely warning me off. He started with the usual caution about patient confidentiality and then proceeded to break all his own rules, telling me that she'd been a patient for many years, suffering from what he called persistent paranoid delusional mania, and even reading directly from her file, like he really had a point to prove. Of course, didn't tell him I've already started interviewing her!

His secretary came and whispered something in his ear, and he asked me to excuse him for a few minutes. He was gone for much longer, so I started wandering around his office, looking through the windows, etc., till I noticed he'd left M's file open on the desk.

I had a quick flick through, but it was all a bit technical and there was not enough time to make proper notes. Then remembered I'd brought my camera, so took photos of a couple of pages, then got jumpy. Dr. W. came back after about quarter of an hour, all bright and breezy, we chatted a bit more, and I said good-bye.

New problem: how to get the photos developed without revealing personal information? Can't take them to Boots the Chemist, can I?

4.

THAT VERY WEEK, DESPITE MY IMPECCABLE ANSWERS to those consultants' crass questions, I was laid off. "Pack up your desk within the hour" laid off. And although I knew that the immediate dismissal was nothing to do with their assessment of my honesty and everything to do with protecting commercial secrets, it felt as though I'd been kicked in the teeth and all my hard work for them over the past few years was entirely wasted.

"I just don't know who I am anymore," I moaned, pouring myself a third glass of Pinot, when Jo arrived that evening. "It sounds so stupid. It was a hellish, boring job, and I couldn't wait to get out. But getting laid off makes you feel as though they haven't valued a single thing that you've done for them in four years. I walked out of there feeling like a nonperson."

Jo and I had been best friends since fashion school. We shared several small, grubby apartments in the early years and were virtually inseparable until relationships and careers took us on different paths. I still had a photograph of us on graduation day, snapped by my proud mum. Jo is squinting at the camera in an attempt to please, and I am gazing into the distance, perhaps daydreaming or simply bored by the whole event. Neither of us would wear a traditional gown and mortar board for the occasion, of course, being far too cool for that sort of thing. We opted instead for some of our more outlandish fashion statement outfits, all torn edges and spray-painted patterns—we'd dubbed it graffiti chic, as I recall. Now I'd cringe whenever I looked at it. She is tall and angular, with an unkempt mop of hair blowing into her eyes; I'm a head shorter, slightly built, my round face topped with a rebellious retro-punk hairstyle like a blond pincushion. It was not a flattering look and soon got discarded once I started job hunting and saw the disdainful glances of the slick-suited bosses I was trying to impress.

She was always fascinated by historical fabrics and went to work as a textile conservator, while I spent my first year out of college living on sofas and struggling as an unpaid intern for various interior design companies until landing a menial job. But I hated the cliquey, hothouse atmosphere of the studios and the arrogance of their rich, self-obsessed customers. Before long, I was deeply disillusioned and decided to get out.

When I joined the bank, I'd had to adopt the uniform of the city—dark suit and heels, bleached hair in a neat elfin cut, and a mask of makeup reapplied several times daily. Jo still disdained such conformity. She went to work in skinny jeans and a T-shirt, artfully embroidered, dyed, or painted perhaps, but still a T-shirt. I never envied her temporary contract hand-to-mouth existence, but respected her for hanging on with fierce determination, despite everything, to her long-held passion for textiles. The respect was not reciprocated: Jo had never disguised her disapproval of my "selling out" to the banking world and her disgust at the bonus culture which, for me, was its only real attraction.

Despite our divergent lives, we'd remained the best of friends. Although I'd been devastated when Jo and her boyfriend Mark moved to distant south London for more affordable house prices, we met as often as we could, and she was still the only person in the world in whom I could confide really personal things, the person I turned to when everything was going wrong. This evening, she'd decided to stay over, because Mark was away on business.

She sat on the floor hugging her knees, dark curls falling in front of her face, reminding me of our student days, before we could afford chairs. "Looking on the bright side, perhaps it'll be the spur you need to get you back into interior design," she said. "You can do whatever you want. Something you really enjoy."

She was right, of course. It had always been my plan to save enough to set up my own business, but even with the generous payoff, how could I do this with no job to fall back on, plus a massive mortgage? Once upon a time, I'd had talents and passions, but they'd been so neglected recently that they'd probably packed their bags and emigrated.

"And that, on top of splitting up with Russell…" I croaked.

Russell and I had parted more in sorrow than in anger. He was a man of such absurdly perfect features that when he entered a room, every female glance was drawn involuntarily toward him. As if that didn't make him desirable enough, he also had a starry career, having just been made the youngest-ever partner in his law firm. We were the perfect match, or so our friends believed, but appearances can be so misleading. Couples may seem enviably united and loving on the outside, but who can tell what goes on behind closed doors?

Apart from our sex life, which was great, Russ and I had little in common. He wasn't the slightest bit interested in art or interiors, and I'd rather watch paint dry than go to a rugby match, which was his grand passion outside work. He was a massive carnivore and never understood why meat could be so repugnant to me; in his world, vegetarians were there to be converted or, at best, baited for their whimsical ways.

His ideal holiday was skiing, hang gliding, or white-water rafting; I usually wanted to visit galleries and old houses, or simply crash out on a beach in the sun and read. Apart from law tomes and the occasional trashy thriller, I never saw Russell with a book in his hand. For him, relaxation was getting hammered in the bar on a Friday evening, shouting to fellow lawyers. He didn't do chilling out, and he wasn't too fond of my alternative ex-university friends either. I think he was terrified I might one day give up being a banker and revert to my artsy roots, take up painting again, dig out my eighties tie-dye and big earrings, and start serving organic quinoa with every meal.

Despite our differences, we got along fine for a few years, but eventually the sparkle just wasn't there anymore, and though we'd tried hard to revive it, deep down we both knew we weren't right for each other. One tearful evening last November, we found ourselves admitting it, and although we were both devastated, agreed to spend some time apart.

I calculated that my salary would just about cover the mortgage payments on the flat, so he'd moved out just before Christmas. Apart from a drunken sentimental night together on New Year's Eve, we were still officially separated, and on New Year's Day, once I'd guzzled enough painkillers to kill the hangover, I promised myself that this would be *my* year, a year for rediscovering my sense of adventure, my independent spirit. I might even request extended leave from work and go on that around-the-world trip I'd always been too broke, or too timid, to do in my twenties. When I returned, I would start building a business plan for the design company I'd always dreamed of setting up, but never had the courage.

Jo had already spent several evenings consoling me about the breakup; unfailing reserves of mutual sympathy had always been the currency of our friendship. Now, she crawled across the floor and climbed onto the sofa, wrapping her arms around me.

"You're having a really crap time, but in a few weeks, you won't believe you were saying these things. You'll get another job, start meeting other people. You're so talented you could do anything you want."

"High-class escort, perhaps?"

"No, idiot, something in design," she laughed. "Something you really enjoy, for once, and not just for the money. Plus, there are plenty of men out there for the taking. You're so funny and gorgeous too, you won't be single for long, I know it."

I gulped another massive swig of wine. Jo seemed to be on water. "But I've just taken on the mortgage. How will I ever afford it? I can't bear to lose this place."

Russ and I found our airy top-floor flat, in a quiet, leafy north London street, two years ago, and I knew from the moment we stepped through the door that this was the one. We'd redecorated in cool monotones of cream, taupe, and dove gray, restored the beautiful marble fireplaces and plaster ceiling roses, furnished it with minimalist Scandinavian furniture, and spent a fortune on wood flooring and soft, deep carpets.

"I'm so sorry to be such a moan. I really appreciate you coming over."

"It was the least I could do. You *will* survive, you know."

I took a deep breath. "Anyway, what's new in the star-studded world of textile conservation?"

Her face brightened. "I've had my contract renewed at Kensington Palace. Another two years of security, at least, and I've been given some cool projects. There's a new exhibition planned, and they need all hands on deck, which is good news for me." She smiled mysteriously. "We're going to need all the money we can get."

"Go on. What haven't you told me?"

"Now Mark's got a permanent job and my contract's been renewed, we think we can afford it." She paused and lowered her eyes. "We're trying for a baby."

"Ohmigod, Jo. That's sooo exciting," I squealed. "I thought he hated the idea of a stroller in the hallway? I'm so glad he's come around."

Even as I congratulated her, I could feel the familiar ache of melancholy in my own belly. Each time a friend announced the "big news," I had to steel myself to enter the baby departments in search of an appropriate gift. It was the tiny Wellington boots that really twisted my heart.

Jo knew all this, of course. "I'm sorry. It's hard for you, just when you've finished with Russ."

"No worries," I said, more breezily than I felt. "I'm just thrilled for you. And I'll be the best babysitter in the world."

As I went to put away the glasses, she called from the spare room, "I haven't seen this quilt before. Is it yours?"

"I've just brought it back from Mum's. We found it in the loft at the cottage. It belonged to my granny. Look at this," I said.

"How bizarre. I've seen sampler verses incorporated into quilts, but never sewn into the lining like that. Do you know who made it?"

I shook my head. "Mum thinks it might have been made by a friend Granny met in the hospital. It's a bit of a mystery."

"Let me show you something else. See these?" She pointed to the background behind the embroidery in the center panel of the quilt. "And this one? Can you see the motifs, the sprays of flowers woven into the brocade?"

I peered more closely.

"I'm not certain, but it reminds me of something I read recently, about the May Silks," she said, stroking the fabric with a reverent fingertip.

"May Silks?"

"They were designs created for the royal family around the turn of the twentieth century—George and Mary, that lot. Mary was particularly keen to support British designers and manufacturers, and these designs were commissioned from a London studio run by a man called Arthur Silver. They were quite famous in their time."

She handed me a tiny brass magnifying glass. "Take a look. You can see the rose, thistle, and chain of shamrocks—symbols for the nations of the United Kingdom."

"What about the Welsh daffodils—or is it leeks?"

"These flowers in the center look a bit like daffodils. It's hard to tell. But more important, can you see those silver threads? Isn't it extraordinary?"

Looking closer now, I could see what she was talking about. The pale cream silk seemed to have metal threads running through it, and woven into it were delicate designs of flowers and leaves, linked together as a garland.

"Raise-a-fortune-at-Sotheby's extraordinary?"

"It won't pay off your mortgage," she laughed. "But it would be really interesting from a historical perspective." She took back the magnifying glass and ranged over other parts of the quilt. "Quite apart from the interesting fabrics, the stitching is amazing. I expect you've noticed?" She pointed to the maze design, a double row in the finest of chain stitches, perfectly even throughout its complex twisting pattern. "And the appliqué stitches are so tiny. I've never seen such neat needlework. Whoever made it was a brilliant seamstress," she said, straightening her back. "Was it your granny, you said?"

"Granny did dressmaking, but we never saw her doing embroidery. Mum thinks it might have been made by a friend of hers."

"Whoever it was, I'd love to know how they got hold of those fabrics. They were unique and very closely guarded because they were only to be used by the queen. Did she have anything to do with the royal family?"

I shook my head. Granny was always rather antiestablishment and certainly no royalist. She'd always been angry about the hardship my grandfather had endured, fighting in the First World War. "Lions led by donkeys," I'd heard her say once, and when I asked what it meant, she explained that the generals leading the war were upper-class twits who had no idea what it was like for what she called the "cannon fodder" in the trenches.

"You mentioned a hospital?"

"She was a patient at a mental hospital for a short time, probably just after the war. The only thing Mum can remember is that the quilt is somehow connected to the hospital, or perhaps someone she met there."

"I wonder whether the hospital had a royal connection, perhaps, or a link with the factory that wove the silk?"

"Let's have a look." I turned on my laptop and searched for "mental hospital, Eastchester." Almost at once, an archive site came up: *A History of Helena Hall*. "This must be it!"

Jo peered over my shoulder as we read:

This website is dedicated to the doctors, nurses, consultants, and other staff who worked at Helena Hall Mental Hospital, as well as the many thousands of patients who were cared for there during its eighty-four years of serving the community.

The hospital, first named the Helena Hall Asylum, was opened to patients in 1913. At its peak, it housed over 1,800 patients, as well as medical and academic staff. The site demonstrates the changing approach of asylum layout through the early part of the twentieth century, incorporating large ward-style buildings typical of the echelon style, yet having outlying villas typical of the colonial style.

The hospital began to release patients into the community in the 1970s and finally closed its doors in 1997. Since then, the building has suffered from a number of arson attacks, especially on the main hall and the superintendent's house. The site is to be regenerated, with the main administration building and wards being restored and converted to housing.

In the grainy black-and-white photographs, Helena Hall looked for all the world like a well-staffed stately home. Groups of pin-neat nurses posed proudly on the steps in front of a grand entrance with pillars on either side, and gardeners in three-piece tweed suits worked among meticulously manicured lawns and precision-edged flower beds. But there was also a harsher reality: shots of long, empty wards furnished with plain, white iron bedsteads ranged on either side in military rows, bewildered women patients in baggy dresses grinning toothlessly at the camera, and men with ravaged faces and slumped shoulders blinking into the sunshine from a garden bench.

"Jeez, look at this." Jo pointed to a photograph of nurses and doctors gathered by a bedside with an alarming-looking machine sprouting wires toward an invisible patient.

"Looks like electroshock," I said, shivering at the thought that Granny might have endured such treatments.

A section on "Patient Life" showed more recent, reassuring scenes: color photographs of dances in the Great Hall, an arch-roofed affair decorated in blue and gold, hung with chandeliers with a large stage at one end bordered with ruby-red velvet curtains. Smiling people played cricket, badminton, tennis, and lawn bowling, and interior shots featured spacious rooms with gleaming parquet flooring, Persian rugs, and comfortable three-piece suites. In one of the photos, entitled "Ladies Needlework Room," women sat at tables in a sunny room working on embroidery and knitting.

"Is it patchwork that lady's sewing, do you think?"

I squinted closer at the screen. "Could be. It's hard to tell. Can't recognize anyone." The faces were largely concealed, and certainly none looked anything like my grandmother.

It seemed that controversy over closure of the place had been raging for several decades, and future development plans were still keeping it in front-page headlines in the local newspaper. The most contentious issue was the planned demolition of the Great Hall, which had been in use by local amateur dramatic groups and choral societies long after the hospital wards had closed. Many of the articles were bylined: "Our chief reporter, Ben Sweetman."

"This guy seems to be a bit of an expert," Jo said. "He might be able to tell you whether the place had any royal links, or put you in touch with someone who might know, someone who used to work there, perhaps?"

"You think it's really that important to find out?"

"A family heirloom with what looks like unique royal silk in it? It's amazing. It's up to you, of course, but whatever you decide, I'd really like to show it to my curator."

"The head of royal costumes? I thought you told me she was a dragon."

"She is, but I've warmed to her a bit since she renewed my contract." Jo checked her phone and yawned. "Ugh. It's already past one, and I've got to be at work early tomorrow."

"Thank you so much for coming over. I feel a lot better."

"You'll be fine, you know," she said sweetly. "This could really be the start of something exciting."

"Finding the quilt, you mean?" I said, momentarily misunderstanding her.

"That too," she laughed. "What I really meant was you could have a whole new career ahead of you. Move over Moschino and Stefanidis, Meadows is on your tail."

"I'm more excited about your new venture." I gestured toward her stomach.

"Don't hold your breath. It's early days," she said, as we hugged good-night.

❦

My sleep was threadbare that night, like cheap curtains letting in too much light, as my mind tried to make sense of the events of the past couple of days. Despite the shock of getting laid off, I couldn't help feeling a sense of anticipation and elation. Jo was right: this could be the start of an exciting new phase of my life, an opportunity to do something completely different.

I dozed briefly and then, in my half-awake state, from the deepest part of my subconscious, came a powerful memory. I must have been about four years old, staying the night at Granny's house and sleeping in the spare room in the big bed with the shiny brass bobbles at each corner. It was so wide that I could easily fit into it sideways and so high off the floor that I needed a stool to help me clamber onto it, like a miniature mountaineer. Her house always seemed enormous, especially in contrast with the low ceilings and doorways of my parents' cottage.

The quilt had been spread across the bed, and that night,

ding a bedtime story, she told me all about how
is made from scraps of material sewn together
different ways to make beautiful patterns. She also
described how quilts were sometimes made by people because
they were so poor they couldn't afford proper blankets or,
more often, by people who just enjoyed sewing something
beautiful. She told me that some quilts were made to mark an
occasion, like the birth of a baby, a wedding, a coronation (I
wasn't sure what that was, but didn't like to interrupt), or in
memory of friends.

As she talked, I traced my finger over strips and squares and
triangles of fabric. Some were so smooth to the touch it was
like brushing my own skin, but others were rough and catchy.
Some seemed to glitter like jewels, the patterns pulsing almost
as though they were alive, the threads shimmering as they
caught the light.

She showed me how the quilt had been designed as a series
of squares, each one larger than the last, like a painting within a
painting within yet another painting, each one framing the one
inside, and each one so different from the next, in the complex-
ity of its patterns and colors and the types of fabrics used. We
wondered, together, how many tiny scraps of material had been
used to make the quilt, and I tried counting them, but gave up
at twenty, the limit of my numbers. Then she suggested that we
play a game of "match the scraps," discovering that a section
of triangles near the head of the bed was repeated at the other
end, and the row of printed cottons sewn into squares were in
the same order in the opposite corner.

The design of the outer panels were just shapes and colors,
as far as I could see, sometimes in patterns like sticks or steps,
what looked like rising suns along the sides and ends. I liked
to run my fingers along the curly pattern of embroidered

stitches in the central panel, imagining myself to be in a maze of tall hedges.

But it was the panel of appliqué figures that most intrigued me. In a row along the top was a duck, an apple, a violin, a green leaf, and a dragon with fiery flames coming out of its mouth, and at the bottom, another row with a mouse, an acorn, a rabbit, a lily-like flower, and an anchor.

"Why is the duck trying to eat the apple?" I asked.

Granny chuckled in that easy way that always made me feel safe. "Have you ever watched a duck trying to eat an apple? They can't pierce the skin with their round beaks, so the apple keeps running away." She mimicked the action with her hands, the fingers of one bent over the thumb like a bird's bill, the other a round fist in the shape of an apple. "They have to wait until another bird with a sharp beak has cut into the apple, then they can eat it."

I pointed to the dragon at the end of the row. "Why's he got flames coming out of his mouth?"

"Perhaps he's trying to scare away the duck so he can eat the apple."

I'd chattered on brightly, desperate to prolong the conversation and postpone the inevitable lights out. "Mummy says I can have a real-life rabbit, like this one, when I am a bit older."

"That's for her to decide, my little Caroline," she said. "Now it is time for sleep. Tomorrow's a big day. Someone special is coming to meet you."

In the middle of the night, I sat up in bed and tried to write down as much of that memory as I could. Some details were still clear as a spring day, but there was something else I couldn't

quite grasp, a foggy incompleteness, as if my mind associated
with that moment something important but which was, long
since, too deeply buried to bring back to the surface.

5.

IS THAT THINGY WORKING AGAIN?

The clink of a cup being placed into its saucer.

That was a nice cuppa, wasn't it? Where had we got to?

"You were going to alter the prince's breeches…"

That smoky chuckle again, rattling in her chest and catching her throat till it becomes a full-blown coughing fit. She struggles to regain her breath.

It do sound a bit unlikely, don't it, when you say it out loud like that? It's no wonder they thought I was making it up. Most of 'em didn't believe me, you see. And why would they, when they was surrounded by crazy women with all kinds of weird imaginings? There was Ada, for example, who believed she was the pregnant Virgin Mary and used to stick a pillow up her dress whenever she got the chance. They'd tell her off too, just like they did with me. "Stop putting on airs," they'd say. The psychiatrist was the worst, sitting there like a pudding with that question-mark face on him. "This is in your imagination, dear," he'd say to me. "None of it is real, and the sooner you understand that, the sooner we'll be able to release you."

Then there was poor old Winnie, who got locked up that many times for climbing into bed with other women and stealing food off other people's plates. She always claimed it was the voices telling her to do it, but they never believed her neither. Well, I'd try to argue back like Winnie, of course, but after a while, I gave up trying to prove that what I was telling them was the truth. What was the point? In the end, I figured it was best to keep quiet and let them think it'd all been in my imagination.

But if you are happy to hear me out, I'll carry on.

"Please do. That's what I am here for. When you're ready. The prince's breeches…"

Ah yes. Hrrrm. Well, I don't know what I imagined a royal bedchamber to be like, but that room was so enormous, if there hadn't been a carpet on the floor, I'd have taken it for a ballroom. Besides, there was no bed—must be next door, I thought to meself. On the far side was a person preening himself in front of a long mirror dressed in what I took to be a pantomime outfit—not that I'd seen a pantomime in me life, you understand, but I'd seen the posters outside the music halls. He had white satin breeches with great rosettes at each knee, with a doublet which barely came down to his thighs and a coat and cape in purple velvet with furry trimmings—I later found out it was called ermine—and a floppy velvet hat on his head.

"At last, Finch, you're back," the prince said, and as he turned to us, his face twisted into an angry frown. Finch bowed and I made my best curtsey. I'd been practicing since last time.

"This is Miss Romano, Your Highness, the best seamstress in the palace, come to make the alterations you require," said Finch in his oily voice, making me shimmer inside at the compliment.

"Excellent, excellent," said the prince, looking at me so curiously I began to wonder whether I'd put my apron on back to front. I kept my eyes fixed to the ground as I'd been told, but through my eyelashes I could see that the frown had been replaced with a teasing smile.

"Your curtsey is much improved since we last met, Miss Romano," he said. "I only hope your needlework skills are as good."

He smiled at me then, that smile that seemed to light up the room, just like he did that day when I'd botched my first attempt at a curtsey. I could feel my cheeks burning, and my heart begin to beat a little faster just recalling that moment, and realizing that he, too, remembered it.

"Now, sir," said Finch, all brisk and businesslike, "perhaps you could describe to Miss Romano the work you would like her to undertake?"

"These bloody breeches," the prince grumbled, and he pulled out the sides of them below the doublet so that they stuck out like angels' wings either side of his thighs. "They're like something a ruddy ballet dancer would wear. There's not much we can do about the rest of this preposterous rig, but at the very least I want these taken in. Not too tight, mind."

"Would you care to show Miss Romano exactly how tight, Your Highness," asked Finch, "so that she can place a pin for marking?"

I rummaged in the basket of necessaries to find Miss G's pot of pins. Then, as the prince held the fabric either side, I knelt down in front of him, with my hands trembling so much that I could hardly hold it, doing my best to place the pin close to his fingers through the fabric on both sides, and all the while trying not to have hysterics at the extraordinary turn of events which had brought me kneeling with my face only inches away from the most personal parts of the future king of England.

She breaks out into that smoky cackle and the interviewer laughs along with her. They are growing easy in each other's company. It takes some time for them both to gather themselves.

Oh dearie me. I'll remember that night till I die, I tell you.

Thinking about it has helped me laugh through the blackest of times since, and there have been plenty of them, let me tell you.

Anyway, I managed to pin the fabric without sticking a pin into the royal nether regions, and then stood back while he regarded himself for a long time in the long mirror again and finally pronounced that the shape of the breeches was now much improved. He turned to me, said a brief thank-you, and then, without so much as a by-your-leave, undid the hooks at the waist, dropped the breeches to the floor, and stepped out of them, in his undershorts alone.

Of course I turned my eyes away, blushing to the roots of my hair and the soles of my feet. A man in his underwear wasn't something I'd ever seen before, but Finch took no notice, as if it was perfectly normal to see the prince in a state of undress. When I thought about it later, that was probably how a valet sees his master most days. He just pointed to me again to pick up the breeches and said, "Thank you, sir, we will return these first thing in the morning. Just to remind you, it is a six o'clock start, sir, for the rehearsal at Carnarvon tomorrow afternoon. Will that be all?"

"That will be all, Mr. Finch," said the prince, "and you too, little Miss Romano." Finch bowed and I curtseyed again, and I copied him as he shuffled crabwise out of the chamber so's not to turn his back on His Royal Highness. I was that elated about the whole business that I seemed to glide along the corridors and downstairs to the sewing room without touching the floor. What a red-letter day it turned out to be. I had just been within inches of my heart's desire, the boy who will be king of England. *And* Finch said I was the best seamstress in the palace.

After that, I was so determined to prove it, I spent most of the night on the alterations to the prince's breeches. First I had to remove the knee band and the satin rosette on each leg and then take in both side seams. The satin was so delicate that every stitch threatened to rip the fabric unless I used the very finest of needles with a single strand of silk thread and sewed the tiniest of fairy stitches. Knowing that if I had got it wrong there would be no going back and my job at the palace would probably end here and now, I cut away the excess fabric and oversewed the seams to stop them fraying. Then I had to re-gather, with a double line of tacking stitch, and sew back the below-knee band and fit the rosette in exactly the right place. It wouldn't do for it to hang out at the back or stick out at the front, or—nightmare of nightmares—to fall off in the middle of this investi-wotsit.

After all that, I pressed the seams flat with a very cool iron ever so carefully—imagine if I had singed them—so that they would sit perfectly on the prince's beautiful limbs. The big clock on the sewing room wall ticked around at an alarm-ing pace, but I was finished at ten minutes to five o'clock, so I wrapped the breeches in some white cambric, picked up my sewing kit again, and went in search of Mr. Finch in the servants' hall.

I heard nothing more for quite a few days, and so I had to assume that my work had been to the prince's satisfaction. Gossip in the servants' hall was that the event had been a great success, that the rain had held off, and the prince had said his lines in Welsh correctly and the king had been very pleased. There were photographs in the newspaper, and to be honest, he did look a bit of a ninny even with the slimmed-down version of the satin breeches I'd created, but at least I had done my best. After all the excitement of that night, I felt a little let down that my efforts had gone unnoticed and unthanked.

Until Mr. Finch arrived in the sewing room one afternoon and passed me a note. He stood in the doorway while I opened it, my fingers trembling terribly as I'd given a bit of cheek to the housekeeper the day before and feared I might be for the sack.

It was unsigned, but had the Prince of Wales crest at the top: *"Dear Miss Romano, I have some further sewing for you to do. Please come to my chamber at ten o'clock this evening."*

We went through the very same rigmarole as before. Finch called for me at five minutes to ten precisely. From his silence and the set of his shoulders as we made our way to the prince's chambers, I could tell he was dreadful put out, having to escort the needlework maid around the palace at this hour.

This time, the prince was in a red velvet smoking jacket and Harris tweed trousers and seemed a deal more relaxed, resting on a chaise by the fireplace with a cigarette and a newspaper in his hands. When we entered, he looked up with that smile like spring sunshine.

"That will be all, thank you, Mr. Finch," he said. "Miss Romano will see herself out once we have finished. There is no need for you to wait."

I could feel Finch hesitating beside me, shifting his weight from foot to foot. He cleared his throat and said quietly, "Excuse me, sir. Are you sure? It's just that…" He struggled to find the right words. "Miss Romano may not be too familiar with the route…"

The prince looked at me with a mock-serious frown and a little smile on his lips. "I am sure you can find your own way back to the servants' quarters, Miss Romano, can you not?"

What was I supposed to say? I could not disagree with the prince, whatever trouble that got me into with Finch later, so I mumbled, "I think so, sir," and he said, "Very good, very good," before waving his hand at Finch. "Thank you for your concern, Mr. Finch, but that really *will* be all. See you in the morning."

The next few hours was like a dream. Even now I cannot really merit that it really happened, and believe me, I have thought of it almost every day of my life. In the Hall, they give you drugs to forget, and I didn't want to forget a moment of this time, so after a while I refused to take them. What else did I have but my memories?

I asked what it was he wanted me to sew for him, and he laughed and said, "There's no mending to be done tonight, little one, except perhaps my poor life. It's been so dreary since they made me leave naval school and all my pals. No, I've invited you here because I want to have a conversation with someone normal. And you have such a charming smile, I felt sure you would be fun to talk to."

I hesitated then, I really did, and my heart started banging in my chest at the unusualness of the situation I found myself in. It was not my place to go around having casual conversations with princes, let alone at night when everyone else was asleep.

"Are you sure, sir, I mean, Your Royal Highness," I stuttered. "I am a very ordinary girl, you know, not even needlework mistress. When Miss G gets back to work, perhaps…"

He interrupted, "But that, little one, is exactly why I want to talk to you. Now come and sit down beside me and tell me about your life." He wanted to hear about everything, he said.

Well, I barely knew how to start, not being in the habit of having conversations with princes, but I knew better than to string it out too much, so I just told him briefly about the nuns and his mother the queen, when she was a duchess, coming to The Castle, about how we arrived at the palace and how me and Nora liked to have a laugh together. He sat quiet, as if he found my every word fascinating, and those blue eyes was on me the whole time, smiling with amusement or frowning in sympathy. He must surely be the best listener in the world, I thought, not that anyone much had ever listened to me before.

I told him about Miss G and how she needed a prince's kiss to cure her warts, and he hooted so long and loud I was afraid it would rouse the rest of his family, wherever they slept. When he stopped, his beautiful soft eyes went serious and he put his hand on mine, leaned forward, and gave me a kiss on the cheek. I nearly jumped away with the shock of it.

"There," he said, "a prince's kiss to make Miss Romano even more beautiful."

"Oh sir," I gasped, blushing to the tips of my toes.

He lifted my chin with his finger and turned my face toward him, then planted another kiss—this time on my lips. It was my first proper kiss, imagine that, and so delicious. He tasted of marshmallows, vanilla, and icing sugar, and I wanted it to last forever, but after a few seconds, he pulled away, stood up suddenly, and walked over to the fireplace, stopping with his back to me. I must have been holding my breath the whole time, for my head started to swim, and I thought I might faint clean away, so I kept my eyes to my lap to stop the room from spinning around.

After a long moment, he spoke. "I am so sorry, I got carried away. Please forgive me."

"There's nothing to apologize for, sir. It's surely *my* fault for being so impertinent, sitting here and going on about my ordinary little life."

"But that's just it, don't you see?" he said, walking back across the room toward me, taking my hands in his and shaking them with every emphasis. "I *want* to know what ordinary lives are like. My family is not *normal*, never will be. But I want to know how it *could* be."

He let go of my hands and suddenly pulled me to my feet, wrapping his arms around me so our bodies were touching from top to toe. My hands seemed to take matters into their own, clasping themselves around his waist. Though he was not a tall boy, my cheek rested on his chest, and I breathed in his smell of expensive shaving soap and clean-washed tweed and tried to get my head around this extraordinary turn of events.

I could hear his heart beating and feel his breathing, fast and strong. As his fingers stroked the back of my neck, my legs went to jelly with the joy of it all. I wanted to stay there, close to him, for the rest of my life. Apart from Nora, he was the only person in the world who had ever held me so tight.

After a very long time, he drew away. "You had better go, little one," he said, "or I might be tempted to kiss you again. You know, don't you, that you must not whisper a word about this evening to anyone, even your friend Nora? Rumors get about like wildfires in this place."

"Yes, sir," I said, remembering who he was, and made a little curtsey even though it seemed too formal, when moments before we had been so close as to feel each other's heartbeats.

He went to the door. "Go left, then right, along the corridor to the third door on the left, down the stairs, turn right again, and you will be back in the servants' hall." He smiled. "Got that?" As I turned to go out of the door, he caught my hand again and kissed it.

"Sweet dreams, little one," he said. "You will come to see me again, won't you?"

My hand burned where he had kissed it. That night, I climbed into bed and tried to relive every blissful moment of that encounter—the easy conversation, his laughter, the sweetness of our kiss, and the long, tender embrace. Each time I thought of it, my body ached with longing to be close to him once more, and I became almost choked with the fear that it might never happen again, might have been a one-off.

But I need not have worried. He asked for me several times after that, sometimes during the day, and the footmen came to recognize me as I made my way along the palace corridors to his chamber. Perhaps for the first time in my life, I felt important.

Each time, when I walked in, his smile bathed us in its sunshine, and he made me feel as though I was the most special person in the world. We would have a small sherry while we were talking, and though the taste of alcohol was strange and tart at first, I soon began to enjoy the way it helped me to forget the oddness of our situation. We talked for hours, he held my hand, we kissed and a bit more besides, if you get my meaning.

Don't think badly of me, miss. Each time he went just a little further, and I knew it was wrong but I was that hungry for him I never tried to stop it when he unbuttoned my top and put his cheek to the rise of my breasts, or when he stroked my backside through the cotton of my uniform or pulled my skirt up to feel the bare leg above me garter. Naive as I was, I couldn't help but notice the effect I was having on him, and it made me want even more.

I did my best not to tell Nora, I honestly did. But we had been friends for years, and she knew me too well.

"Don't say a word. I don't want to know," is what she whispered to me when, for the second night in a row, I'd crept into our room in my stockinged feet, trying to avoid the creaky boards, well after midnight. In the morning, as we started into our sewing, she said, "It's *him*, isn't it?" When I said nothing, she went on, "You're *not* to go again. You know how gossip gets around, and if anyone finds out what you've been doing, you'll be on the streets before you can even try denying it."

"I can't refuse him, can I, the future king of England?" I said, all snippy. Consorting with the prince was giving me airs above my station, I see that now.

"If he calls again for a seamstress, I'll go instead. That'd put a stop to it," she said firmly.

I was about to say he wouldn't want to kiss a great tall thing like Nora—she'd tower over him—but all I said was, "If he asks for me, I'll have to go."

"Be it on your own head, then," she said, throwing down her sewing and stomping out. We didn't talk for the rest of the afternoon, and the atmosphere in the sewing room was frosty for days afterward.

A week or so later, I was summoned again, but this time, when I entered the bedchamber, his smile failed to light up, and I immediately knew that something was wrong.

"Dearest girl," he said, holding me in his arms for a brief moment and then pulling away.

"What is it, sir?" I asked, with my heart in my boots. "You look unwell."

"Sit with me a moment," he said, patting the chaise beside him. He took my hands in his. "You know, do you not, that my fate is not my own to decide?" he said, with a sorrowful face. "The king has decreed that I should go back to the navy. I leave for Southampton tomorrow."

"But that's not too far away, is it?"

"I shall not be in Southampton, dearest, but on a ship, traveling who knows where. Then, when I get back, I must go to Norfolk to study in preparation for Oxford. Father seems to want me out of his way. Or perhaps he thinks I will get up to mischief if I stay in London." His eyes twinkled again, briefly.

It seemed as though my world—as I had come to know it—was unraveling like a loose seam. But he pulled me into his arms again and whispered, "But I will write, as often as I can, and I will surely be back in London from time to time. So let's have a little tipple and make this a night to remember, shall we?"

And so we did, dearie, so we did. After what seemed like hours of kissing and cuddling, long past the time when the clocks chimed midnight, he pulled away, took a deep breath, and looked me straight in the eyes. "Can we?" he asked, and I nodded, knowing exactly what he meant and wanting it so much but at the same time fearing I might faint with the terror of it all. He asked me to unbutton him, and my fingers were that shaky I couldn't get a single one undone, so he took over himself. What happened next was clumsy and hurried, but the look of pure joy on his face afterward will stay with me forever. He held me in his arms and kissed me so tenderly it felt as though I was melting pure away.

It was his first time too. He was eighteen and I'd just turned sixteen.

I knew it was wrong, of course I did. I should have kept myself pure for my future husband. I can see you're smiling. You must be thinking what a little trollop I was.

"No, Maria, I'm not judging you. I'm smiling because I'm glad you had some fun while you were young."

Oh yes, it was fun all right, and I found I could lock away me conscience easily enough. I was already head over heels in love with my beautiful blue-eyed boy, and he was going away for months, perhaps years. Who knew when we would have the chance again?

Besides, who was I to say no to the future king of England?

The tape clunks off.

6.

————

O N MY FIRST DAY OF JOBLESSNESS, I WOKE WITH A
new sense of purpose and wrote a list:

> *— sort out finances & talk to mortgage adviser*
> *— write business plan & create website*
> *— appointment with bank re loan?*
> *— Lewis, James, Suze, and Fred lunch dates re*
> *interior design contacts*

I took a long luxurious shower, then pushed aside my city
uniform on the wardrobe rail and grabbed my weekend gear:
comfortable black skinny jeans, T-shirt, and a hoodie. "That's
more like it," I said out loud, as if needing to convince myself.
"This is the upside of getting laid off." I usually spent a good
ten minutes in front of the mirror each morning, making sure
that the person presented to the world was immaculate. Now,
none of that mattered—I could just be me, whoever that was.
With a bit of luck, I was about to find out.

So I ended up spending time in front of the mirror anyway,
wondering what the new me might look like. Those roots in
my hair needed doing, but why go to the expense? Why not
allow it to return to its natural mousy blond? My eyebrows

were a bit bushy—but actually I quite liked the slightly fuzzy shape, a relief from those starkly waxed lines.

Without the weight of mascara on their lashes, my eyes felt lighter and more alert and appeared to be brighter blue without the carefully applied shadows and highlighter that usually framed them. Okay, my wrinkles were more obvious without foundation, the odd chickenpox scar from long ago more prominent—but I decided there was nothing too scary.

I straightened my shoulders, looked myself directly in the eye, and took a deep breath: this was the new me, the natural, unadorned, take-me-as-you-find-me Caroline, a strong, independent, and yes, about-to-be-successful self-employed interior designer. Yes, that was the plan.

But it was strange having no job to go to, no appointments to rush between in the usual manic way, no one breathing over my shoulder asking when the report would be ready. My calendar was blank.

I pushed the living-room table over toward the window so that I could have a view of the small park from my new "office," phoned the bank for an appointment with their business adviser, and emailed several friends still working in the interior design field, casually suggesting that we might lunch. I sorted out my filing system, cleaned the flat, and made several more cups of coffee.

When I changed the sheets on the spare bed, I brought the quilt into the living room, hanging it over the back of the sofa. Low sun streamed in, as it always does in winter when the branches of the plane trees outside are bare of leaves. The beams fell onto the quilt, and the silver threads in those silks that Jo had been so excited about seemed to come alive, gleaming in the light.

I read the little verse again, even though I already knew it by heart. Who had written it, and who was her lost love? How did the maker get hold of those royal silks? How did they know Granny? And was there any connection, as Mum seemed to suggest, with the mental asylum? Then I peered at the appliqué figures for a few moments, willing them to yield up any clues, but the duck and rabbit were stony silent.

The mysteries were too intriguing to ignore. I added a final bullet point to my list:

- *Contact journalist to find out about quilt/
  hospital/royal connection?*

I was in the supermarket later that afternoon when he phoned.

"Could I speak to Caroline Meadows?" the man said.

"Who's this, please?"

"Ben Sweetman, from the *Eastchester Star*."

"Hello, yes, I'm Caroline," I stuttered, startled by his speedy response. It must be a quiet news day at the newspaper. "Thanks for getting back to me."

"What can I do for you?"

"I'm hoping you might be able to help me with some information about Helena Hall? As I said in my email, I gather you're a bit of an expert?"

"Journalists know a little about lots of things, but we're never experts." His voice was baritone, his laugh a deep rumble. I visualized an overweight man, maybe balding, probably in his later years, who'd been at the newspaper for decades. "Do you mind me asking why?"

"My granny was a patient there. She died quite a few years ago."

"Aah." There was a slightly awkward pause. "I'm sorry to hear that. What exactly are you trying to find out? It's just that records are always confidential, of course."

"I inherited a patchwork quilt from her, which I believe she or someone else may have made while they were patients. I was hoping to discover a bit more about the sewing and needlework they did there."

"Is this quilt something special?"

"Special to me." I hesitated, a little uncomfortable under such direct questioning. "Look, thanks so much for offering to help, but…"

"I know," he filled in after my pause. "You think I'm after a story?"

"Yes, I suppose I do," I conceded. "You are a journalist, after all."

"Local newspapers are pretty parochial, but patchwork quilts are hardly likely to make the front page, even here in Eastchester." He laughed again, with that easy chuckle. "Look, I may be able to help. I know a former nurse who worked there who might be prepared to talk to you."

"That's very kind. I really don't want to put you to any trouble. It's probably a wild goose chase anyway."

"Not to worry, wild geese are a local hack's stock in trade. I'll be in touch again shortly."

He phoned again two days later.

"My contact is happy to talk to you," he said. "Her name's Pearl Bacon. I interviewed her some years ago, when Helena Hall finally closed. She's an old lady now, but she used to work on the women's wards and she's got some interesting memories. Would you like me to arrange it?"

"Perhaps you could just give me her number?"

"She never answers the phone, too deaf, I'm afraid. But she

lip-reads well. You'd need to visit her in person. Do you come from around here?"

I hesitated, still cautious, but then thought to hell with it, I've nothing else to do with my time. There was little to lose, and I might just find out something interesting about the quilt.

"I'm in London, but my mum lives not far from Eastchester. I'm going down to visit on Saturday. Is that any good?"

There was a short pause, and then he said, "Saturday's fine for me. I've got to take my son to football in the afternoon, but I'll be free from about four o'clock. I'll see if that's convenient for Pearl."

When Mum's dementia was first diagnosed two years ago, I'd been devastated, but she seemed surprisingly sanguine.

"At least now I know what's going on," she'd said on the way home from the hospital. "It's got a name. Don't you worry about me, my darling. We all have to go sometime."

But not like this, in a slow, depressing deterioration and erosion of her personal dignity. At the time, she was still living an active, independent kind of life, driving herself all over East Anglia to visit friends, doing yoga, reading voraciously, and singing in the church choir. Now, she was losing confidence: she had stopped driving because she was afraid of losing her way, found novels no longer satisfying because she could not remember who the characters were, and even forgot to feed herself from time to time. But she refused to give into self-pity and was determined to remain independent, refusing most of my suggestions for making her life easier.

Russell and I talked about relocating to a house with a granny annex, but neither of us could face the ruinously expensive daily nightmare of commuting. Besides, we had no desire to give up our city life, and Mum would not contemplate moving away from the village where she had lived for fifty years, her friends, and the few regular activities she was still able to enjoy.

Last winter, when she'd become very ill with a chest infection, we'd visited a couple of residential homes nearby which had been recommended by friends. Both places were perfectly pleasant, warm, and comfortable with kindly staff and only the faintest whiff of incontinence. Mum had shown polite interest but refused, point-blank, to discuss the matter any further.

So for now, the daily telephone calls and trips to Essex every Saturday had become part of my routine. Our conversations often turned to past memories, but this time I had a specific agenda: to discover everything she could remember about Granny and the quilt. After lunch, I pulled out the family scrapbooks kept in a cupboard under the television.

The earliest photographs, in black and white, are so small that you have to squint closely to see faces.

"There's my darling Richard when he was a baby, and look, there he is again," Mum said, "with Jean and Arthur." The angelic boy with the shock of blond hair and a lacy dress was about three years old, beaming at the camera with a wicked grin while his parents, holding his hands on either side, stood stiffly still for the photographer.

There were snaps of his first day at school, posing with trophies for various sporting triumphs, and perhaps my favorite, as a moody teenager affecting a look of James Dean, lounging against a sports car with a cigarette hanging from his lip. He'd tidied up for graduation day, peering out uneasily from behind the tassel of his mortar board, white knuckles clutching a roll of fake parchment the photographer had probably thrust into his hand at the last moment.

I paid special attention to the photographs of Granny around this time—a tall, serious-looking woman with only the occasional hint of a smile. She appeared serene enough, certainly not the look of someone who might have had, or was about to have, a breakdown.

As we turned the page, Mum yelped with recognition, "Oh look, there's me. That was our wedding day, dear." The girl on Dad's arm, in her registry office wedding dress, looked young enough to be his daughter—as indeed she was.

"You look so much in love, Mum." I couldn't help feeling a twinge of envy.

"We were, dearest. I couldn't believe my luck. He was such a handsome man. And those eyes! Bluer than the Mediterranean and so deep you could drown in them."

More recent albums were crammed with photographs—in color now—of my own childhood, and for a while, we reminisced happily about my first tooth, first day at school, my gang of friends, and the surly, rebellious adolescent that I turned into.

"You were such a worry," she murmured.

"I didn't turn out so badly after all, did I?" Apart from no boyfriend, a huge mortgage, and no job.

"No, dearie," she said, patting my hand. "You turned out just fine."

As I closed the album, on the very back page after several blank sheets were two color snaps I'd never seen before. They must have been taken in the midseventies; one of them showed me as a child aged about three, sitting on Granny's knee. Although you can't see her face, she was holding a book, apparently reading to me. In the other, Granny was alone on the sofa, looking directly at the camera with a notebook in her hand. Something bright in the corner of the photograph caught my eye—slung over the back of the sofa. I squinted more closely.

"That's the quilt!" I nearly shouted. "The one we found in the loft, Mum."

"She was very attached to it," she said. "Used to have it on the spare bed most of the time. Wonder what it's doing there?"

Behind Granny, in the doorway, was the shadowy shape of an elderly woman, as if the photographer had caught her just entering or leaving the room. The figure was so slight that she could be a child, were it not for the gray hair cut in a simple, straight bob. Her hand, lifted to the doorknob, was also tiny, and her face half-turned away from the camera, looking at something in the corridor beyond. Even so, it was possible to make out an expression of lively amusement, as if she was reacting to a joke.

"Who's that, Mum?"

She squinted more closely and sighed. "The face is familiar, dear, but the name's gone missing." Another long silence and then, "It might be Maria."

"Maria? Granny's housekeeper?" I'd never paid much attention to the person who'd lived with Granny for a while and then seemed to disappear as quickly as she had arrived.

"Queer old thing, not really a housekeeper, more a houseguest. Pretty hopeless she was, couldn't even make a proper cup of tea," Mum said. "Jean met her at the hospital, as far as I remember, but she wouldn't hear a word against her, said she'd had a hard life. Always had a needle in her hand…" she tailed off.

"Perhaps it was her who made the quilt?"

"Could be, love. She was a bit of a mystery, that Maria. Only lived with Jean for a few years till the heart attack carried her off."

She yawned, her shoulders starting to droop. "Are we finished now, dear? I think it's time for my afternoon nap."

I tucked her up in a rug on the sofa, left a sandwich for her tea, and headed off for my appointment with Ben Sweetman.

⌒⌒

The café in Eastchester was packed with weary shoppers. Past the queue of people waiting to be served, toward the sofa area at the back, I spied a man sitting alone, his head in a newspaper.

I cleared my throat tentatively. "Mr. Sweetman, erm, Ben?"

"Caroline?" He stood up and we shook hands. He was younger than I'd expected, with less belly and more hair. "Pleased to meet you. Have a seat and let me get you a drink. What will it be?"

He was an imposing man, well over six feet tall, and broad-shouldered too, clean-shaven and, while not as overweight as I had imagined, certainly well-covered. I guessed he was in his early forties with a full head of thick, wavy brown hair going to pepper-and-salt at the temples, in a style I could only describe as *au naturel*. Definitely not my type, although there was boyishness, and something open and unguarded in that face warmed me to him.

I watched him in the queue and wondered what his wife was like. Probably petite and pretty, who loved to feel protected by this big bear of a husband. I visualized the family together, the sporty son in his early teens and perhaps a younger daughter. The perfect family unit.

"It's good of you to see me on your day off," I said, as he returned with the drinks.

"I'd only have been at home depressing myself, watching Eastchester United lose again." He laughed in that genial, open way. "Anyway, it's just exchanging one sofa for another—no great hardship there."

"How did your son do in his game?"

The proud father's smile lit up his face, crinkling the lines at the corners of his eyes. "Thomas's team lost, but he's only ten so he bounces back soon enough. I've just taken him back to his gran's for tea, and she'll spoil him rotten."

I caught my reflection in the glass behind. In the harsh uplighters of the café and without makeup, I looked pale and tired, my roots a dark stripe along my scalp, and I was dressed for housework in a scruffy T-shirt and my oldest jacket. Why hadn't I taken more trouble before coming out?

He took a sip of coffee and sat back. "So, Caroline—can I call you that?"

"Of course."

"Why are you so keen to find out about Helena Hall?"

"My granny left me a quilt when she died, which she, or someone else, sewed when they were patients there. I just want to find out a bit more about it and who made it." I hesitated, the direct gaze of his flecked hazel eyes bringing me back to full alert. "I hope you don't think this is going to make some kind of story for you?"

He looked back at me, one eyebrow slightly raised, his lips in the start of a smile. "I admit that I probably wouldn't have offered to meet you if I wasn't a little intrigued." He held out his hands. "But look, no recorder, no notebook. All off the record for now."

He was a persuasively good listener and, ignoring the whisper of caution in the back of my head, I found myself telling him more than I had intended: that Granny had been a patient at Helena Hall for a short time, and toward the end of her life, a woman called Maria, a seamstress, came to live with her as a sort of housekeeper. That my forgetful mother said she thought the quilt was somehow associated with Helena Hall. I pulled out the photograph. "This is my granny. You can just see a bit of the quilt in the corner, and this is probably Maria in the background."

He perched reading glasses on his nose and peered at the snapshot. "Tell me more about this quilt. There must be something special about it for you to be so curious." As I hesitated, he cocked his head to one side with that slight smile again. "There is, isn't there?"

It was a good question: *why* was I so interested in the quilt? Yes, there was the strange little verse, Jo's interest in the royal silks, and Mum's intriguing snippets of information about Maria and the mental asylum. But there was something more, something I couldn't yet put my finger on, which drew me to the mystery, made me want to know more, brought me to this crowded café, talking to a stranger.

"Look," he said, checking his phone. "You don't have to tell me now, but this person I mentioned who worked as a nurse at Helena Hall is expecting us at four-thirty. Her name's Pearl Bacon. Shall we go and meet her?"

We took a short cut through a soulless modern shopping center, down a graffiti-splattered underpass, across a small scruffy park, and into a quiet residential area of Victorian terraced houses. As we walked, Ben talked passionately about how generations of town planners had managed to destroy the medieval town center that had been built on the street lines of an important Roman settlement.

"I lived here for eighteen years and never noticed any of this stuff," I said. "And you're not even from around here, are you?"

"You can probably tell I'm originally from oop north." He exaggerated the flattened vowels for effect. "But I've been here years, too long really."

"How long?"

"Twenty years or so. Started here as a cub reporter, did some shifts on the nationals when I was young and energetic, became disillusioned by the corruption and the backhanders, saw the job here as chief reporter, got married, and settled down. It's not a bad life."

"What's kept you here?" I'd spent my teenage years desperate to get away.

"Everyone gets bored with their job sometimes, but when you work for a local rag, you tend to get involved with people's causes, and before you know where you are, you're passionate about them too. Like Helena Hall. Of course the place had to close, but they should have kept the buildings in better shape so they could be restored into flats or whatever, and lots of people cared deeply about that, so I got pulled in. There was a beautiful function room and theater, with a stage and sprung floor and chandeliers, the lot, but it's been pretty much destroyed by vandals and fire. It's a sad sight these days. You'll have to take a look one day, before they knock the place down completely."

We turned into a street of small terraced houses, stopped at a door which led directly onto the pavement, and rang the bell. A cat glared at us indignantly between lace curtains in the front window as we waited. Eventually we heard a bolt being drawn, and the door opened to reveal a round, rosy-faced old lady, squinting at us with a perplexed expression.

"Hello, Pearl, it's Ben Sweetman. From the *Eastchester Star*, remember?" he said loudly. "I work with Julie, and she said she'd asked if I could drop by this afternoon? This is my friend Caroline."

Confusion slowly transformed into recognition and she smiled, revealing brilliant white dentures far too large for her mouth. "Ah yes. Julie said you were coming." She turned to me. "Are you his girlfriend?"

"Oh no," I stuttered. "We only met an hour ago."

"I won't have to fight you for him then." She giggled girlishly. "But what are we doing here on the step? Come in, come in, you are both very welcome."

She let us into a tiny front parlor like the stage set for a forties play: flowery wallpaper, the cast-iron fireplace with an embroidered fire screen, and an art deco clock on the mantelpiece. In the corner was a glass-fronted cupboard crammed with china animals. My vintage-obsessed friends would have shelled out a fortune for it.

"Would you like tea or I've got lemonade?" She began to hobble toward the kitchen.

"Why don't you let me get it?" Ben said.

"That's very kind. A glass of lemonade would do fine for me." She lowered herself with a grateful sigh onto an overstuffed chintz sofa, complete with lace antimacassar, and patted the seat beside her. Then she reached for a pair of dusty bifocals, put them on, and peered at me as I sat down. "What was your name again, dear? You'll have to speak up, you know, and let me see your face. I'm a bit deaf these days."

"It's Caroline, Mrs. Bacon. Caroline Meadows," I said, enunciating as clearly as possible. "Ben tells me you were a nurse at Helena Hall."

"Call me Pearl, please," she said, taking off the glasses. "Yes, worked there for decades. Knew the place inside out. What do you want to know?"

"I've inherited a patchwork quilt from my grandmother. She was a patient at Helena Hall for a short while, and we think that she, or someone she knew, made the quilt while they were in the hospital." I handed her the photograph. "That's my Granny Jean, the quilt is over the sofa, and in the background is someone we think she met at Helena Hall, called Maria."

Pearl put her glasses on again and squinted at the photograph. "Sorry, dearie, don't recognize either of them. In any case, I don't think I remember a Jean, or a Maria, my dear. Did you know their surnames?"

"My grandmother was Mrs. Jean Meadows."

She shook her head again. "Rings no bells, I'm afraid. Of course there were thousands of women there in my time. I can't remember them all."

Ben returned, bearing a tray with glasses of lemonade, handed them around, and perched on a chair which seemed altogether too small for his frame.

Pearl peered again at the photograph. "You're quite sure they were patients at Helena Hall?"

"That's what my mother told me. Granny suffered some kind of nervous breakdown and was only an inpatient for a few weeks, but we don't really know why Maria was in there or for how long."

"Lots of them like that, stuck there for no good reason, only that their husband or their family didn't want them anymore," she mused, shaking her head sadly. "It was a convenient place to hide them away."

I'd heard about this sort of thing in Victorian workhouses, but it was shocking to learn that it was still going on within Pearl's lifetime, perhaps even when my granny was a patient. It was a chilling thought. "What did they do all day?"

"The ones who got it bad—who really *did* need to be in there—did very little apart from an hour of exercise in the airing courts each day. Drugged up to the eyebrows, of course," Pearl said.

"Airing courts?" Ben asked.

"Fenced areas the patients were let out into for fresh air," Pearl said. "Like animals in a zoo, I always used to think, poor buggers. But the lucky ones got work in the laundry, on the cleaning teams, or in the workshops, the sewing room, that sort of thing. Some of them said they quite enjoyed the life they had there. It was safe, you know, from whatever they had been afraid of outside, warm, regular food, and they had friends. I knew a few who refused to leave when the time came."

"Tell me about the sewing room," I prompted. "What sort of work did they do?"

"They made clothes, mostly, for the other patients but also for sale," Pearl said.

I began to fear we'd reached a dead end when her face brightened. "Ah, now I remember, dearie. There was one woman who they said did exceptional needlework. What was her name? Come on, brain." She tapped her temple with a frail finger. "That's it…Queenie! That was it."

She took a sip from her glass, scratched her head again, and muttered to herself with the effort of remembering. Finally, she said, "She had delusions. Lots of 'em had delusions, you understand. No one believed her, of course. It was part of the illness. Some thought that they were the Virgin Mary, or Boadicea. Then there was Lady Godiva, who took her clothes off all the time. But we didn't take any notice, 'cause talking about it only encouraged them.

"But Queenie? Let me try and remember—that's it, she was called that 'cause she believed she was a queen. No, that's not right. She'd *worked* for the queen." She gave a wheezy giggle. "Or at least that's what the voices seemed to be telling her, the funny old baggage. That's why everyone called her Queenie."

A shiver started at the top of my head and traveled down my spine. "Tell me a bit more about her," I asked, trying to keep my voice calm.

"She was quite a character, but no trouble. Had a couple of

friends she hung around with, and of course, they went to the sewing room every day to earn a penny or two for smokes and nylons, that sort of thing. It was a quiet kind of life, but they seemed happy enough. Of course in later years, the ones like Queenie were allowed out into the grounds for walks and that."

"Didn't they try to run away?" Ben asked.

"Where would they run to?" Pearl said with a gentle smile. "They had no families, not that we could tell. No, they liked it at the Hall. It was their whole lives, for some of them."

"If Queenie was a nickname, do you know what her real name was?" I asked.

"Sorry, my dear, it's such a long time ago." She shook her head and sighed quietly. Out of the corner of my eye, I could see Ben gathering up his jacket.

"One last thing," I said, choosing my words carefully. "Did the hospital ever have any royal visitors, or any other kind of royal connection that you remember?"

She snorted. "Huh, not much chance of that, dearie. Out of sight, out of mind, that's what mental health was in those days, probably still is today. We never had so much as a visit from the local mayor, let alone royalty." She handed back the photograph, took off her glasses, and rubbed her eyes. "Sorry, my dear, I haven't been much help to you, have I?"

"It's been fascinating." I leaned over to shake her hand. "Thank you so much."

"Would you like a drink or something to eat before you head off?" Ben asked as we walked back down the road from Pearl's house. I was hungry and had a two-hour drive ahead of me. It seemed like a good idea.

The Victorian pub at the junction of three streets of terraced houses had been ruined by a cheap gastro makeover and was now bereft of any character it might once have had. Matching mock-oak tables and chairs were tightly packed and uniformly arranged, a flame-effect gas fire spluttered ineffectively in the hearth, and a blackboard offered the usual unimaginative items clumsily repackaged as local fare: Essex ham and field-grown eggs (whatever they were), Blackwater Island Fisherman's Pie, steak and chips. Barely anything for a vegetarian.

Apart from an elderly couple in the corner, Ben and I were the only customers.

"Sorry about this. I didn't realize it was quite so grim," he whispered as we waited to be served by a spotty teenager engaged on his mobile phone in a conversation of apparently international importance. "Must have been revamped since I was here last. Shall we go somewhere else?"

"It's fine." I gave what I hoped was a reassuring smile. But it wasn't really all that fine. This place was exactly why I'd been so determined to escape from Eastchester and never wanted to return: the dreary resignation of it all, the low expectations, the small-town pretentiousness. It just capped my low mood: Pearl's stories of Helena Hall had saddened me, especially the thought that my granny might have had to endure such treatment, even for a short while. And I was no closer to discovering anything which might have led me to Maria. There was an uncomfortable silence as we sat down with our drinks.

"I'm sorry Pearl wasn't a lot of help," Ben said. "Have you got any other leads?"

"Only Mum's memories and the photograph."

"What was that you mentioned about a royal visit?"

I skirted around the question. "Pearl is a lovely lady, and her stories were fascinating, but I'm afraid I've wasted your time. It's only an old piece of patchwork, after all."

"That's not what you suggested in the café earlier." He smiled sweetly enough, but there was a catch of irritation in his voice. "You said it was a precious heirloom."

"It is," I stuttered, wrong-footed. "Don't get me wrong, I'm really grateful for your time, Ben, but I don't think I'm going to find out any more through the hospital connection."

"Sorry, too many questions. It's a bad habit of mine."

"Let me ask you some then," I said, trying to fill the awkward silence. "Tell me about your family. What does your wife do?"

He mumbled something about "not a lot to tell," and "it's a bit complicated," then fell quiet again. After that, we struggled to make desultory conversation about the closure of the mental hospital, Victorian architecture, and his passionate support for the failing local football club until finally our food arrived.

The cheese in my toasted sandwich was bright orange and smelled like rubber, and a pathetic few leaves on the side of the plate looked wilted and vinegary. His fish pie had clearly been microwaved, burned at the edges and glutinous-looking in the center. I watched him poking it suspiciously with a fork, and then, as I picked up my sandwich, the cheese slithered out from between the slices of soggy white toast into a gloopy mess down the front of my sweater.

"Oh, for God's sake." I cursed my clumsiness, pushing the plate away in disgust and trying to scoop the cheese out of my lap. I grabbed a bunch of paper napkins and managed to clear up most of the mess, then took myself off to the ladies' washroom to clean up.

Ben looked up with a grin as I returned to the table. "Not really your day?"

"Too right. I give up." I laughed, finally managing to see the humor of it all.

"Me too," he said, grimacing. "This is possibly the worst fish pie I've ever tried to eat. I'm so sorry this has been such a disaster. Shall we try somewhere else?"

"Thank you, but I've got a long journey," I said. "If you don't mind, I think I'll hit the road."

In the doorway, we wavered, struggling to find the appropriate parting gesture: handshake, hug and/or cheek kiss? My face only came up to his chest, so a hug would have been embarrassing unless he stooped, and a handshake felt too formal. Eventually he resolved the dilemma by leaning forward as I stood on tiptoe, and we managed an awkward single cheek kiss.

"Keep in touch," he said. "Let me know how you get on with your quilt search."

7.

ANOTHER CASSETTE, MISS? I CAN'T IMAGINE WHY you want to go to all this trouble and expense to record the ramblings of a crazy old woman.

"Your story is important for my research, you know. To help us understand the historical context of mental health care."

Historical context, is that what it is? I call it the story of a sad little life, but if you insist. Now, where did I get to?

"You'd just had a night to remember with the prince."

She laughs, with a hoarse, asthmatic chuckle.

All the years and all the drugs and treatments have so addled me brain it's sometimes hard to recall me own name, but nothing blots out the memories of that night. Call me a silly old fool, but I believed him then and have no reason to doubt what he told me, even all these years later.

A long pause, and then: "What was it you believed?"

The answer comes in a dying phrase so soft it is almost inaudible.

That he loved me, dearie, like he said.

Even the squeak of the cassette rolling in its spindles cannot conceal the profound silence that follows. Then the voice starts again, a little cracked at first but becoming stronger, more defiant.

Oh yes, I can see that look in your eyes. Just like the rest of them, the trick-cyclists and the nurses and the therapists; they all think it's some madwoman's crazy fantasy. I don't blame you. If we was sat in different chairs and you was doing the telling, I'd probably be thinking the same. Even Nora, who knows the truth because she was there, says I was duped by a boy whose only thoughts were for himself and his own desires. "Look at how he turned out," she would say. "Let down the country and sided with the enemy."

All I can say is that perhaps for the first time in my short life, I felt loved, genuinely loved, for myself. And it's hard to let go of that feeling, even when you find out it was all a sham.

He was true to his word, at least for a while. He wrote to me a few times—the envelopes were addressed in a different hand, of course: he must have asked a mate to do it for him. He talked about his sea voyage and being bored at Sandringham in Norfolk, which sounded a long way away. In the spring of 1912, it must have been, there was a letter from Paris where he was learning French.

I found out from dining hall gossip that he had spent a few days at the palace in September, but there was so much going on upstairs, I reasoned that he hadn't been able to find an excuse to call for me. Then the news was that he had "gone up" to Oxford—which I later found out was not a town on top of a hill, but a university—and the letters stopped. Nora had got friendly with the chambermaids and spent her time off with a different crowd, which left me lonely so I just hung about between our bedroom and the sewing room, nursing my broken heart.

Months went by, and then a whole year. Miss G never returned to work, and the week I turned seventeen, I was promoted to the position of chief needlewoman, which was a very big event in my life, let me tell you. I'd always been a nobody, but now I was a somebody, a *chief* somebody. But it made it even harder with Nora; she didn't like the fact that I had been raised up over her, and I'd have felt the same if the boot had been on the other foot. She was so distracted with her new friends that her work became shoddy and slapdash, and once or twice I had to pull her up, which went down like a lead balloon, and after that she spoke to me even less.

While all this was going on, I was very, very lonely. I even thought about running away. But what could I do outside? I'd end up a streetwalker, more than likely. And though you might doubt it from what I've told you, I wasn't that kind of girl.

One day, I was hunting in the sewing cupboard for a piece of bias binding in a particular color when down at the bottom, under a pile of uniform fabrics, I found a box of scraps. There was wools and cottons, satins and velvets, even silk brocades with little flower designs and silver threads running through them. Miss G must have kept them for some reason, but most of the scraps was so small I couldn't think what they'd've been useful for. Then I remembered the quilt I'd started at The Castle, what got left behind. Looking through these beautiful strips and squares, I got the notion that perhaps I could start a new quilt, to keep me hands and thoughts busy in the lonely times.

I was just about to stuff some of the fabrics into my pockets so's I could get started on something when I got an attack of the nerves.

"What if someone notices?" I thought to myself. "I could be accused of theft."

But after a few days, I got to thinking that by the time Miss G got back, she'd never remember what was there, so I started taking a few scraps at a time, hidden under my uniform, back to the bedroom and hiding them in the kit bag under my bed. All over that long winter, I got a bit possessed by it, working on the design in every spare moment—it was a way of escaping my loneliness. Then I set to cutting out the fabric shapes, tacking them onto paper templates, ready for sewing them together in the right patterns.

By the time spring 1914 arrived, I'd completed the central panel, an embroidered lover's knot, a double row of pale lavender chain stitch in twelve-strand spun silk twist onto a square of beautiful cream silk brocade, made up of four smaller squares. I turned the square onto one point, cut eight more triangles of brocade, and sewed them together in pairs to create four larger triangles which would fill in the corners to complete a new square. I got it into my foolish head that by creating a symbol of my love for the prince, I was keeping it alive for the future, and even dreamed, poor mug that I was, that we might one day sleep together beneath my quilt.

Nora had been stepping out with a footman called Charlie for about six months, and she was so brimming with happiness she couldn't keep it to herself. At work, she talked about the lad all the time. He seemed nice enough, even though he had an outbreak of spots on his face like a raisin pudding and had to wear pancake makeup when in uniform to avoid upsetting them upstairs.

I was ever so glad to have her friendship back, even though I now played second fiddle to Charlie. Being a footman, he ate in the main servant's hall and heard a higher level of gossip than us lowly maids, which is how I learned that the prince was back in London to enjoy his first "season." The only time I'd ever heard that phrase used before was about rutting dogs, and Nora soon confirmed it was a similar thing for humans. "It's when posh boys are introduced to posh girls and matched up for marriage," she told me, and it was bitter news to my ears, hearing about the endless round of balls and parties and many tales of how the prince loved to dance and the beautiful young ladies who flocked to his side.

The cracks in my heart were well and truly broken and then, at the end of July, when we heard that Britain had declared war with Germany, the rest of the world also seemed to be falling apart. Charlie talked about signing up to fight, and Nora was desperate to stop him.

In November, quite out of the blue, I was on my own in the sewing room when Finch appeared at the door and ordered me to report to the prince's chamber immediately. Well, of course, I went into a spin, flapping around to make sure I had everything I might need in my "basket of necessaries."

This was not the usual time—it was the middle of the afternoon—and as I stood outside his door pinching my cheeks and biting my lips to give them a little color, my heart was like cannon fire in my chest and my nerves jangled so much I was afraid I might faint before I could step over the threshold. The only thing keeping me on my feet was sheer bloody-mindedness. I refused to have him open the door and find me passed out in a heap on the ground.

Nearly two years had gone by since we last met, but he never even batted an eyelid.

"Dear Maria, my favorite seamstress," he shouted. "What a splendid sight. Come in, come in, I am so pleased to see you." He was handsomer even than before, less boyish and more manly. The fuzz around his chin had thickened into a bristly afternoon shadow.

As I tried to curtsey, my legs went to jelly.

"What can I do for you, Your Highness?" I kept my eyes lowered, afraid to meet his. I knew that if I did, I would be lost again.

"Drop the formality, please, little one." He took my hand and led me to the chaise. "I do have a small task for you, but for the moment, come and tell me what you have been doing with yourself."

"Not so very much, sir, as you know," I said, as primly as possible. "Apart from being promoted in my work, my life is very unexciting compared with that of a prince. We servants do not go to many parties and balls as you do, sir."

He heard the edge in my voice, I suppose, and mimicked a sad face. "Ah, my little one, you have been listening to gossip, have you not?"

I nodded, a little shamefaced now, for my cheek.

"Then you must know that I am not the master of my own destiny. It is expected of me to attend these functions, but it does not mean that I enjoy them. The women—ah, the women— they are very beautiful, but they are so *vacuous*." He paused while I wondered what this could mean. "They do *fawn* so. Yes, that's the problem, because of who I am, they cling to me, simpering and giggling. It makes me want to run away to sea again, back with all my sailor mates. They couldn't care a bugger who I am." His great guffaw got me giggling and broke the ice.

"Don't you see?" He was suddenly serious again, turning my face to his and giving me both barrels of that gaze. "They are not real people like you, my pretty girl. Those society girls are like little actresses, being just what their mamas want them to be, so they can snare themselves a wealthy husband."

For a moment, I thought he might kiss me, but he gave a little sigh before letting go of my hand. "Alas, much as I would wish to, I cannot dally today. I have a rather urgent sewing task for you." He went to his closet and returned with three pairs of khaki trousers.

"It's the bugger of being so short," he said, passing them to me. "Not that you care, my dearest, but it's a matter of pride for us chaps, and I could never admit it to the official tailor. All these need shortening, by two inches. It must be invisible, impossible to tell that any alteration has been made. Can you do that?"

"Of course, sir." I tried to keep my voice businesslike even though I was sick with disappointment inside. "That is a perfectly straightforward task. I will get onto it straightaway. When do you need it by, sir?"

"This evening, is that possible? After dinner? Ten o'clock, say?"

"Consider it done, sir," I said, making hasty calculations in my head.

"And will you deliver the work in person, please, as I would like to check that it is correct?" Though his voice was formal, there was that little smile at the corner of his eyes that I recognized of old, and it raised my foolish hopes once again.

"Indeed I will if that is your wish, sir." I bent my face to hide the blush burning my cheeks.

"And we shall have a little talk like the old times, shall we?" he said with a wink. Two long years had passed without word, and now he seemed to believe that we could fall into our old ways. No, I would remain cool and distant, I told myself, not allow any further intimacies which would only break my heart once more. Even so, I nearly skipped down the corridors on my way back downstairs.

When I entered the sewing room, Nora gave me a long, fierce look, pointing at the trousers. "Whose are those?"

I said nothing and started hunting for my tape measure.

"You're flushed," she said. "Where have you been?"

Again I held my tongue, but of course she knew.

"There's only one person upstairs who's going off to war." She glared at me. "It's *him*, isn't it?"

Then I realized: of course, these were *army* trousers. Why hadn't I made the connection? The panic rose in my throat; he was going off to fight.

"For goodness' sake, don't let it happen again," she snapped.

"Let *what* happen again?" I asked, trying to stop myself blushing.

"You bloody well know what. Let *me* take the bloody trousers back." She made a grab for them, trying to pull them from my hands.

"No, Nora, he asked for *me*. I have to go." I hung onto the trousers for grim death. What would he think if Nora turned up instead of me? It would be an unforgiveable snub, and he would never ask for me again.

"Then be it on your own head. Don't expect my sympathy ever again, you stupid, stupid girl," Nora shouted into my face, before stomping out and slamming the door.

At ten o'clock sharp, I knocked on the door, and even before I could show him my careful stitching on the hems, which was so much neater than the army tailor's coarse work, he pulled me to him and kissed me, long and hard. All my good intentions to resist him evaporated in an instant. He'd been practicing on his beautiful women, I could tell, but I wasn't complaining. I was like putty in his hands; the kissing was delicious and I wanted it never to stop.

I was a reckless, foolish girl to let it happen again, but I can't say I regret it. I won't go into details to save your blushes, dearie, but all I can say is I know quite well why that Wallis woman wouldn't let him go, why she fought so hard for him and made him give up the crown. By golly, he'd learned a trick or two since those early trysts of ours.

She breaks in to an asthmatic giggle and has to clear her throat before continuing.

But then, of course, off he went, to war. He told me they wouldn't let him fight in the trenches but he was going to do all he could to get to the front line anyway, and he promised to write every day. What a fool I was to believe it. Every day passed with me barely able to breathe as Mrs. Hardy or one of her minions handed around the post to us servants after breakfast and, of course, nothing arrived for me.

But one day, after six long weeks, she finally handed me a letter, and I blushed scarlet as everyone around the table turned their faces toward me, hoping for a clue. Not bloody likely. I rushed away to the toilets and opened it in there, heart pounding, and sure enough it was from him, though his handwriting was heavily disguised.

It was short and gave little away, but it did say that he thought of me every night and called me "my love"—it was enough to keep up my hope and dreams for many a month. My quilt panel was complete, and I finished a beautiful border of pieced lozenge-shaped hexagons, in silks and satins, that would hold the secret of my love, hidden for ever.

But there was no further word from him and slowly, day by day, crack by crack, piece by piece, my heart was broken all over again. Nora's beau Charlie came home for leave at Christmas and told such tales about what life was like in the trenches as you would struggle to believe. I feared for my love but took comfort in the thought that they would surely look after the future king of England. As the war ground on into its fourth year, my despair reached rock bottom.

Then, around Christmas 1917, the talk was that the prince would be returning to England in the new year for a tour of defense plants and might be in London for a few days. It was a bitter cold night in February, the night Nora received the news about Charlie. He'd been injured weeks ago at Cambrai, they said, but had finally succumbed. She was inconsolable, taking to her bed and refusing to eat or drink, weeping fit to burst for hours on end, till I worried for her health.

When the knock came, I thought it would be one of her house-maid friends or even Mrs. Hardy the housekeeper, coming to check how she was, so I was very surprised to see Finch, stand-ing stiffly outside the door. "His Highness wishes to see you, Miss Romano," he said through gritted teeth.

I was reluctant to leave Nora, but knew I could not refuse the prince.

She lights a cigarette and sighs deeply.

Do excuse me, dearie, but the memory makes me feel a bit wobbly. I've sometimes thought to myself, if only I'd never gone, stayed to comfort Nora like a best friend should have done, my life would have been so different. But I was young and stupid, and of course I went. I knew what would happen, and that it was foolish, but I didn't care.

Another deep sigh.

I will never forget that night. When I first sat down, he placed a small box into my hands and told me to open it.

"It's a gift for you," he said with that melting look in his eyes.

My hands were shaking as I opened the box, and inside was a small round flat bottle, the shape of a pocket watch, with a medallion label with the figure 4711 and some words in a language I did not understand.

"It's a French perfume, called *eau de cologne*, smells a bit like lavender. Dab a little behind each ear—go on." This idea was so unfamiliar to me that he took it from my hands, unscrewed the little gold lid, and dabbed it onto his fingers, then onto my neck. Then he brought his face close to mine and drew in a long breath.

"Perfect," he said. "I knew it would suit you. Lavender always reminds me of a sunny summer's day." Well, you can imagine that put a smile on my face, and I blushed like a beetroot but somehow that didn't seem to matter, we was so comfortable with each other. We drank sherry while he talked about his war experiences, how he enjoyed being with what he called "real people," his pleasure in being recognized for his skills and hard work and not just for being a prince, his frustration at not being allowed to go to the front line. Now the Americans were in the war, the tide would soon turn our way, he felt sure, and the war would be won within the year.

We kissed and then he asked me, would I like to? And, foolish girl, I nodded. Look at what happened to poor Charlie, I thought to myself. We have to take our fun while we can and hang the consequences. Devil-may-care—that just about sums up what I felt that evening. In the back of my head, I'm thinking that, when the war is over, he will have to marry his royal princess. So why not make hay while the sun shines?

This time we did it properly, in his bed, with our clothes off and all. It was as though the months and years had never passed, and though I was already approaching my nineteenth birthday, we were like young lovers again. He was kind and gentle, affectionate and attentive, and took me to another world where our differences did not exist. It felt like standing on a cliff edge ready to jump, to enjoy the thrill of falling, not even considering what might happen when I reached the bottom. I never wanted it to end, but of course I knew that it had to.

I've thought and thought about that night. After all that time when he was away and not even taking the trouble to write, why did I do it? Why hadn't I learned my lesson? Why didn't I face the facts? I wasn't the loose type of girl, but I'd never known life outside of the orphanage and the palace, and I was just naive. Self-destructive, the docs around here would call it, though the idea would never have entered my head at the time. The truth is that he was the only boy who had ever shown me any affection, which is what I craved more than anything, like a drug. And like a drug addict, I couldn't say no.

I never saw him again because, soon afterward, he returned to France. The days slipped by in a fog of misery, and Nora, true to her word and anyway too concerned with her own loss, refused to talk to me.

A few weeks later, I realized that my luck truly had run out. Me monthlies failed to come. Hot baths and gin wouldn't shift it, and I even tried throwing myself downstairs but this only left me with a sprained shoulder, a black eye, and a three-day headache. I prayed hard, too, but by three months, I knew that I had, if you'll excuse the expression, cooked my goose.

There's a long silence, then a gentle voice: "Are you all right, Queenie? Can I get you anything? A cup of tea, perhaps?"

Just give me a moment, dear. Can we turn that thing off while I catch me breath?

PATSY MORTON RESEARCH DIARY
JUNE 10, 1970

Spent the day interviewing M. What a dear old thing! She's so convincing and her story even brought a tear to my eye once or twice, but how am I meant to believe she had an affair with the Prince of Wales? Why in heaven's name would a man who had the cream of London society falling at his feet want to seduce a servant girl?

But she's such a sweetie and very entertaining, and I'm enjoying letting her ramble on. Might even use her as a character in a story someday. Have already decided to include her in my research, whatever Dr. Watts says. Already on second cassette—need to buy more.

Transcribed some of the tapes—a long old job—and befriended technician in the university labs to get my photos developed. Had to pretend I fancied him, and even ended up having to kiss him, just for a set of photos! Still, it was worth it—I didn't want to have to go to Boots.

Here's the first entry from her medical notes:

Miss R. was admitted to Helena Hall three weeks ago and was certified as suffering from paranoid delusional mania. Apparently she was in service (as a seamstress) at a large house, but since it appeared that she had no members of her family still alive, her employer had no option but to request certification. Upon admission, M. exhibited patterns of extreme behavior, making fantastical claims, including attempts at suicide, putting not only herself but other patients and staff in danger, requiring physical restraint and treatment with paraldehyde which has proved initially successful.

Am def. going to carry on with M.

8.

AFTER THE FRUITLESS MEETING WITH PEARL, I decided to concentrate on setting up my new interior design business, but Jo was still determined to prove her theory about the quilt silks and had fixed up a meeting with her boss, Annabel Smythe-Dalziel, Senior Curator of Costumes, Royal Palaces.

The old leather case was too heavy to carry on the Tube, so I hauled down my wheelie bag from the top of the wardrobe, lined it with an old cotton sheet, and then carefully folded the quilt, patchwork side inward, before zipping up the case. It fit perfectly.

It was a bright, cold day, and Kensington Palace seemed to glimmer in the low January sun. I waited nervously in the entrance hall, surrounded by crowds of overexcited schoolchildren and harassed teachers, until Jo arrived. She opened a door hidden in the paneling into the backstairs area and led the way along several dark corridors and into a white, well-lit room with a large table in its center.

Miss S-D turned out to be every bit as imperious as her name suggested. I guessed she was in her midfifties, tall and rangy, with a long face framed by stiffly lacquered hair held firmly in place with the kind of velvet hair band you only ever see in *Tatler* magazine. Her handshake was like a vise, her voice clipped, and I understood immediately why everyone was in awe of the woman.

Jo passed me a pair of white cotton gloves, and out of the corner of my eye, I could see her stifling a fit of the giggles as I nervously put them on back to front, with my little fingers in the thumb side. Then I had to take them off and start all over again as the two of them, already gloved, stood waiting.

"Let's see what you've got then," Miss S-D said briskly.

The quilt looked dull and shabby in the harsh glare of the artificial lighting as we unfolded it across the table, out of place in this pristine environment. I muttered apologies about the state of it as she leaned forward, peering through her magnifying glass.

"Hmm. Medallion design, central square on point, nothing unusual." There was a long silence as she scrutinized the embroidered central triangle and feather designs. Jo and I waited, suspended in anticipation, as the minutes ticked past on the wall clock above our heads.

Eventually, she stood up and stretched her back. "This really is *exceptionally* interesting. Tell me, Miss Meadows"—she pointed at the embroidery—"what do you see?"

"A lover's knot?"

"Most handsomely embroidered it is too," she said approvingly, handing me the magnifying glass. "But, as I think you know, it is the cream damask background fabric that deserves closer attention. Take a look for yourself."

I leaned over the quilt and put my eye to the glass.

"Do you see the rose and thistle, and then at the corner, the curved edge of what would have been a garland of shamrocks?" A self-satisfied smile glinted across her horsey face. Across the table, Jo made a silent "told you so" smirk, then hastily resumed a normal expression as her boss turned to her.

"What is of particular interest, as you have already noticed,

Joanna, is that these sections of background tissue, so beautifully made up of smaller pieces, are very reminiscent of the fabrics woven by Warner and Sons to designs created by the Silver Studio for the Duchess of Teck, for the wedding dress and trousseau of her daughter Princess May. Some of the fabrics were woven with silver threads, and this certainly looks like a metallic weft although it is very tarnished." Miss S-D turned her gimlet eyes to me again. "Tell me, have you any provenance for this quilt, Miss Meadows? Joanna tells me it was left to you by your grandmother."

"That's right. But we don't think it was actually made by her. We think it might have been a woman she met, who had been a patient in a mental hospital and was apparently an excellent seamstress."

Miss S-D's face resumed its default expression of haughty skepticism. "It seems extremely unlikely that whoever it was could have got hold of royal silks in a mental hospital," she said. "Those designs were extremely closely guarded, and I have never seen any trace of them outside our own collections, the V&A, and the Warner Archive."

She leaned over once more to scrutinize the border around the inner square, with its brightly colored appliqué figures that I had so loved as a child. Eventually, she stood up and folded the magnifying glass. "The remainder is not so interesting, except for two points. It is rare for quilters to use velvets because they are difficult to handle, but what makes this even more unusual is that this velvet is handwoven and therefore likely to have been made in the eighteenth or nineteenth century, no later. After that, most velvet was woven on power looms, apart from a very few hand weavers specializing in supplying restoration projects. So it's unusual, certainly, and probably a century old, though not necessarily royal."

"What was the second point?" Jo prompted.

"The quality of the work," Miss S-D said, almost smiling. "It is exceptional." She pointed at the designs running along the outermost panel that I'd rather assumed were depictions of dawn or sunset. "These are grandmother's fan designs, still widely used by quilters today and certainly they are a more recent addition, perhaps the seventies, judging from the fabric, but the needlework is by the same hand and is still remarkable for its quality. I've examined plenty of top-notch craftsmanship, believe me, but I'd go so far as to say it is the equal of any handsewn work that I have ever seen."

"That's quite a compliment," I said.

"Indeed." A genuine smile softened the haughty expression at last.

"If the silks are authentic, would that make the quilt valuable?"

"In financial terms, probably not a great deal, depending on market interest, of course," she said. "But if those silks are what I think they are, then this piece is certainly of great historical interest, so you need to think carefully about what you want to do with it in the future. In the meantime, it would be helpful if you could find out as much as you can about its provenance." She took off her gloves, signaling that our session was coming to a close.

"One last question: do you think it is worth getting it dry-cleaned?"

Jo and Miss S-D adopted matching expressions of dismay. "Any kind of cleaning could be a disaster, Miss Meadows, unless carried out by a fully qualified fabric conservator," the curator said. "Joanna can let you have some details of good freelancers, and perhaps you could get the fabric strand-tested at the same time, just to be one hundred percent sure. Personally, I think this piece is definitely worth the investment. You *will* take great care of it, won't you?"

"I certainly will," I said. "Thank you so much for your time."

By the time we'd repacked the quilt in its sheet and zipped it back into my wheeled suitcase, it was past five, and Jo went to get her coat.

"Shall we have a drink before you head off to darkest south London?" I asked.

❧

"Are you okay?" Jo gave me a concerned look as I brought the drinks to the table—red wine for me, orange juice for her.

"I think so. Why do you ask?"

"No offense, but you look exhausted."

"I've been feeling a bit crap since the weekend. Think I've picked up some kind of tummy bug. Kill or cure," I said, taking a slug of wine. "How's things with you?"

"Get this, we've just booked a week in Morocco—three days in Marrakesh, then trekking in the Atlas mountains," she beamed. "Our first proper holiday together, ever."

"Sounds brilliant. I've always wanted to go there. When?"

"End of the month—they say the temperatures should be in the thirties."

"Lucky sods. Just don't post photos of yourselves in the sunshine or I might die of envy, stuck here in the winter gloom." I took another sip of wine. "Look, thanks so much for this afternoon. Horsey-face seems to agree with you about the silks."

"Makes a nice change."

"She really is a bit of a dragon. 'Let's see what you've got, then,'" I mimicked Miss S-D's plummy brusque tone.

"Your quilt really charmed her though," Jo said.

"It's weird, there really is something a bit bewitching about it. I spend more time thinking about the thing than planning my new business. Not a good sign."

"Have you got any further finding out who actually made it?"

I described my meeting with Pearl Bacon and her story of the patient who claimed to have worked for the queen.

"Any chance they're the same person?"

"I did wonder, but Pearl didn't seem to think so. She said lots of patients had delusions that they were famous historical figures or had connections to them, and it all sounded very unlikely. Not much to go on, I don't think."

"Whoever made it, I'd still love to know where they got those silks from."

"Me too," I said, thinking about Pearl, and Ben, and whether I would ever unravel the mystery.

As we went our separate ways, Jo to the bus and me to the underground station, the streets were still busy and the Tube platforms rammed with commuters. I squeezed myself and the wheelie into a packed car, thanking my lucky stars that I no longer had to endure this torment every day.

As I changed trains at Leicester Square, a woman tripped at the bottom of the escalator, falling to the ground immediately in front of me. Instinctively, I held out my arms to hold back the crush of people behind me and tried to help her up. She scrambled to her feet hastily, insisting in a strong foreign accent that she was not hurt. A man who claimed to know first aid offered to help, but she seemed anxious to be on her way.

Turning around to pick up my case, I thought at first that someone had moved it out of the way for safety. Then, with a sickening swell of panic, I realized that I had fallen for the oldest scam in the world.

The case was gone.

I swore loudly. What an idiot I'd been.

I scanned the crowds for a few frantic seconds, then rushed up to a busker and bellowed over his painfully amplified backing track, "Have you seen anyone with a black wheelie bag?" What a stupid question—there were dozens of people trailing by with their suitcases. He shook his head without missing a beat, as the uncaring crowds pushed past.

Cursing myself, I pushed through the crowds onto the nearest platform, desperately hoping to catch a glimpse of the case. A train thundered in, brakes screeching noisily to a halt, a mass of people climbed off, and hundreds more climbed on. The platform cleared, and I rushed to the other platform and watched the same process for the train running in the opposite direction. As the platform emptied again, the panic gave way to tears. My search was hopeless. The case, and Granny's heirloom, my precious royal quilt, had disappeared.

The transport police, once I managed to locate them, invited me into the relative peace of their control room. Feeling dizzy and faint with the shock of it all, I sat down onto a chair and gratefully sipped the glass of water they offered.

"What would you estimate the value of the lost item, madam?"

"Sentimental only, I'm afraid."

They took a full statement and assured me they would review the CCTV footage and pursue any leads. They would also alert their colleagues in the Met, but warned that my chances of ever seeing the quilt again were slim. Once the thieves discovered that there was nothing of value, they said, they would probably just discard the suitcase and its contents. Short of hunting every Dumpster or garbage can for miles around, there was little they could do.

Even in a few short days, I had grown used to the random colors and higgledy-piggledy patterns of the quilt slung on the back of the sofa, creating a bright focus in the cool cream living room. Without it, the flat looked empty, and the Scandinavian minimalism I'd once loved now felt bleak and soulless. I dug out a large tub of ice cream, the kind with bits of unbaked cookie dough in it, and ate the lot in front of a reality TV show, feeling very sorry for myself. No Russell, no job, no quilt, nothing. My earlier excitement about starting my own business suddenly felt too exhausting to contemplate.

I woke the following day feeling sick and shivery, as if I was coming down with the flu. But I'd promised to visit Mum again to sort out the boxes now that Cozy Homes had completed their work, so I swallowed several aspirin and set off.

When I arrived at the cottage, it was already midmorning, but the front door was locked and the curtains still drawn. I rang the bell and hammered the knocker; there were noises inside, but it seemed to take an age for her to appear. Eventually the latches were drawn, and when the door finally opened, it revealed a woman so changed in just a couple of days that I barely recognized her. She seemed even more shrunken, her face pale and cheeks hollow, gray hair hanging in unbrushed clumps. Her flimsy nightgown was covered in black smudges, and her bare feet were blue with cold.

"Hello dear," she said, as if nothing were wrong. "You look as though you've seen a ghost."

There was a strong smell of burning from the direction of the kitchen, and through the living room door, I could see a steady dribble of water pouring from the central light fixture. A sizeable puddle had already formed on the carpet. The kitchen was full of acrid smoke, and a pan was still smoldering on the stove under a tea towel that had obviously been used to smother the flames. A couple of other charred towels lay on the floor, and there were black cinders all over the countertop and sink.

"I was making porridge," Mum whispered from the doorway. "I'm afraid the saucepan might be a bit tricky to clean. But not to worry, there are plenty of others I can use."

"I'm more worried about *you* than the bloody saucepan," I barked, a wave of irrational anger sweeping over me. "You could have set the whole house on fire." I turned off the stove at the mains and opened the back door to let out the smoke.

Then I remembered the dripping ceiling and ran upstairs. Just as I'd feared, the bath was overflowing, taps still running. I turned them off, plunged my arm into the scalding water to pull out the plug, and threw towels onto the floor to soak up the worst of the water. Finally, I grabbed Mum's dressing gown and slippers and a blanket from her bedroom and ran downstairs again, swaddled her up like a baby, turned on the electric fire in the dining room, and sat her down in front of it.

"Sorry for shouting at you, Mum. Stay there while I make you a cup of tea and something to eat. We'll soon sort you out."

"Thank you, dear." Her face lit up with a childlike smile. "I've got myself into a bit of a pickle, haven't I?"

Much later, after more clearing up and conversations with the neighbors and the daily help, I bundled Mum and a small suitcase of her personal things into the car and set off back to London. She wasn't safe to be left alone overnight, certainly not in that damp, smoky house, so the best thing was to get her home, feed her up, and allow her to recover from what had been a terrible shock for both of us. Then we would worry about what to do next. All thoughts of the quilt were pushed far to the back of my mind.

⟡

The next day, I woke to find her bumbling about the flat in the dark, muttering to herself.

"Mum? It's not morning yet," I said, switching on the light. "What are you doing?"

"My watch says it's six o'clock, time to get up." She peered around, puzzled. "It's very odd. This hotel doesn't seem to have a bathroom."

"It's my flat, not a hotel," I said. "Let me show you."

A few minutes later, she was padding around the living room. "Shall we order tea, dear?" It was no use sending her back to bed; the day had started. She stopped by the window; her eye caught something in the street below. "Why are we staying in this hotel, dear?"

"It's not a hotel, Mum. It's my flat," I repeated, as gently as possible.

She paused in her pacing. "Your flat? Then where's Russell?"

"It's a long story. He doesn't live here anymore," I said, praying she wouldn't ask any more questions.

"I like Russell. Better than that other scruffy lot you used to hang around with." Mum sat down. "Now, what were we talking about?"

"Can you remember what happened yesterday?" I started carefully. "You were cooking porridge and the saucepan burned?"

She looked at me blankly. "I burned the porridge?"

"That's right, at the cottage. And it set off a bit of a fire in the kitchen."

"If you say so, dear."

"The thing is, Mum, it'll take a while to fix after the fire, so we need to think about where you'd like to live."

"Can't I stay here for a few days?" she pleaded in her childlike way. "Please? I like this hotel."

"Of course you can. But perhaps in the longer term, we might need to find you somewhere they can look after you properly, where they can cook your meals and do your cleaning for you," I said, holding my breath as she grappled with the concept.

"No, I don't think so, dear, do you?" she replied at last. "Not my sort of thing. I like my own company."

Winning her around was going to be a long haul. "But you will consider it, Mum, won't you?"

"Of course I will, dear," she said. "Now, what's for breakfast?"

Later that morning, when she was resting, I found a cleaning company to sort out the cottage. It had to be fixed, even if Mum never went back to live there. Although I hated the very thought, I knew that we would have to sell it before long.

The next day, after breakfast, Mum said, "I've been thinking. You know those places people go to live in? That we were talking about before?"

"Residential homes?"

"Yes, those. It's lovely staying with you, dear, but there's nothing for me to do here. And the house is such a worry these days. Do you think they might have somewhere close to Eastchester so that my friends can come and visit me?"

"That's a really good idea. Shall we look at some on the Internet?"

Over the following couple of days, we visited two homes, both within a half-hour drive of Rowan Cottage. The first one was grim from the outside, smelled of stale food inside, and the staff seemed harassed. The next, a place called Holmfield, was far more welcoming. The matron was kind to Mum, the rooms were light and airy, and best of all, they had a vacancy. The room—on the ground floor with French windows onto its own self-contained patio—was available almost immediately.

"What do you think? Would you like to come and live here?"

"Very nice, dear, very nice." Mum had been quiet most of the afternoon, meekly following me around as I talked to staff and surveyed bedrooms, dining rooms, and sitting areas.

By now, she was probably exhausted and had no real idea what a significant decision we were about to make.

"You could always come here for a trial period, Mrs. Meadows," the matron said. "A couple of weeks, perhaps? Look at it as a kind of holiday and see whether you like it." I almost kissed her.

"A holiday, that sounds like a nice idea," Mum said on the way home. "That was a very pleasant hotel, wasn't it?"

"It's not a hotel, Mum. It's a residential home. Yes, it is very nice."

"Can we afford it, dear?"

"No problem," I said, trying to reassure myself as much as Mum. The weekly fees were terrifying, and it was clear that her pension would never cover it, but we could worry about that later. "You deserve a little holiday."

"I'll give it a try then, shall I?"

For the first time in days, I felt the weight of responsibility beginning to lift from my shoulders. Perhaps things would work out fine after all.

Returning to the cottage to collect Mum's belongings was a gloomy affair. The builders had not started work yet, and our once warm, lively family home felt dismal and abandoned. Almost as soon as we were inside, she began to weep.

"I want to come home," she whimpered. Then she stood at the bottom of the stairs, chilling my heart as she called out, "Richard? Where are you, Richard?" Then she turned to me with a pitiful face, her eyes brimming. "Why isn't he here? Where's he gone?"

"Dad died years ago, Mum," I said, blinking back my own tears. "You're going to see those lovely people at Holmfield for a couple of weeks, remember? They'll keep you company."

Back at the residential home, everything seemed to run smoothly until the time came for me to leave. As we settled Mum into her new room, I tried to point out all its benefits: the private patio with the bird table, the wide windows which would bring morning sunshine, the pretty curtains and bedspread. I avoided mentioning the stains on the carpet and the inescapable fact that just beyond the patio was a parking lot.

She appeared to be content, or at least uncomplaining, as we unpacked her clothes, displayed her photographs and ornaments on the dressing table and windowsill, and then went to the conservatory for coffee. The place was busy with visiting families talking too loudly to their elderly, and obviously very deaf, relatives. We drank overbrewed coffee, and I chatted with brittle cheerfulness as we moved toward the dreaded moment when I would have to leave.

"Would you like to go back to your room for a little rest?" I asked.

She gave me that vague, puzzled look which had become so familiar. "Yes dear. This has been lovely, but it is probably time we went home now."

"This is your home now, Mum," I said, more brightly than I felt, "and the wonderful thing is that you've got your own room just down the corridor."

"But I want to go back to the cottage," she said firmly, "for Richard."

I took a deep breath. "Dad's not there now, Mum. He died years ago. You need to live somewhere else so that other people can look after you, remember?" It was all wrong, the singsong voice I found myself using, like talking to a child. I hated myself for it.

"I've changed my mind," she said, her face resolute. "I would like you to take me home now, please."

I can't do this on my own, I thought; it's just too painful for both of us. In her office, the matron was on the telephone but motioned to me to sit down. When she finished her phone call and asked how she could help, I started to sob, and by the time I'd explained what was happening and we got back to the conservatory, Mum had disappeared. She wasn't in her room either. The matron muttered into her pager, and panic rose in my throat as we searched the long corridors, knocking on doors and entering rooms. Then, as we went outside to check the garden, I caught sight, through a ground-floor window, of Mum chattering away to an old man in his bed.

As we entered the room, she smiled cheerfully. "Poor old thing, he's not feeling too good, he says. We were having a lovely conversation."

"I'll call someone to look after Eric, Mrs. Meadows," the matron said, taking her arm with practiced calm. "You can see him later, but it's probably time to get ready for supper now.

Come with me and your daughter and let's see if we can find your own room, shall we?"

She whispered into my ear, "Probably best to give your mother a kiss and head off now. Don't you worry, I'll take over from here. She will be fine."

❧

By the time I got outside into the parking lot, the tears were streaming again, and the sense of guilt was like a rock in my gut. What right did I have to take away my mother's freedom? She had given so much to me. Surely I should be prepared to look after her, now that she needed me?

But living together at the flat would be difficult, if not impossible, and the only other choice would be for me to live at Rowan Cottage. I'd go mad buried in the countryside without any friends, or a job…well, I had no job keeping me in London anymore, of course, but all my contacts were there for the new interior design business I hoped to build. Moving out to the countryside would never work. And besides, much as I loved my mother, I simply could not imagine becoming her full-time caregiver.

Lots of old people live very happily in residential homes, I tried to convince myself. We just had to get over the difficult first few weeks, until everything settled down.

9.

IS THAT THING RUNNING AGAIN? WHERE DID WE LEAVE off, can you remember?

"You discovered that you were pregnant, and you were trying to get rid of the baby."

Oh my Lord, what a place to start.

She sighs and clears her throat.

I was three months pregnant, out of wedlock, and he'd disappeared back to France with never a word. I knew that I'd lose me job and had no one to turn to. Each night I lay in bed weeping silently so as not to alert Nora or the maids. I could not imagine how life could go on, and the thought of ending it all was never far from my mind.

The River Thames was quite close by, and it wasn't uncommon to read in the newspapers of them poor souls who'd jumped from a bridge into the cold, dark water, their corpses discovered downstream several days later. But in truth, I was too much of a coward to attempt anything so drastic, so I just tried to blank the whole thing out of my mind and got on with work. I was nearly five months gone when Nora noticed.

"For Christ's sake, look at you. Whatever have you gone and done?" she whispered one evening as we undressed for bed. The maids were asleep already, of course, so we ended up sitting on the floor outside the door, with me sobbing on her shoulder.

"Have you tried to get rid of it?"

"I've tried everything," I wailed. "Nothing works. I'm done for, Nora."

"Have you written to him? You never know, he might take some responsibility, help you out somehow."

"There's nothing he can do, Nora. He's away at the war."

"The bastard," she hissed.

Even then, I still loved him so much that I made excuses. "I did write and tell him," I lied. "The post from France is very unreliable."

"You poor bloody fool. When will you ever learn?"

"But what am I going to do now, Nora? No one will ever employ me in this state."

"What you are going to do, my love, is go back to The Castle and ask the nuns if they will look after you till you've had the baby," she said firmly. "Then you can get it adopted and go back to work."

Even as she spoke, the baby fluttered in my belly, and I knew I would never give it up, no matter how hard life might become. Nora stopped badgering me after a bit. As the child moved more and more, I fell in love with it and was glad now that my efforts to lose it had been unsuccessful.

I started the next panel on the quilt, holding in my heart a picture of the child wrapped in it, sleeping sweetly in his crib. Such love went into those tiny embroidery stitches, that fine appliqué! I still think it's the best work I have ever done.

Meantime, of course, my belly went on growing, and although careful adjustments to my uniform helped to conceal the bump for a few more months, by September it was really starting to show. The day would come soon enough.

A few weeks later, Mrs. Hardy called me into her room and looked pointedly at my bulging belly. "Miss Romano, as you will probably appreciate, your condition makes it impossible for us to continue employing you," she said with a pinched voice. "You will pack your bag and meet me here in twenty minutes."

"Where…?" I started, but she held up her hand.

"You will be looked after," she said, and my heart lifted, poor fool that I was, thinking that I might be sent away to have the child and then allowed to return. "No further questions. Now go."

I ran to the sewing room. Nora's face told me that she already knew. She'd eavesdropped Finch and Hardy talking about me. They'd clocked that it was the prince's child, she said, and she'd heard Mrs. H say "we'll have to take care of it," but nothing more.

"She says I've got to leave now, but they won't say where I'm going," I blubbered. "Oh God, I am going to miss you so much, Nora."

She took me in her arms, stooping down for me as usual, and stroked my hair. "It'll work out, you know. It always works out somehow. You've survived plenty of bad things in your life and you'll survive this one too. Write when you get there, and I'll come and see you on my days off." I nodded, mute with misery, and then ran upstairs to pack.

My belongings were precious few, but what I had was truly precious: the panel of quilting that I'd started for the prince, along with the scraps of silk that I'd half-hitched from Miss G's box, was already in the old kit bag I'd brought from the orphanage. I had kept it there, under the bed, for secrecy and safe storage. On top of this, I threw in my few belongings: some socks and boots, the single dress for Sunday best, my hairbrush and the cherished bottle of the lavender water, along with the barely opened Bible the nuns had given me when I left The Castle.

When I got back to Mrs. Hardy's room, Finch was standing at the door.

"You're to come with me, Miss Romano," he said, in a somber voice.

I thought this a little odd, for a lowly seamstress being chaperoned by the prince's valet, but assumed that as his master was away, he had little else to busy himself with.

"Where are we going, Finch?" I asked.

"I am not at liberty to divulge the location," he said formally. "But you will be quite safe there, don't you worry."

We took a motorized cab, which was alarming enough in itself, and when we reached the station, the sight of all those train engines, steaming like great angry metal animals in their pens, was terrifying. But once we climbed into the carriage and set off, I became so fascinated watching the houses and factories and fields go by that I forgot my fears and even my worries about the future. After staying silent for the whole journey, Finch finally declared that ours was the next stop, and we climbed out and took another cab.

Well, as you know, I've lived in large buildings all me life, but I'd never seen such a huge, rambling place before, nor anything in the world like it in the newspapers or penny magazines. Helena Hall looked like a mansion when we pulled up, only brand new and more spread out than Buckingham Palace, what with its guard house, the grounds reaching as far as I could see, the large central building with its high clock tower, and all the other villas in the distance. There was trees and lawns and flower beds being planted, all new, with gardeners tending them.

"You've fallen on your feet again," I said to myself. How little I knew.

It was a bit of a shock to be met by a man in a white coat, but he shook my hand all civil-like and introduced himself as the medical superintendent and told me not to worry because I would receive the best possible care. I asked his name, and he said Doctor Wallis and looked at my belly, and poor fool that I was, that's what I took him to mean.

I turned to Finch and was about to tell him that I didn't need to be in a hospital as I was only having a baby, but at that moment, he pulled out a large brown envelope from the inside pocket of his greatcoat and passed it to the doctor with an odd glance that I couldn't read.

"The terms we agreed?" he asked.

The doctor nodded and put his finger to his lips. "It will all be taken care of, sir," he said, "with the greatest discretion."

I got all flustered then, saying I was perfectly well and didn't need a doctor, thank you, and anyway I didn't have any money to pay for one, but the doctor calmed me, saying again that I would be given the best possible care and it wouldn't cost me a penny. I turned to Finch again, but he was already back in the cab, closing the door with a slam and looking straight ahead as the tires spun on the gravel driveway. I never saw hide nor hair of him again, but what did I care? He was no friend of mine.

"Come this way, my dear," the doctor said, taking my elbow. He took up my bag, and we climbed the steps through the main entrance doors and an echoing hallway. We walked for what seemed like miles along a wide, straight corridor with gaps for windows but with no glass, all open to the fresh air. The floors and walls were tiled in shiny green, up to about head height, and above that, the red brick this whole hospital is made of. Heaven knows, they must have kept the local brickworks going for years when they first built the place. All the time, he's talking to me, telling me how this was the best hospital of its kind in the world, with all the top doctors and the best possible care, and I'm beginning to think the prince has organized this for me, so I can have our baby in comfort and safety and will be looked after until the time we can be together again.

The mind can play terrible tricks, you know. Every so often, as we walked, we would pass heavy metal doors, painted in the same sickly green, and from inside, we could hear the most terrifying howls, like dogs baying at the moon, what set my skin tingling with fear. And even then, I wasn't suspicious: I just supposed they was crying out with pain of childbirth.

Finally we stopped at one of the doors, and he took out a heavy key. As it opened, the first thing to hit me was the smell, a stench of piss and carbolic, enough to make you faint. Ahead of us was a long room with dozens of beds arranged along either side—around thirty in all—and in them, or wandering between them, were women so shabby and in such a state that they seemed barely human. Their clothes were baggy sacks of rags, worn and soiled, and some were barely covered. Madness has no respect for modesty, one of the nurses said to me later, and I've remembered it to this day.

As we went in, the women nearest turned to look at us, their faces either terrifyingly blank or screwed up in agony, then some of them set up wailing like I'd never heard before—the sound that chills your soul. The nurses was trying to settle them or get them into bed, and even in that brief moment, I could see it was a hopeless task, like herding cats. This was not the sort of hospital I had expected. I started to panic and looked around for somewhere I could run, to escape, but the doctor gripped my arm like a vise.

The door clanged shut behind us. I will remember that sound as long as I live—it was the sound of my freedom being taken away.

One of the nurses came toward me with a smile pinned to her ugly face and said hello and welcome. Being a well brought up convent girl, I started to say good afternoon and my name was Miss Romano, and they seemed to have got it wrong as I didn't really need to be in the hospital to have my baby, but I could see her face not listening and even as I was speaking, a kind of animal survival instinct seemed to take hold of my legs. I took off down the ward as fast as I could run, between the rows of iron bedsteads, weaving between the women and their white faces like rows of moons, throwing myself against the door at the end of the room.

Of course it was locked, and they soon caught up with me, pinning me down as I shouted and snarled, scratched and tried to bite anything which came into range, like a trapped rat. They picked me up and held me down onto a bed as I felt my skirt being lifted and then the fierce pain of a bloody great hypodermic being stuck into me bum.

After that, I knew nothing more.

It must have been the shock of it all, but just a few days later the pains started, and before I knew it, I was in labor.

There's a sharp intake of breath as if she is being pricked again by that needle, and then she clears her throat a few times.

"Are you all right? Can I get you a glass of water?"

Just give me a moment or two, to catch meself up again. They're painful memories and all, the worst.

"Please, take your time."

Another long moment passes before the voice starts again, lower and more somber now.

They never let me hold him, did you know that? By God, that labor was so long and agonizing I felt sure I was going to die. The only thing what kept me going through that terrible night was the thought of holding my child, our child, in my arms. But they took him away, and though I swear I heard him cry, they told me he died shortly afterward, poor little mite. A boy, they said. Just think of it, he would have been heir to the throne had he lived, because the prince never did have any other children, not that anyone knows of at least. If only they had let me hold him, I might have been able to accept it better. But they didn't.

It was the day they declared peace, Armistice Day, though I only learned that later. It brought me no peace, no peace at all.

Her voice fades away and there's a long pause, then she sighs deeply and starts again.

Have you got children, dearie? No, you're too young just yet. But let me tell you, once you have carried a baby in your belly for nine months and felt its every movement, the little leaps of surprise at loud noises, the way it wriggles getting itself comfortable for sleep, the little bumps in the skin of your belly its knees and elbows make as they press from the inside, you are already completely in love with the little scrap even though you have never seen it with your eyes and it has never yet taken breath. It's a love that's hard to imagine if you've never experienced it, so total it fills you up, drenching your whole body like a wet sponge, so there's no room for feeling anything else.

Then, in a moment, all that is gone and it feels like they have torn your heart out, along with the baby. I've known despair in my life, and plenty of it, but that was the blackest...

Another long pause is interrupted by the familiar sounds of the cigarette pack rustling, the click of the lighter, the outgoing sigh of smoke.

Looking back, it turned me into a wildcat. I was fearless with anger, crazy with grief. I come into this place a sane woman, but by now I was just as mad as the rest of them, just as unkempt and disheveled as those lost souls I'd seen on my first day. They kept me drugged, of course, stop me trying to escape or attack the nurses. I spent years moldering in the fog of phenobarbital, or the alternatives, which was shouting at yourself in a padded room or being tied up in strong clothes.

"Strong clothes?"

Sorry, love, that's loony bin language, ain't it? That's what they used to call the straitjackets, made out of canvas, with arms that tied up. It's no fun, I tell you. Several times, I got close to killing meself, I was that miserable and that desperate. I figured that there was nothing left to live for, and anyway, life in this place wasn't worth living. But when you're being watched night and day, and your head is fuzzy with drugs, it's not that easy to do away with yourself. It takes some planning and effort, I can tell you, and it was never that successful.

One time, I managed to wangle myself a bed in the corner of the ward, furthest away from the nurses' station. To kill myself, I needed to stay awake and somehow avoid the nightly sleeping pill they would force you to take, standing over you until you had swallowed it down. This time, I stuck it in between my teeth and my gums so that it didn't go down with the water, and then spat it out under my pillow once the nurse had moved on to the next bed. It felt like a small triumph, just managing that, taking control of my own destiny.

Then, in the middle of the night, when the nurses was snoring at their desk, I started to rip up the sheets into narrow strips to make a kind of rope. By God, in a silent ward, the noise of tearing cotton is as loud as a crack of thunder, and I was sure it would wake the whole hospital. It took ages, doing it slow to keep it quiet, and when I'd got a few strips, I knotted them together and put a chair onto the bed so as I could reach the light fixture to tie the end of the sheet around it.

It was a wobbly business, balancing on that chair, and I was that worried I might fall off before I was ready to hang myself. But the knot was soon tied around the metal light fixture, and all I had to do was tie the other end around my neck and jump off the bed. That'll show them, I was thinking to myself. In a twisted kind of way, the thought made me feel happier than I'd been for a long while. I wasn't afraid; I was that desperate I'd have done anything to escape the place. Even death could not be worse than my half existence here on earth.

But after all that struggle and effort, it wasn't to be. I suppose someone up there wasn't ready to have me. The light fixture was made of metal and looked perfectly strong enough to hold, but just as soon as I slipped my feet off the bed there was the sound of tearing wood and plaster, and I fell into a heap on the ground beside the bed with the light fixture and the flex falling around my head followed by clumps of plaster and a snowstorm of dust.

Of course, I was put on the red list then: the strong clothes, the padded cell, knockout injections every twelve hours. They won't let you die, oh no, that'd be too easy. They just let you live in despair instead.

She sighs wearily, and a long pause follows.

It's a sad old business, remembering those times, dearie. There's a good bit more to tell, the most important events still to come. But I'm getting tired now. Can we call it a day?

"Of course."

The tape clicks off.

PATSY MORTON RESEARCH DIARY
JUNE 20, 1970

Phone call from Dr. Watts's secretary, he wanted to see me urgently.
Took the bus (two changes, what a nightmare!) back to the Hall

again to meet him, and his face was like thunder. He's somehow found out I've been interviewing M when he had expressly recommended (his words) that she was an unsuitable research subject on account of her persistent inability to accept that what she recalls of her "life events" is almost entirely delusional, with no basis in reality.

Tried to reassure him I fully understood that mental patients, even those that have been out in the community for years like M, may not be the most reliable witnesses, that this would be taken fully into account in my analysis, etc. etc., and suggested that if he had any concerns about my research methodologies, he might like to talk to the Prof again. He growled that it would not be necessary if in future I followed his advice.

Did more transcriptions this evening and listening to M made me sad all over again. It's almost impossible to separate the truth from fantasy because she believes every word she's saying—and I can see that she feels it too—genuinely, with every part of her being, poor love. It's emotional stuff, and none of it really relevant to my research, but I can't resist her.

I can't expect her friend's son to drive her all the way up to Eastchester again, so have arranged to visit her in London next week. Must warn Prof that Dr. Watts may be in touch again.

10.

H AD I BEEN GOING TO WORK EACH DAY AS USUAL, I
would have been keeping closer track of my dates and
how long had passed since the last time, but these days, my
appointments were so few that I rarely needed to consult the
appointments diary on my phone. In all the mayhem of recent
days, I had missed something glaringly obvious.

It was in the middle of a call to Jo, pouring out my woes, the
theft of the quilt and my guilt about Mum, when I had to run
to the bathroom.

"What was all that about?" she asked when I called her back.

"Still got a bit of a tummy upset. Must be coming down
with something."

"Still? Are you getting sick all the time?"

"Isn't that too much information, first thing on a Sunday
morning?"

"So you *have* been sick?"

"Yup. Since you ask so sweetly."

"It's the morning, and you're getting sick? Is there something
you're not telling me?"

"Oh, Christ..." was all I managed before dashing to the
bathroom again.

She was horribly right, of course. I checked the dates: four weeks since Russ and I drunkenly ended up in bed on New Year's Eve, six weeks since my last period. When we split up, I'd gone off the pill, of course, to give my body a break from the daily hormone drench. Whoever said that getting older means getting wiser was deluded. It certainly doesn't seem to have had that effect on me.

As the pretty double blue line lit up inside the plastic tube, I burst into tears. "You stupid bloody idiot," I screamed out loud, throwing the tube across the bathroom. It hit the door and fell to the floor, its contents leaking out, but I didn't care. "How could you get your life so wrong?"

I collapsed onto the sofa and howled, loud wails shaking my shoulders, sodden tears gushing out, snot streaming from my nose. After a while, I was sick again, and afterward, rinsing my face, I looked up into the bathroom mirror at an apparition I barely recognized: a haggard crone with bloodshot eyes and a nose red and raw from wiping.

"Pull yourself together," I said to myself, hearing the echo of Granny's voice. After nibbling gingerly at another piece of dried toast and sipping some water, the sickness began to pass.

I texted Jo: You were right. Aargh. What the hell am I going to do?

Her reply was almost instant: Hang on in there—whatever happens I'm here for you. I'll come straight from work. Love you loads xox

Although my mind was already whirring ahead to the abortion clinic, out of nowhere an alternative choice seemed to present itself. At thirty-eight, this could be my last chance of motherhood. What if I kept the baby and co-parented it with Russell? At the very least, he ought to be given the option. I gazed around the flat with new eyes, imagining toys on the floor, the spare room decorated in pastel colors with a crib and changing table.

Running my own business would allow me to work flexibly and have time to spend with my daughter—as I already thought of her. Through my newly acquired rose-tinted vision, everything seemed perfectly possible. My body seemed to relax and become unusually at ease. Lots of women bring up children on their own these days, I told myself, making another piece of toast.

But reality soon reasserted itself. What an insane idea—must be the hormones. I was grasping at straws, desperate for something good to happen. With a resigned sigh, I dialed the number of the abortion clinic.

The receptionist was clearly experienced in dealing with telephone calls from panicky and indecisive pregnant women. In a smooth, reassuring voice, she told me what would happen: an initial assessment and discussion with a counselor, a scan to confirm my dates plus a few other tests, after which I could have the "procedure" in a week's time, if that was what I decided to do.

My head was spinning with conflicting emotions. Termination was the obvious route, quick and clinical, but what if I took no action and let nature take its course? Chocolate box visions reappeared: of me as the serene mother, cradling a contented, rosy-cheeked baby in my arms.

"I've decided to keep it," I told Jo that evening.

"Whoa! That's quite a decision."

It was enough to set me off again. "Oh God, I just don't know what to do," I wailed. "I'll be forty in a few years. I might never get the chance again."

"You've had such a crappy few weeks." She unwrapped the

box of luxury Belgian chocolates she'd brought and handed them to me. "But you need to take your time and not jump into drastic decisions."

"But I have to *decide*. I've got an appointment at a clinic tomorrow and then I need to make up my mind before next week."

"Okay, let's write down the pros and cons," she said. After ten minutes, we had two columns on the back of an envelope:

PROS	CONS
– Want a baby	– No partner, no job
– Might be too late to try again	– My life is a mess already without more chaos
– Want someone to love	– Baby will make it harder to find perfect man
– Russ's baby—good genes	– Links me to Russell forever
– Could work flexibly	– How will I work with a baby around?
	– Ummm…Flat has too many stairs for stroller, etc.
	– Expense of having baby, child care, etc.
	– Exhaustion of being a single mum

"So you're right. We have scientifically and conclusively proved that having a baby right now, without a partner, is a stupid idea," I said at last. "But it doesn't stop me feeling sad and broody."

She hugged me again. "Of course you're upset at the moment, and your hormones are all over the shop. See how it goes tomorrow, and then ring me. Promise?"

⁓

Monday dawned gray and cold, and it matched my mood perfectly. En route to the clinic, every woman I passed—and even some men—seemed to be pushing a stroller or clinging to the hand of a small child. It was like being hit in the stomach, time and time again, each one an aching reminder of what I might be sacrificing.

I hung around outside for several minutes, shivering with miserable apprehension, knowing that by the time I emerged, my fate would probably be decided. When it became too cold to linger any longer and I was starting to attract curious glances, I took a deep breath and went in. The receptionist handed me a small booklet entitled *Unwanted Pregnancy, Your Choices* and showed me into the waiting room.

In the corner, by a dusty dried flower arrangement, a teenager nervously chewed her fingernails, and on the other side, an older woman sat utterly still with her eyes shut, as if trying to deny that she was even in this place. I understood how she felt: I would rather be anywhere than here, and even now my thoughts veered wildly between rosy imaginings of loving motherhood and an altogether more alarming vision involving scalpels and the stark white severity of an operating room.

To distract myself, I flicked through the random titles of dog-eared magazines: *Angling World*, *Vogue*, *True Life Tales*, and a medical journal called *Gynecology Update*. I would have preferred to read any of these instead of the booklet, but after a few moments, I pulled myself together and opened it. The matter-of-fact language and simple line drawings were reassuring: it's a staged process and this is just a preliminary assessment, I told myself firmly. Call it a fact-finding mission.

I emerged from the consultation even more paralyzed by the choices I'd been given. But I still had a whole week, even more if necessary, to decide.

The days dragged slowly by. I spent hours on the phone gnawing Jo's ear off and changed my mind every hour. I ate little else but dry toast and tried to stop myself from falling into a mire of self-pity. "It'll turn out right in the end," Granny used to say, and I found myself repeating it like a mantra whenever I began to feel too defeated. I even went out to meet friends—keeping my secret firmly to myself, of course.

I made calls to Holmfield every other day. Mum was doing fine, the matron said, but probably best not to speak to her on the telephone just yet. She was still a bit confused as the result of the fire and the move. I promised I would visit next week and tried not to worry.

Meanwhile, though my heart really wasn't in it, I started trying to write a business strategy and launch plan for my interior design consultancy.

The finance bit I could learn about or get advice on, but what I really needed was an interesting, unusual, and preferably unique design idea, a vision which would help my pitch stand out from the crowd. My imagination seemed to have gone into hibernation, suffocated into an early grave by those long years at the bank. Perhaps, I wondered at my worst moments, it never really existed in the first place? As a student, I had received praise and even won prizes for originality, emerging with a first-class degree and professors convinced that I had a bright future ahead of me. Now, all that confidence had evaporated. Talking to friends in the business was even more depressing—all seemed to agree that the industry was going through a terrible time, struggling with overseas competition.

Desperate to kick-start my imagination, I bought every interior design magazine on the shelves and browsed the web pages of all the top companies. I dug out sketch pads, my pens, and paints, and set up a studio at the dining room table. There I sat, for hours, looking out of the window and doodling ideas. They all seemed drab and derivative. There's no spark, I thought gloomily. I'm past it. I'll never make it.

A former colleague from the bank rang to say he had moved to another organization and they were hiring. With a heavy heart, I updated my CV and forwarded it.

Each day, I called the police station, more to reassure myself that I was doing all I could to recover the quilt than with any expectation of good news. They received me politely, taking my "incident number," and searching their databases diligently, all with no result. But one day there was a new voice—change of shift, perhaps.

"Sorry, no news," he said. "But the stolen item is only described here as a colored quilt, Madam. Have you got a more detailed description, perhaps, or a photograph, to aid our search?"

At least this was a positive suggestion. Regretfully admitting that I had no photograph, I offered instead to make a sketch and drop it off at the police station tomorrow.

The quilt had become so familiar to me, but now that I was faced with a large blank sheet of creamy white cartridge paper, recollecting its complex design in sufficient detail to draw it turned out to be surprisingly difficult. The scale of each section was relatively easy to remember, and the scrutiny of Jo and her curator meant that the shapes and colors of the central square and frames were imprinted on my brain. But the patterns of the outer panels were much harder to visualize with any accuracy. Two hours later, the table was thick with pencil dust, but I had at least managed to create a reasonably accurate sketch.

It wasn't just the patterns but the brilliance of the colors and the texture of the fabrics that made this quilt so unique. I ferreted around in cupboards and dug out my old acrylic paints and a palette, untouched since leaving college, and started to mix and apply color to the squares and triangles, circles and appliquéd figures, as close to the originals as my memory would allow. Of course it was only the general likeness, colors, and main distinguishing features that the police would be interested in. But it had come to matter very much to me.

When my recall became too hazy, I tried to visualize the quilt in its most recent home, slung over the back of the sofa. As I mixed and painted, using a blow-dryer to speed up the drying, I became fascinated all over again with the way that it had been constructed, the techniques used to join the pieces together, embroider, or overlay them, and how the colors of the patches clashed with or complemented each other—sometimes both at the same time.

As I worked, I found myself humming. I was rediscovering something that I had lost: the thrill of using color to create dramatic effect, the way that two tones placed next to each other could battle so fiercely it could actually make your heart beat faster, or blend so beautifully that it made music sing in my head. In my teenage years, nothing mattered so much as using paint, or dyes, or fabrics; I covered almost everything I could lay my hands on in vibrant colors and patterns, not just paper and canvas and fabric for making clothes, but also my bedroom walls, my chest of drawers and curtains, my fingernails and hair, and my schoolbag.

I completed the colored sketch in far greater detail than the police would ever need, photographed it, and then wondered what to do next. I'd enjoyed the process so much I didn't want to stop. This time, I found myself sketching the living room around me, with the sofa at its center. But in my drawing, instead of dove-gray velour, the sofa and chairs were upholstered in patchwork, the cushions a blending set of hues, the curtains striped in the same colors. Even the lampshades were patchwork in effect.

Only the carpet and walls remained cream; the rest of my design used shocking combinations of vibrant greens, sapphire blues, and cherry reds—and it seemed to work. I sat back, hugely satisfied with my evening's achievements, and understood what I had been missing all these years. I'd been hungry for color.

I took a quick photo of the room design and texted it to Jo: Gone a bit crazy! What do you think?

Wow, brilliant. Amazing colors! Good start. What news on decision? J xox

No decision yet...xxx, I replied.

The following afternoon, I returned to Marylebone Police Station with a copy of my quilt painting, carefully labeled with the incident number, my name, and the date of the theft, and then wandered back through the darkening streets toward Tottenham Court Road Tube. The weather forecasters were predicting a cold snap, suggesting sleet or even snow, and workers poured out of shops and brightly lit offices in a purposeful stream, desperate to reach home before night set in.

The homeless are almost invisible in London, until you start

looking. Then they appear everywhere, men and women, old
and young, drunk, drugged, or just miserably sober, and some
with dogs always in far better condition than their owners.
As evening approaches, they lurk close to ventilation outlets
and covered porches, ready to claim their pitches just as soon
as office doors are closed, the lights are turned out, and the
security staff are safely tucked inside. As they waited, so did
I, for the moment when they would unravel those elaborate
constructions of cardboard, plastic sheeting, and scraps of
blanket under which they hoped to survive another night.

As I scrutinized each encampment and its owner, trying to
remain inconspicuous, I wondered what I'd do if I saw my
quilt. I should have brought another blanket or covering, just
in case, to offer in exchange. They'd accept money, of course,
but more booze or drugs would never keep a person warm on
what was predicted to be the coldest night of the year so far.

Tentatively approaching a couple of men hunkering down in
a doorway, I said, "Can I ask you a question?"

"Depends what it is," one of them muttered in a broad
Scottish accent, distracted by the contents of his luggage, contained in several plastic bags.

"I've lost a quilt," I said, "and wondered if it might have been
picked up by someone."

"A kilt? That'd be yours, Jock," he slurred, with a bronchitic
laugh that turned into a ferocious coughing fit.

"Who'd wear a feckin' kilt in this weather?" his mate replied.
"Freeze your balls off."

"It's a *quilt*, you know, patchwork," I persevered. At least
they hadn't told me to get lost. "Like a bed cover."

"Aye, a *quilt*," the Scotsman said. "Naah, haven't seen such a
thing in a long year, lassie."

There was an awkward pause.

"Well, if you see such a thing, would you let them know, down at the police station?" I asked. The suggestion was received with stony silence. "Sorry…I mean…" I stuttered, realizing how naive I'd been. "But perhaps you'd look out for it anyway?"

"Fair enough," the other one said. "Spare a tenner, miss?"

Flustered now and knowing that it was probably the wrong thing to do, I fumbled in my wallet and handed each of them a ten-pound note before dashing for the warmth of the Tube station.

On the way home, I got a text from Jo: Mark's sent your design to Justin! Woohoo J xox

This made me smile, even though I was certain nothing would come of it. Jo's boyfriend Mark was just being kind. He also worked in interiors, though not as a designer, and we both knew Justin, a fast-rising hotshot who had recently been featured in the trade media for having picked up several celebrity clients.

My patchwork upholstery idea was fun, but it was not entirely original, and in the ephemeral world of interiors, no one could ever predict what might catch on next. Everything depended on the name and the network. I had neither.

That night, I dreamed of my patchwork room. The sofa grew stumpy legs and began to shimmy around the room like a starlet, singing an unmemorable nightclub song through fat, cushiony lips as the yellow-and-white-striped curtains at my window drew back to reveal an audience of bedraggled homeless people outside in the street, pressing their noses to the glass, enjoying the cabaret. The sofa threw a cushion at the window, mouthing something angry but unintelligible, and I

I was that desperate, if Satan himself had come in offering me a new treatment, I'd've taken it. So when they said they'd found a new drug that could put me into a coma for weeks on end and I'd wake up sane, I went for it. Narcosis therapy, they called it. It was so weird—you'd be put to sleep in the height of summer, but when you woke up, the leaves on the trees were already starting to turn. When I come around, I was so bewildered it took me a few weeks to get my bearings again, and of course then the terror and despair came back just as bad as before.

You wander around in a daze for weeks, meek as a lamb, and then just as you're getting back some of what you've forgotten and start to be a bit more lively, they do it again. I tried to deceive them into thinking it had cured me by staying docile, whatever was going on in my head. The ploy didn't work, and I must have had half a dozen doses when one day I come around and discovered that my power of speech had gone. I knew what I wanted to say and could hear the words in my head. I could move me lips and make some sounds, but they was not words, not like anyone could understand. It made me mad with frustration, not being able to tell people what I wanted, but I suppose it was a bonus for the staff. They'd always been telling me to shut my gob, and now they'd drugged me dumb, and that's how I stayed for quite a few years. The foggy years, I think of 'em now, because it was like walking through one of those old East End smogs, when you could hold your hands up in front of your face and barely be able to see them. Only this fog was inside my head, if you get my meaning?

Looking back, perhaps it was better that way, because otherwise I'd have literally died of boredom. Every day was exactly the same: dragged out of bed at seven, stripped naked and showered with all them other women naked as Eve—an ugly lot we was and all, in our pale baggy skins. The nurses would sometimes sponge us with the carbolic but otherwise the only cleaning was what the water washed away—so we wasn't ever that fresh, if you get my meaning, not in the hidden bits. We'd then be wrapped in sheets and dried down. That was the worst bit, because some of them nurses was angry souls, and they took it out on us sometimes, rubbing you down so roughly you felt your skin was coming off—they'd pull your hair and all.

We always wore regulation hospital clothes in them days, dresses like sacks that went over your head and didn't need buttons, made of stripy materials so they'd know you was a patient. No bras in case you tried to hang yourself, and "open drawers" so you didn't have to pull 'em down to go to the lavvy. There was no dignity for us poor lost souls in them days, though it got a bit better after the second war.

Breakfast was porridge with bread and margarine, every day of the year, then we'd sit around the ward for an hour or so till they shoveled us outdoors into what they called the "airing court," which was a huge paved area with chain-link fencing all around. Can you imagine, hundreds of women, all padding around like caged animals, for exactly an hour and a quarter, rain or shine? We didn't mind even if it was snowing; at least we was out of doors and in the fresh air, away from the stink of disinfectant and other people's bodies. Some of 'em even used to scream and try to rip their clothes off with the pleasure of it.

It was best in summer, of course. I'd spend my time peering through the chain links, watching to see how the trees and flowers was growing. Even the daisies and dandelions in the grass just beside the fence was a special little pleasure to me. Men were strange creatures to us because there was absolutely no mixing in that hospital, but some of the less crazy ones was allowed to work in the gardens, and they would come and talk to us until the nurses shooed them away.

After lunch, we'd get out into the courts again till teatime, and you'd be starting to feel a little more like a human being by then as the drugs wore off, but come seven they'd bring around the pill trolley and then it was off to la-la land for the rest of the night. Some of 'em will tell you of cruelty, of forced enemas and the rest, though it was never that bad in the wards where I lived.

But there wasn't any kindness, neither; no one spoke to you in a friendly way or called you by your first name, you know. We was regarded like dumb animals in the main, subhuman at best. That is what I had become, and I'd stopped caring any more. Even if I'd had the gumption to complain, I had no voice to do it with from all the treatments I'd been given.

Well, I'm not sure exactly when it happened, but things started to get better at some time during the thirties. Perhaps we had a new medical superintendent, who knows? Either way, that was when I first got invited to work in the sewing room, and I'm not exaggerating when I say, looking back, that it saved me, dragged me back to life. I was mute, drugged, and out of it most of the time under the old regime, and I suppose they started to understand that doing something useful actually helped patients get well.

The sewing saved them money because we made everything the hospital needed: bed linen, curtains, aprons, clothes for patients, uniforms for staff, the lot. It made us feel human again.

The sewing room was in the central block—which meant I got a good walk there and back through the gardens from my ward each day, an extra bonus because fresh air always seems to help clear my brain. It was a long rectangle, lit with windows all along one wall and electric lightbulbs hanging over each of the tables—about eleven of them in rows from front to the back of the room. Along the front was ten treadle sewing machines what the more able women worked on, and at the back was the cutting table. We wasn't allowed to use scissors ourselves, in case someone took a mind to killing themselves, or someone else, with them. Of course, we had to use needles and pins, but these were counted out and counted in again at the end of each session.

Now I think about it, we even sewed for stage sets when the staff put on plays in the great hall and bunting for the dances. Did I tell you about the dances? Yes, for patients too, that was another of the things they introduced—they wanted us to have a bit of fun.

The first time they put a needle into me hands, the fingers just seemed to know what to do without me telling them, and after a few moments, the tears was pouring down my face so much that I couldn't see me work.

The supervisor gave me a hanky and waited a moment till I'd sorted meself out, then she tried to show me again how to make a stitch. "It's not difficult," she says. "Have another try." She thought I was crying out of frustration, you see, because I didn't know how to do it, and how was she to know that it was out of happiness, that having a needle in my hand was the most natural thing in the world? I couldn't tell her, of course, because I was still dumb at the time. After a while, she got the measure of me, because I'd fly through the work and she'd give me harder and harder tasks to do—buttonholes, darning, gathering, and piping—the more complicated it was, the more I loved it. I started to smile and even laugh again, in that place. Three hours every weekday it was, and they was the best hours since I'd arrived in the place.

⌒

One day, a new woman turned up, and the supervisor told us she would be helping out once a week. She spoke in a posh voice, not like most of the nurses who was real Essex girls in the main with a few foreigners thrown in. She was tall and well-dressed, severe-looking, like one of the head nuns at The Castle. At first I thought her stuck up and kept clear of her, but over the weeks she relaxed and became more friendly and took a special interest in me—she seemed to have set herself the challenge of getting me talking again. She spoke like I was a real person, quite a novelty as you can imagine, trying to get me to answer her questions: what was my name, where did I used to live, how I come to be in here and suchlike. She was so kindly that I became determined to talk again, if only to please her. I started practicing, in private, like, shaping my lips to the words and making sounds to fit.

My first out-loud word in six years was "David," which made her very happy, and she shushed the rest of the room and asked me to say it again.

"David," I said again, and everyone else all put down their sewing and clapped, which made me proud.

"Is David your husband?" she asked, and I shook my head.

"Not my husband," I wanted to say. "My lover. The father of my child." But I didn't have the words, not just yet.

"Perhaps your son?"

It had always troubled me that he'd never had a chance to be christened, but I was so out of my mind with the sadness and the drugs when he died that it never struck me that I could have named him anyway. So now I realized that I should give him a name. "David, my son. My son, David," I said to myself, over and over. He had lived in this world, if only for a short while. Getting my speech back returned his memory to me. It made the loss sharper but somehow easier to bear.

A little later that day, she praised my sewing, and out of nowhere, the word came into my head and out of my lips. "Quilt," I said, but my mouth and tongue was that out of practice the word didn't sound right, more like "kilt."

"I didn't quite catch that. Can you say it again?" she said, and I repeated the word, but it still came out fuzzy.

"You mustn't upset yourself," she said. "There's nothing to feel guilt about and even if there was, I am sure David would understand."

Her misunderstanding made me even more desperate to explain, and I managed to say the word "quilt" again till she recognized it properly. The following week, she came in with a bag of fabric pieces and started showing me how to make templates and the rest, sweet soul that she was. What I wanted most in the world was to find my old quilt again, the one that I started in the palace before the baby was born. I was sure it had come with me in my old kit bag, but I'd never seen it since that day that Finch dumped me here. It was the only thing that I had left of my former life, my only connection with the prince, and now that I was getting back to some kind of sanity, all I could think about was finding the quilt again, to continue the next panel in memory of my son. In my mind, it became a sort of life raft that would help to save me, by some kind of magic, I suppose.

Strangely enough, looking back, that's pretty much what happened.

Over the next few weeks, my lips managed to form more words, enough to explain about the kit bag, and I must have gone on about it so much that eventually the woman said she would ask the authorities and try to find it for me.

What a red-letter day! The sewing room supervisor arrived,

with Margaret—did I tell you that was her name?—and they had my case, would you believe it? The battered old brown canvas bag that the nuns at The Castle had given me—oh, it would have been twenty years before. My name still on the label and untouched, as far as I could see.

"Is this the one?" she asked, and I nodded with my heart pounding fit to burst, and right then and there, in front of all the other women in the sewing room, she untied the canvas straps and opened it up for me.

Inside it, still there after all that time, was my few belongings from what felt like another lifetime, what I hadn't set eyes on since I'd packed them hurriedly that day at the palace, not since I arrived here nearly fifteen years before, that simple chit of a girl eight months pregnant, the day Finch disappeared in the cab without a word of good-bye. A short length of pink ging-ham ribbon wrapped around the handle of a mirror reminded me of what I had lost: once I had been a young woman with nimble fingers and ambitious dreams. Now I was a hopeless wreck of a crazy woman, unable to speak and likely to end my days in a madhouse. I was weeping fit to burst over the sadness of it all when the bell rang for lunchtime, and instinctively I grabbed the bag, holding it tight in my arms—I wasn't about to let anyone take it away from me again.

"You can't take it to lunch with you," the supervisor said, trying to lift it out of my arms. "I'll keep it safe for you," she said, but I didn't believe her and held onto it even more tightly, starting to kick off with me noises as usual. After a bit, I recognized what I was yelling—it was "no, no, no," over and over again. I had found another word.

In the end, Margaret managed to persuade me that she would make sure the bag was kept safe, and I had no choice but to hand it over, join the queue, and file out with the others.

✐

The following day, Margaret was there again, though she usually only came once a week.

"I came especially to make sure your bag was kept safe for
you," she said, holding it out to me. "To make sure no one
snooped or stole anything. We'll unpack the rest of it at break
time, shall we?" I'd been on the machines for several weeks
now, what I disliked most of all because it was boring sewing
long seams in sheets and other large items. There was no craft
to it. That day, the machine seemed to sense my impatience
and frustration—the shuttle jammed and the thread twisted and
knotted itself. I broke several needles.

At last, break time arrived. It was usually when the women
got together to have a smoke and gossip about what was going
on in the wards, though of course I could never take part in the
talking and usually just hung around on the edge of the group
to listen.

This time, Margaret took me to the side, away from the rest,
and together we opened the case, taking the items out slowly,
one at a time: two flowery cambric blouses and a woolen skirt,
a pair of sturdy leather shoes, a hairbrush, and a tortoiseshell-
backed hand mirror. There was my bottle of *eau de cologne* what
the prince had given me, though it had gone all yellow with
the years, and the Bible the nuns had given me when I left The
Castle—I don't think I'd ever opened it.

Then, at the bottom of the case, was the small linen bag like
what we used to keep our shoes in. I untied the drawstring and
pulled out the panel of quilting that I had started in my long
lonely hours at the palace, all those years ago, when the prince
disappeared and broke my heart.

And there, wrapped inside a bundle of fabric scraps, along with

my design scrawled on the back of a laundry order and an envelope with the paper templates inside, was another piece of paper,
which I didn't recognize. With my hands shaking, I ripped it open.

Dearest M, it said. *I put some extra scraps in so you can finish this
for the baby. Let me know where you end up, and I will visit. I'm
going to miss you so much. Love and kisses, Nora*

I sat down with a bump and started to howl like an
animal—oh yes, I could still make a noise, just not words. The
supervisor and some of the other patients rushed toward me,
but Margaret sent them away and drew up a chair, putting her
arm around my shoulders. At first I pulled away, I was such a
stranger to human contact. I'd not known a gentle touch since
my final hug with Nora, that day I left the palace. Where was
she, my childhood friend? What had the years brought for her?
Suddenly I so wanted to hear her voice, to laugh again with
her. "Nora," I said, out loud. "Want to see Nora." It was the
first sentence I had spoken for six years.

"Who is Nora?" Margaret said gently, keeping her arm
around me. The warmth of her helped me relax and focus my
brain on forming words.

"Long ago," I said, amazing myself with the sounds that came
out of my mouth, without even trying. But it stopped as suddenly as it arrived. I struggled and stuttered my hardest, but no
more words would come. She seemed to sense this and tried to
change the subject, to distract me.

"What beautiful silks, and delicate embroidery," she said, pick-
ing up the scrap of quilt and looking at it closely. "I've never seen
anything like them before. Did you make this?" I could only
nod. "Perhaps you would like to complete it sometime?" she
carried on, and I nodded again. The notion of finishing the quilt
for my lost child seemed the most obvious idea in the world.
Now that I had named him, I was going to treasure him with

every stitch. I took a pencil from the supervisor's desk, unfolded the laundry order, and started to add new detail to the designs I had started all those years ago on the second panel, for the baby.

The room seemed to disappear as I got wrapped up in drawing flowers and animals, shapes and shading, but I could feel Margaret beside me, watching in silence. At one point, I stopped and looked up at her and felt the smile spread across my face before turning back to the design. I was happier than I could remember.

A long pause.

"Would you like me to stop the tape now?"

Yes please, dearie. I could do with another cuppa.

"That'd be nice. Let's take a break."

I had to do my shifts of sewing for the hospital, of course, but after that, I spent every spare moment designing, cutting, preparing templates, and quilting. Margaret would sit with me as I worked, praising the delicate embroidery or the neatness of my appliqué, asking questions. At first, I would only nod or shake my head, but every now and again a word would come out: "template" or "daisy-chain," then I'd blurt out sentences, odd thoughts that might be running around my head at the time, like "daffodils for David" or "rabbits have such sweet noses."

After a few weeks, I began to trust her, almost like a friend. The sewing room manager cut us some slack too, allowing us to use the sewing room outside of the usual shifts, so long as Margaret was there to supervise the scissors and needles, making sure I didn't try to smuggle them out afterward. She even offered to do some of the more straightforward sewing, although at first she made great clumsy stitches and I had to make her undo it and show her the way I wanted it. "These long fingers were not made for holding needles," she'd laugh. "They're more suited to holding a pen."

Over the months, me talking improved, and the more questions she asked, the more I found the words to tell her about meself, about my childhood, and the whole rigmarole just like I've told you, dearie. She wanted to know why the staff and patients called me Queenie, and I told her it was 'cause Nora and me had got chosen by Queen Mary as her special orphans and how I went to work at the palace.

To be honest, I don't think she believed me, but she played along, like all the rest of 'em did—just like you're doing, bless you, dearie. I dare say they'd told her to, so as not to anger me. That was the new thinking in them days—they'd stopped trying to deny our fantasies and just let us rage on. Old Ada wore a pillow under her dress most days and told us several times a day that baby Jesus would soon arrive—blimey, that must have been the longest pregnancy in the world—and Winnie got away with stealing food because she genuinely believed that was what she was being told to do. My foot.

I didn't tell Margaret nor anyone about the prince, of course, because I didn't want to get him into any trouble or cause a scandal. She offered to try to find Nora for me, and I believe that she did write to the palace but there was no reply. Anyway, I was sure that by now Nora would have married and left service, so it would be impossible to trace her.

When she pressed me about how I came to be in the Hall, I couldn't find the words at first. There was no making sense of it, you see. Why would I have got locked up just for getting pregnant? It was only the grief of losing the baby that sent me mad, that and their so-called treatments. And now I felt saner than ever, but there was no way of proving it, and in any case, I reckon they'd told the medical superintendent to keep me shut away, in case I told my story.

In the end, there was no hiding, because my first word had been David, and she soon twigged what the stitched swirls of the central design represented. She was a clever lady, that Margaret, who knew how to look things up in books.

"That's a lover's knot, isn't it?" she asked one day, and I couldn't stop myself blushing crimson and giggling. "Was this for David, the name you spoke, your boyfriend? Or was he your husband?" she pressed, and eventually I had to admit it.

"I loved him," I said, "and I think he loved me, once. But…" I stumbled over me words and wished I'd thought about it before blurting it out. "…I didn't come from the same background."

"Poor you," she said. "You're not the only one to have fallen in love with the wrong person. But how come that landed you in here?"

We were alone in the room, I could hear the birds singing outside as it was nearly spring, my speech had returned to nearly normal, and I felt saner than I had in years. It was time to tell her the rest of my story.

"I was a poor foolish girl," I said quietly, "and I got pregnant. They told me I would be taken care of when I had my baby and they brought me here."

I could feel her go stiff and still beside me and assumed she disapproved of my morals, but when she spoke, her voice was gentle. "They locked you up for getting pregnant?"

I nodded.

"And what happened to the baby?" I could hear the sympathy in her voice, the sweet lady.

"It was a long labor. I thought I would die," I said, the howls of that night replaying themselves in my head. "In some ways, I wish that I had." I paused and took some breaths to steady meself. "The baby died. I wasn't mad before, but it was that night what properly unhinged me."

She seemed to stop breathing. "How long ago was all this?"

"A long time ago…a long time," I said, gulping back the tears. "What year is it now?"

"Nineteen thirty-six," she said. "We have a new king, have you heard?" Of course I hadn't heard; we didn't get to read newspapers or listen to the radio. I suppose they thought that knowing what was happening on the outside would unsettle us, show us what we were missing.

"The old king, George the Fifth? Has he died?" My heart did a little somersault. I knew what this meant, of course: David, my David, would now be king of England.

"Yes, it's now King Edward," she said, confusing me for an instant, until I remembered that was to become his official name. It all seemed so long ago. In my head, I knew, of course, there was no chance that I would ever see him again, but we had been lovers, I'd had his baby, and though in my heart I knew that I'd been just a passing plaything for him, I still held onto a foolish woman's fancy that one day he might come to reclaim me. Now that he was king, all chance of that had definitely disappeared.

David, the shy, golden boy who was now king of England, smiled at me that day. How would my life be now, I wondered, had I never set eyes on him, nor he on me? What could I have made of myself, do you think, dearie?

"What would you like to have made of yourself?"

I'd like to have been able to change the world, to make it a fairer place and give women an equal say in things. A politician, perhaps? Or the queen?

They laugh together.

I've forgotten where we'd got to, dearie. Where was I?

"Margaret told you that Edward—David—had become king. But it wasn't for long, was it, because he resigned to marry Wallis Simpson?"

Yes, that came later, but I wasn't bothered no more. No, the terrible thing what happened to me around then was that just a few days after this conversation, Margaret disappeared.

I thought we had become friends, and over the weeks as my talking got better, she seemed to enjoy my company, but I don't suppose I'll ever find out why she never come back to Helena Hall. I've run it over and over in me mind, again and again. Was it something I said, out of turn as usual, what offended her? Or perhaps she got unwell, or something else in her life went wrong?

At least she could have sent a message, I thought. But there was nothing, just silence, and it laid me low for weeks. That last day I saw her, we'd both been working together on my quilt, as had become our habit, with her doing the plain stitching and me working on the design for the baby's panel. She looked over at what I was drawing and asked me what it was.

"The date of his birthday, do you see?" I'd decided to embroider the date as part of a border of wild flowers, so that the numbers were woven into the stems and flower heads. The shape of the numbers, all uprights and circles, made this quite easy.

She peered at it more closely then. "Eleven, eleven, one eight?" she said, running her finger over the shapes. "Your baby's birthday was the eleventh of November, 1918?" She quizzed me as if there was something wrong with my numbers. "Are you sure?"

I should know, surely? "I'll never forget it," I said. She went quiet then, and a bit pale. Perhaps she was remembering her own labor, or maybe there had been a tragedy. I realized I'd never asked her whether she had any children of her own.

"Margaret?" I said, after a moment. "I hope I haven't said something to upset you?"

She shook herself and sighed. "It just reminded me of something—I'm sure it's nothing to be worried about. Now I need to finish this last seam before I go."

She bent her head over the work and made a few stitches, then she put it down again. "I'm sorry to ask you this again, but did you say your baby died that night?"

"That's what they told me," I said. "They never gave me him to hold." I kept my face to the stitching and pinched my lips tight together to stop meself from saying it, the thing I had been trying to hide from myself all these years. But the words came out anyway.

A long pause, and a prompt. "What words did you say?"

"I'm sure I heard him cry."

More silence, a few sniffs and throat clearings.

"Can I get you a glass of water?"

That would be nice, dearie, thank you.

Who knows what those words meant to Margaret? I'm sure I'll never know. She sat there, stock still, hardly breathing, and her face white like she'd seen a ghost. Then she stood up suddenly, scattering the fabric, threads, and needles onto the floor, grabbed her handbag, and said, "Sorry, I have to go now." Everyone else in the room looked up at the kerfuffle as she rushed out of the door.

"Bye, Margaret. See you tomorrow," the supervisor called. And that was the last I ever saw of her.

The tape clicks off.

MISS M. R. PATIENT PROGRESS REVIEW MAY 1935

Somniphine treatment (two-week narcosis, repeated monthly over six months) applied successfully, resulting in significant improvement in patient's mental state. Patient still refuses to speak, but seems otherwise well. There appears to be no further agitation or paranoia, and she no longer expresses the delusions which hitherto have obsessed her, although this may be the result of her aphasia (see note*).

No further bouts of aggression toward staff or patients have been recorded, and no further attempts at suicide or self-harm have been noted for the past three years.

Now that Miss R is considered to be low risk, she has been moved to Belstead Villa, where she continues to improve. She is employed on a regular basis in the Ladies Sewing Room where she has demonstrated excellent needlework skills and is considered to be making a significant contribution.

*The aphasia appears to be selective, thus ruling out fears of any long-term damage, and is considered to be a condition imposed by the patient herself.

12.

THERE WERE JUST TWO MORE DAYS BEFORE MY appointment for what the clinic called "the procedure," forty-eight hours in which I needed to keep every moment fully occupied to stop my resolve from weakening.

The worry over whether to tell Russ played over and over in my head like a catchy pop song. Did I have a moral duty to tell him of his potential fatherhood? I was afraid he might go all soft and suggest that we could co-parent, but it would only be out of kindness and loyalty to me, and the last thing I wanted was to feel indebted to him. And what if he insisted that I keep the baby?

In the end, I decided that it was my body, and a moral duty only applied if someone knew about it, so it was best all around to leave Russ in blissful ignorance. The only person I'd shared the news with was Jo, and I knew I could trust her.

Also weighing on my mind was the cottage, which I had neglected since the fire. Builders had been in to fix the ceiling, but the paintwork, both inside and out, was badly in need of a touch up. I'd sent Ben Sweetman a polite thank-you email and at the same time asked whether he could recommend a trustworthy local decorator, but so far he hadn't responded. A little part of me worried that he was grumpy with me for wasting his time, but I tried to convince myself that I wasn't really bothered, either way.

There was much to do: put on the central heating to dry out the living room, clean up the kitchen, and make a start on sorting out the boxes in the spare bedroom. On my way home, I would call in at Holmfield. Mum had been there just over a week, and although the matron assured me all was going well, I was anxious to hear her say for herself that she was happy there.

The next morning, dawn never quite seemed to arrive, and as I set off, the sky had taken on a leaden sheen. Last night's forecast had threatened snowfalls in some areas, but it wasn't expected for London and East Anglia. A little adverse weather was not going to deter me from today's mission, and anyway I needed positive activities to take my mind off the impending appointment.

The journey to North Essex was straightforward—the traffic seemed lighter than usual—and I was soon off the A12 and driving carefully down the narrow lanes leading to Rowan Cottage. As I climbed out of the car, breathing the cold country air and stretching to relieve tense shoulder muscles, a few light flakes of snow circled slowly to earth, melting as they fell.

The house was cold as a tomb. The kitchen was still smoke-blackened and smelled of charred tea towel, and the living room carpet was very damp. I investigated the central heating controls; their sixties technology had always been a mystery to me, but I did my best to decode them, without success. The radiators remained resolutely frigid, and when I checked the "monster"—Mum's name for the enormous oil-fired boiler that lived in its own little outhouse—there was no reassuring roar of the burners, no fragrant smell of warm oil.

Oil? I went outside to check the gauge, a "Heath Robinson" contraption created by my father that had worked surprisingly effectively for decades. A couple of heavy metal nuts acted as a weight tied to a piece of string which in turn went through a small pulley and was attached to a float inside the tank. The metal nuts were riding high, a sure sign that the oil level was low, and when I hammered on the tank with my fist, it resounded emptily. That'd be it then, no bloody oil. Swearing loudly, I grabbed a handful of kindling from the box in the boiler house and an armful of logs from the pile and headed indoors.

The ritual of lighting the fire calmed me down. I've always loved the craft of building a fire: those screws of newspaper, not too loose and not too tight, on top of which you lay a nest of delicately placed kindling topped with the smallest of logs, preferably the split kind, so that they catch light more easily. The reward for all this careful work is applying the match and sitting back with satisfaction as the kindling starts to catch, then the logs, and the whole thing bursts into flames and becomes a furnace, transforming the room with beams of heat and light. The rosy flicker of a log fire, with its ever-changing colors and aromatic smells, never fails to cheer me up.

I could have spent all day snuggled on the sofa with a mug of tea, but there was work to be done. After a satisfying hour or so wiping the soot stains from the walls and every other surface in the kitchen, I sorted out the bathroom, throwing all the wet towels into the washing machine and mopping down the floor tiles. Order was quickly restored. I went upstairs and set to work on the pyramid of boxes and cases Mum and I had piled high in my old bedroom.

There was no time for sentimentality: I worked quickly and decisively, opening boxes and judging their importance. Charity, toss, keep. Charity, toss, keep. I hefted at least twenty boxes and black sacks outside into the garage ready for a garbage run and a similar number stacked next to the front door for the charity shop. I got especially excited when I discovered a suitcase of old curtains and furnishing fabrics in abstract patterns and bold colors, which looked to me like the work of sixties designers like Marianne Straub and Eddie Squires. Definitely for keeping: not only might they be valuable, but they would certainly be inspirational for my future design work.

The rest—still a large pile—needed more careful investigation.

It was time to take a break. Although the fire had helped to lift the chill, I had neglected it in my fervor of efficiency and needed more logs from the pile outside the back door. It had stopped snowing, but toward the west, the sky was slate gray, the wind had dropped, and the birds were strangely silent, as if the world was holding its breath. I stacked the basket high—it would be a while before I could organize a delivery of oil—and went to lift it. As I did so, a sudden pain stabbed in my lower stomach so fiercely that for a moment it took my breath away. Must have pulled a muscle, I cursed, putting the basket down and stretching, taking a few deep breaths to see if the pain would go away.

It didn't help. The pain was getting worse, coming in waves now, as if my stomach was being squeezed by huge clamps. My breath came in ragged rasps, and I began to whimper involuntarily, light-headed with the effort of trying to breathe through it. For a moment, I was afraid that I'd faint. I had to get inside and sit down, get warm, take some painkillers. My legs felt like lead weights, but I forced them to move and somehow made it back indoors.

As I collapsed onto the sofa, there was a warm gush between my legs. I put my hand there and my fingers came up red. Everything now was starkly, frighteningly clear: I was having a miscarriage. I hobbled out to the hall and ripped open one of the bags to pull out some old towels, grabbing whatever came to hand. My first thought was that I should drive myself to the hospital, but the waves of pain were so intense I knew it wouldn't be safe. I dialed the emergency number and asked for an ambulance.

Tension exacerbates pain, I'd read somewhere, so I closed my eyes and tried to relax. A few minutes later, my phone rang. Thank God, I thought, answering without checking the number; it'll be the ambulance crew to tell me they're on the way.

It wasn't. "Caroline?" At first I didn't recognize the voice, but then I figured it out.

"Hello, Ben." A call from him was the very last thing I needed right now.

"I've got a couple of decorator suggestions," he said cheerfully.

"Thank you," I said, trying to breathe through the pain. "Listen, could you email me instead? I'm a bit busy right now."

"What's up? You sound dreadful."

My throat seized tight with the effort of controlling my whimpers.

"Caroline?" he said again. "Are you all right?"

How could I tell this virtual stranger that I was having a miscarriage? "I'm fine," I gabbled, before the next wave clamped itself around my stomach, squeezing the breath out of me. I bit my lip to stop myself crying out.

"You don't sound at all fine. Tell me what's going on."

"Don't worry," I said, trying to sound brave and in control. "I've called the ambulance."

"Have you had an accident? Where are you? Is there anyone with you?"

"It's okay, honestly. I'm at my mum's house."

"Is she with you?" he persisted.

"It's not a problem, Ben." I tried desperately to convince

myself as much as him. "I'll be okay when the ambulance gets here."

"How long ago did you call them?"

"Twenty minutes or so," I guessed.

"If past performance is anything to go by, it could take them hours," he said. "I'm on my way."

"No, Ben. Please don't…" I managed before he rang off.

I texted him. **Please don't worry about coming. I'm fine. Really.**

Weirdly though, from the moment he arrived ten minutes later, I felt so much safer. He banged his head on the living room doorframe, and although I'm sure it hurt, the slapstick of it— the way he clamped his hand to his forehead and swore loudly as he staggered through the doorway—made me laugh.

When he recovered, he pressed me to tell him what was going on, and of course I tried to avoid having to tell him—why would I share that with someone I barely knew? In the end, I had no option, and he responded quite calmly, just saying "poor you" and asking how long it was since I'd called the ambulance.

I checked my watch. "About forty-five minutes."

His brow furrowed with concern. "Let me drive you to the hospital."

"That's kind, but I'd rather wait, to be honest." There was no way I was going to bleed all over his car. "Let's give them another fifteen minutes."

He didn't press me then and just got on with finding a blanket to wrap me in, feeding me painkillers, bringing in logs, and stoking up the fire. Then he boiled the kettle and brought me a cup of strong sugary tea.

"You look a little better now," he said, setting it down beside the sofa. "You were white as a sheet when I got here. How are you feeling?"

"Still horrendous," I groaned through gritted teeth. "I'd no idea how painful it could be."

"You poor thing. Louise had a miscarriage before Tom was born. I know what she went through."

There was something about his awkward attempts to sympathize which set me off, fat tears brimming out of my eyes and dripping onto the blanket he'd wrapped around my shoulders. He went out of the room, returned with the roll of paper towels, and sat quietly beside me.

"It's the irony of it," I sobbed. "I was booked in for an abortion tomorrow."

"You don't want the baby?"

"It's my ex's. We had a messy breakup, and I can't face being a single parent." Hearing myself admitting it just made the tears run more freely.

He put an arm along the back of the sofa and then around my shoulders, and I was so grateful for the comforting gesture that I rested my head on his chest. He smelled clean and fresh, like washing drying in the sunshine. The spasms were still agony, but easier to cope with now that I was able to relax, and soon afterward, the ambulance arrived.

The rest of the night was a blur of pethidine, which doesn't so much remove the pain but somehow removes you—as if you are observing someone else in agony. There were long, uncomfortable hours on a gurney in emergency before I got moved to a ward. At some point in the early hours, my womb went through its final throes of expulsion, and after that, I slept.

In the morning, I woke feeling weak and light-headed, but mercifully free of pain. My phone battery was almost dead but lasted long enough to make a call to the clinic. The reception-ist was sympathetic and asked how I was feeling. Right now just numb and confused, I said, it hasn't really sunk in. She reminded me of their counseling services, in case I needed any psychological support in the coming weeks.

I was waiting impatiently for the doctor to visit, hoping they would discharge me and allow me home as soon as possible, when Ben came striding down the ward.

"I've just texted to thank you," I said, feeling conscious now, in the cold light of day, of my raddled state. "You were great."

He flushed awkwardly, in the way of a man unused to com-pliments. "I wanted to see for myself that you were all right," he muttered.

"I'm okay now, thanks to you. All sorted. They say I can go home this morning. Can't wait to get out of here."

"Hmm. Have you looked outside?" He pulled aside the cubicle curtains so that I could see out of the window. Fat flakes of snow were falling purposefully to the ground and the parking lot was already white.

"Not to worry, I'm sure taxis are still running," I said uncertainly.

"Let me drive you. The main roads will be salted, and my old Volvo's built for snow."

Why was he being so kind to a virtual stranger? "Aren't you meant to be at work?"

"Humor me. Just so I know you are safely back there. Just to put my mind at rest?" he said, smiling so sweetly that I relented.

The snow was still falling in heavy globs and the fields were white, but the main roads were still reasonably clear, and Ben's big car seemed to handle the slippery lane with ease.

"Thanks so much for the lift, and for everything you did yesterday, Ben. You should get back before it gets any worse," I said as we arrived.

"Don't be silly." He switched off the engine. "At least let me make sure you're okay, perhaps make up the fire. And I deserve a cuppa, don't I?"

The house was perishing, and he started laying the fire while I went to make coffee, feeling surprisingly normal. But as I filled the kettle, the room started to swim, and the next thing I knew, I was on the floor with Ben crouched over me.

"What happened?" I asked.

"You fainted, gave me a hell of a fright. Sit up gently, and we'll get you back by the fire."

I was soon feeling a lot better, installed on the sofa with a cup of coffee in my hands and the logs roaring away like a furnace. Outside, the sky had darkened, and although the snow seemed to be falling even more thickly, Ben was showing no urgency to leave.

"This is a lovely cottage," he said, poking the fire.

"It was a great place to grow up, although I hated being stuck out in the countryside as a teenager," I said. "But today reminds me of childhood Christmases, with the fire and the snow outside."

"Where *is* your mum, by the way?" he asked. "Looks like she's been having a clear-out."

"Oh God! I was supposed to see her yesterday. I completely forgot. Just a second, Ben," I said, and then remembered my battery was dead. "Could I use your phone, possibly?"

After I made the call, I explained to Ben about moving Mum

into Holmfield and how I hoped she was going to settle in there, but that to pay the fees, I would probably have to sell the cottage.

"How could you bear to get rid of it? I'd give my eye teeth for a place with a bit of character like this," he said, looking around the living room with its low beams and wonky shelves.

"Sadly I don't have any choice. Mum's pension will never cover the costs, and I got laid off recently. It's been so crazy the past couple of weeks that I haven't even started looking for another job yet."

"What are you looking for?"

"I was working in a bank. Great money, but it really wasn't my thing."

"Hmm, I can see why—not the most popular people at a party these days, bankers," he laughed. "But what really *is* your thing?"

"I trained in interior design and I still hanker after doing something creative," I admitted. "I'd really like to set up my own company."

"Go on."

I pulled out the photos I'd taken of my patchwork room design, and he studied them for several long moments.

"You think I'm crazy?"

"Yup," he said with a broad smile. "Crazy in a good way, though. It's extraordinary. I've never seen anything like it before. Was it by any chance inspired by that quilt you were researching?"

"Kind of," I said. "I'm sorry. It's just that…"

"Just that…?" he prompted

When I'd finished recounting the story of its theft, he said, "You must be devastated. Have you checked with the police recently?"

"Yup, every day, but no luck. They've got more important things to worry about than quilt thieves."

He fell quiet, steepling his fingers in thought.

"Look, I'm feeling fine now," I said. "Surely you need to get back to work, or at least tell them where you are?"

"I've told them I'm working from home. I'll give it another hour or so to see if the snow eases a bit. They'll get in touch if they need me."

"What about your wife? Won't she be concerned?"

"Louise and I are separated." His voice was flat and unemotional, but his neck flushed pink. Trust me to put my foot in it.

"I didn't mean to pry," I stuttered. "I just assumed…your son?"

"I'll spare you the gory details," he said quietly. "We've reached an amicable agreement. I collect him after Saturday football and he goes home on Sunday afternoon. It's been tough on the little chap, but I think he's coping."

"Have you got other children?"

He shook his head, looking down at his hands. For the first time, I noticed how long his eyelashes were.

"I'm so sorry," I said. The only thing I could say.

"We get through these things somehow, don't we?" The break in his voice made it clear the emotions were still very raw. "You've had plenty on your plate too, by the sound of things. We just have to get by the best we can, make the most of it."

"Make the most of it." Another of Granny Jean's favorite phrases—usually in response to one of my teenage moans. I didn't tell him, of course; that would have been weird, likening a forty-something man to my grandmother. But it made me smile all the same.

With the snapping of the logs in the fire and the click of Ben's fingers on his laptop blurring into a gentle rhythm, I allowed myself to close my eyes. The anesthetic must have affected me more than I thought, because by the time I woke, it was almost dark outside.

"How long have I been asleep?" I yawned, to cover my embarrassment. I'd probably been snoring, with my mouth open.

"Nearly three hours. How are you feeling?"

I did a mental check: nothing seemed to hurt. "Fine now, I think. What time is it?"

"Just after four."

"That late? What are you still doing here?"

"Look outside."

It was dark, but beams of light from the house fell across the front lawn like yellow stripes of paint on a blue-white canvas. Beyond that, both cars were concealed under piles of snow at least twenty centimeters deep. "My God, I haven't seen it this thick in years. How am I going to get back to London?"

"You're not," Ben said. "Not tonight at least. They're reporting mayhem out there." He showed photos of traffic chaos on his laptop. "Is there anything you have to get back for?"

I shook my head. It was only the clinic appointment, but that was all over now, thank heavens. Nothing else. And I had no desire to face real life again, not just yet. "What about you?"

"I'll worry about me later," he said. "I'll just finish this bit of work, then we'll have something to eat, perhaps?"

"There's no food here, other than a couple of tins, and they're probably well out of date."

Ben smiled. "As it happens, I did a bit of shopping yesterday lunchtime and got so distracted by your crisis that I totally forgot to take it out of the trunk. This afternoon I remembered and brought the bags in—I was afraid the food would be frozen and inedible, but it seems okay. There's not much, I'm afraid, just staples like bread and butter, ham, some cheese

I think, stuff like that. A few bottles of beer and some wine—well chilled."

"Sounds perfect," I said. "We can have a picnic."

❦

We made sandwiches and returned to the warmth of the living room. For a while, we ate without speaking—it felt curiously comfortable, sitting in silence with him.

Then he said, "While you were sleeping this afternoon, I got thinking about your stolen quilt. I know that it means a lot to you, and from what you say, it is very distinctive and of no real value to anyone else. Have you checked with homeless charities and shelters?"

"No, I haven't, but it's a really good idea. Why didn't I think of it?"

"They might put an article in their newsletters, offer some blankets as a reward, that sort of thing," he went on. "If it's being used by a homeless person, the quilt's quite likely to be getting wet and damaged in this weather, so it'd be a good idea to get a move on. I've done some research and emailed you a couple of leads."

They were reporting blocked roads and jackknifed trucks all over the southeast, and it was obvious that neither of us was going anywhere. So we opened a bottle of wine and talked—about his work, my getting laid off and my ambitions to set up my own company, his childhood in Yorkshire, and my childhood in Eastchester.

"Apart from spending time with Tom and watching football, what else makes you happy?" I asked.

"You're going to think me a bit weird, but my dad was an artist and was always dragging us around galleries as children," he said. "I hated it then, but as an adult, I've rediscovered the pleasure of it. Since, you know, the business with Louise, I've started to visit galleries again. Even started to draw a bit too."

Oh my God. A man who liked art. Was he heaven-sent? "Who's your favorite painter?"

"I'd have to say Constable, coming from around here. There was a great exhibition of his at the Royal Academy last year." So far, so predictable, but then he continued, "But I like abstract works too. Don't really understand them, but the colors and shapes just make me feel happy—or sometimes sad."

"Anyone in particular?"

He scratched his head. "Jackson Pollock? Howard Hodgkin?"

"Howard Hodgkin—he's almost my favorite artist in the world," I said. "Those India pictures—how he gets the mood of a place just with three stripes of paint across a canvas. It's brilliant."

As we chatted about art and color and how it affects our moods, I found myself taking surreptitious glances at his face, side-lit by the firelight, suddenly becoming aware that he was really quite attractive, in a cuddly kind of way. And I could hardly fault his generosity and thoughtfulness over the past twenty-four hours.

We'd been thrown together, the two of us, so we'd had to make the most of it. There was nothing else to be done, no more decisions needed. I found myself more content than I'd felt for a long time.

꩜

Waking in my childhood bedroom the next morning was disconcerting. Apart from the pyramid of boxes still occupying half the floor space, little had changed since my teenage days: every surface was covered with my juvenile attempts at interior design: zany wallpaper, stenciled woodwork, and a truly dreadful painting of mine, a gritty urban street scene of which I was once so proud, behind the door. Pony Club rosettes hung around the dressing table mirror, and a sagging boy band poster was pinned to the side of the wardrobe, as though I had never left. It felt as though, any moment now, Mum would yell up the stairs about breakfast being on the table, and she was refusing to drive me into school this time if I missed the bus.

Then I remembered the nightmare of pain, the ambulance and the hospital, the cold and the snow, the quiet peace of sitting by the fire, and Ben's kindness. I carried out a brief examination of myself: I was still tender, but the bleeding had almost stopped, there was no more pain, and otherwise my body felt remarkably strong. I felt none of the aching loss that I'd anticipated, more a sense of blessed relief. I felt curiously carefree, even happy.

The world outside had changed too; the sun beamed blindingly through the gaps in the curtains, and when I looked outside, the snow was dripping off the roof in small cascades through the leaky old gutters. Ben was already clearing soggy gray slush off the cars.

As I watched his broad back, I remembered our awkwardness at the end of the evening. He'd insisted on sleeping downstairs on the sofa, and I'd brought down blankets and pillows. He'd seen me at my most vulnerable and we'd spent hours together, chatting comfortably, warmed by wine and firelight. We should have been able to end the day with a companionable hug, but something was still coming between us. We stood facing each other for an uneasy moment, neither ready to make the first move. Eventually, I reached up and gave him a quick peck on the cheek.

"Good night, and thank you for everything," I said.

13.

W HEN I GOT BACK TO LONDON, THE SNOW HAD almost disappeared, and a snowman was melting into a melancholy gray pile of slush in the little park opposite my flat.

My stomach was sore, my head still fuzzy from the drugs. Worst of all, my earlier sense of being freed from a burden had disappeared, replaced by a deep, aching emptiness and sadness about the loss of the little life, however unwanted, that I had been carrying inside me for nearly eight weeks. It took me by surprise, this drab sense of mourning: not so much for the bundle of cells that would have become a child, but more for that part of myself—motherhood—which might now never happen. Perhaps that really was my last chance, I thought, miserably.

When I plugged my phone into its charger, it clattered with incoming messages.

Are you ok? I'm thinking of you. What time is clinic? J xox

Your current account is overdrawn. Please contact 0800 156748 immediately.

Justin's interested and wants you to contact him. Yay! Ring me. J xox

Where are you? I'm getting really worried now, please call me. Jo xox

Hope roads not too bad and you got home safely? Ben

"You poor thing. It must have been a nightmare," Jo said when I rang.

"It was bloody painful," I started, then remembered that I should be careful not to scare the life out of her. She'd probably be going through the real thing before long.

"How are you feeling now?"

"A bit sorry for myself," I said, struggling not to buckle. "It's probably just the hormones, but I keep blubbing at a moment's notice. It just feels as though someone's got it in for me this year."

"I wish I could give you a big hug," she said, "but we've got this exhibition deadline and I promised Annabel I'd work through this evening till it's done."

"Please don't worry. I'll be fine," I said. "In a weird kind of way, it's a relief. I was trying to decide whether or not to tell Russell, and this has taken the decision away from me."

"I thought Russell was with you?"

She'd cornered me. "It was Ben, you know, the local hack we contacted about the quilt, remember?"

"The *journalist*? How did *he* get involved?"

"It was so random. He rang out of the blue when I was waiting for the ambulance. I tried to put him off, but he insisted on coming to the cottage and staying until the paramedics arrived."

"What a gent. Is he married?"

"Separated. He's got a son."

"Tell me more," she said. "Don't leave anything out."

I found myself smiling in spite of myself. "Not much to tell, to be honest. Couldn't be more different from Russ if he tried."

"What does he look like?"

"Tall, forty-something, lots of hair. Nice eyes. Wears stone-washed jeans. Nothing to get too excited about…"

"Sounds good to me. You're being very cagey. Is there something you're not telling me?"

Was there? Unlikely, but not impossible, I thought, trying to interrogate my response. Back here in London, the events of the past couple of days at the cottage felt unreal, like an interlude from everyday life.

"He's a lovely guy, but honestly I don't think anything's going to happen. It was such a strange set of circumstances," I said firmly, as much to myself as to Jo. "I've hardly had a moment to think."

"Are you sure you're all right?"

"Promise. I've got lots to get on with, to keep myself busy."

"Text me tomorrow when you've spoken to Justin? I'd love to know what he says."

"Will do."

I made an appointment with the bank, sent a reassuring text to Ben, emailed the homeless shelters that he'd sent details of, and then, feeling more nervous than I'd been for a long time, plucked up the courage to dial Justin's number. I remembered him only vaguely from my design studio days—a very influential supplier who dealt in bespoke, slightly off-the-wall schemes for high-end clients, just the sort of people who might go for my wacky patchwork.

To my surprise, he answered at once and was typically effusive: "Caroline, darling, it's been years. Fab that you're back on the scene." We arranged to meet early the following week, which would give me time over the weekend to work up a broader portfolio of ideas.

Finally, I made my usual call to the police—it had been several days since I last checked. Perhaps, just perhaps, there might be news. The man on reception was distracted and dismissive; I could hear in his voice that he wished I would just give up on my stupid quilt.

Then I got to work on my portfolio, making several detailed sketches of individual items of furniture upholstered in patchwork and two A3-sized sheets with worked-up full-scale living room designs showing how these pieces worked together, set against plain walls and carpets in dark blue or light ecru. I raided the bag of sixties design furnishing fabric remnants I'd brought back from Rowan Cottage and traipsed to charity shops to gather further materials for swatches. My presentation was simple, with no fancy mounts or bindings, and the designs had a slightly thrown-together effect; I hoped the air of casual spontaneity might strike a special chord with Justin.

On Saturday, I was back on the A12 to see Mum, worrying about how she might react when I arrived. What if she cried and begged me to bring her home? Happily, my worst fears were unconfirmed. I found her in the sitting room overlooking the golf course and the lake. Her cheeks had filled out, and she had a good color. In the distance, brown fields and bare trees were beautifully illuminated by a low wintry sun, and I began to feel optimistic that she was settling in.

We drank tea and I encouraged her to talk about Granny in hopes that she might have remembered something more about the quilt, but she ended up reminiscing about Dad with stories I'd heard before: how overawed she had been by his intellect and how astonished she was when he had asked her out to "the flicks," what a gentleman he had been when she'd lost her purse. Her memory of events long ago seemed undimmed, but when it came to the present, she seemed even more confused than ever.

"How are you enjoying things here at Holmfield?" I asked.

"Things?" she repeated, looking at me vaguely. "What things do you mean?"

"Are you settling in okay? Remember, we said you could come for a holiday and decide whether you wanted to stay longer."

"It's a lovely hotel," she said, "but I do miss home. Need to get back for Richard," she said. It felt like a little stab to my heart.

"Let's see what happens when the cottage has been repaired," I said, trying to be positive.

"Repaired?" she repeated vaguely. "Have I ordered any repairs?"

❧

On my way out, I went to see the matron.

"Your mother's getting on rather well, don't you think?" she said. "She's got friendly with some of the other ladies and they're talking about setting up a whist tournament. How did you find her?"

"She certainly looks well," I admitted, "but she seems more confused, and she's still talking about going home to see Dad, how she misses him. He died thirty-something years ago. It makes me so sad that she's so confused and disoriented."

"It's not uncommon," she replied. "When ladies who have been widowed first come to live here, the presence of men reminds them of their lost loved ones. She'll soon get used to it. And the confusion is not surprising either. A move often does that, but she'll recover soon enough, the longer she stays." Her calm, no-nonsense explanation was a relief, but it raised the stakes. Should Mum decide she really didn't want to stay, moving her again would cause yet another setback.

"On the upside, she keeps saying it's a lovely hotel," I said.

"That's a good sign," the matron said, laughing. "But, just like a hotel, I regret that there are bills to pay." She handed me an envelope. "There's an invoice in there, payable weekly by card or check, please. If you decide to make it a permanent arrangement, we encourage people to set up a direct debit, but of course we can keep her on a respite footing for another week or so to give you time. Also in there is a whole bunch of other information you probably won't need, about financial assistance and so on."

The envelope felt like a lead weight in my hands. What it meant was that Rowan Cottage would have to go on the market, sooner rather than later.

Justin was as I had remembered him: the tightest jeans imaginable in emerald green clashed crazily with psychedelic patterns on his T-shirt and the crimson in his hair. His earlobes were punctuated with wide holes like tarpaulin grommets, and carefully manicured slivers of facial hair traced his chin. It was the look of someone Mum would probably have called a "waster," but when he started talking, you could tell at once that beneath the peacock and slightly camp exterior was a sharp-nosed businessman who really knew his market.

We met at an über-trendy wine bar occupying the ground floor of a former industrial building in Shoreditch that appeared to have changed little since its days as a sweatshop: it still had the flaking plaster, rough wooden floors, chunks of metal machinery hanging off the walls, and staff who looked deadly bored.

I ordered cocktails which cost the probable equivalent of a week's wage for the poor souls who had once worked in this place, and after the usual "how's things" chat, spread my paintings and sketches out across the table. Knowing how too much talk can so easily destroy a pitch, I said little, leaving my work to speak for itself.

"Love the look," he said after examining my worksheets for a few moments. "Cottage chic comes to the city. Your color combinations are joyous. And this"—he fingered one of the fabric swatches—"is surely a Marianne Straub? Original?"

I nodded.

"Very now, darling," he said. "Impressive. Where do you get your ideas?"

It was a courtesy question; when I began to explain about the quilt, he lost interest after a few moments, his mind already racing forward.

"Have you got anything made up yet, or are these just ideas on paper?"

I'd anticipated this. "I'm planning to commission the work on a few pieces shortly and then set up my own studio in the next couple of months," I lied. Paying an upholstery company to produce such work-intensive items would be pricey, I knew, but it would be worth it. Renting a workshop in London would be expensive, and I'd need to have a few orders already in the bag to support my business plan before a bank would consider any kind of loan.

Justin finished his cocktail, chewing his olive stick thoughtfully.

"They're very original," he said. "Possibly a bit too home-spun to cut it with my clients, but you can never really predict what they'll go for. I'll certainly bear you in mind. Can I keep these?"

"Of course," I said, holding tight to my cheerful smile, even though I feared this might be the brush-off. I'd tried to stay realistic, but a small part of me had nursed a flicker of hope that he might fall instantly love with my sketches and give a kick start to my fledgling company. But that would have been too easy, and it was not to be, not today anyway.

"Keep in touch," he said, air-kissing both cheeks. "And let me know when you've got a few pieces made up."

As I left the bar and checked my phone, there was a text: I've got a new lead! Phone when you're free. Ben. When I returned the call, it went to voice mail. Shortly after I got back to the flat, the phone rang again.

"How are you feeling?" he asked.

"So much better, thanks. I don't know how I'd have coped without you."

"Good. Now, this'll cheer you up even more. I've got a new lead on your quilt-maker."

"That's great," I lied, trying to sound cheered. Finding the quilt-maker had become somehow irrelevant since the quilt itself had been stolen, and this was just another uncomfortable reminder that—perhaps through my own stupidity—it was probably lost forever.

"You were right all along, you know," he was saying. "Pearl's daughter Julie—you know she works here at the newspaper— told me today that her mum had been talking to an old friend, another former nurse from the Hall, and mentioned that you'd been inquiring about Queenie. The friend remembered her real name: it *was* Maria, just like you said."

"I got this strange feeling when Pearl talked about her. It all makes sense now." Maria, the patient Pearl had remembered as being an exceptional seamstress, who had a fantasy about working for the queen. Was this Granny's friend, the one who made the quilt?

"She remembered something else." I could hear the smile in his voice.

"Go on."

"Apparently some sociology student from the university went to the hospital, back in the seventies, to interview staff and patients just as the place was preparing for the big change-over to care in the community. Research for a doctorate or something, she said. They think Maria might have been one of those she interviewed."

"The University at Eastchester?" I asked, stung by the coincidence. "My father was professor of sociology there."

"We can soon find out. Her name was Patricia Morton. Hang on a minute." I could hear the click of his keyboard. "Go to the Helena Hall website and look under publications," he said, waiting as I tapped through. "Got it? See the title?"

"*The Story of Helena Hall Hospital*, by Patricia Morton, University of Eastchester? Oh my goodness, she might even have known my dad."

"Listen, I've got to go. There's someone waiting for me," he said. "I'll call again later to see whether you've made any progress."

"Thanks so much for this. It's a great lead."

"We aim to please."

I searched on the title only to discover that the book was out of print, secondhand copies were selling for fifty pounds, and no library copies were available in my borough. I'd have to ask the British Library. Then I looked up Patricia Morton, now Professor Morton and still at the same university after nearly forty years. I made a quick calculation: she would almost certainly have known my father.

Dear Professor Morton,

I am researching the life of a former patient and believe that she may have been one of the people you interviewed at Helena Hall Hospital in the 1970s. Her name was Maria, also known as Queenie. I have also been trying to trace a copy of your book *The Story of Helena Hall Hospital*, but have not been able to find one. I would be very grateful for any help you can give.

With best wishes,
Caroline Meadows

Later that afternoon, there was a reply.

Dear Ms. Meadows,

Thank you for getting in touch. It is a source of constant surprise that the research I did so long ago (for my PhD) is still being read today. Of course, all my interviews were carried out anonymously and I cannot recall offhand the names of all those I talked to. It was a very long time ago. But I'll ask my assistant, Sarah, to check through the files. As you have discovered, my book is now out of print but there are probably copies in the British Library or in our university library. Do contact me if you need further information.

Prof. Patricia Morton
Department of Sociology

The following morning, when I turned on my laptop, a further email had arrived in my inbox.

Dear Ms. Meadows,

Professor Morton asked me to do some digging into the archives, and I've found a list of people she interviewed for her research. It includes someone called Maria Romano. Is this the person you are seeking?

Sarah Buckle
PA to Prof. Patricia Morton
Department of Sociology

"Ohmigod! What a result!" I shouted, doing a little dance around the living room. Maria really had existed, and now I had found someone who had actually *talked* to her. If she really was my quilt-maker, I might—just might—discover the secret of that little verse and how my granny came to meet her. Who knows, I might even be able to find out how she got hold of those royal silks.

Dear Sarah,

Thank you so much for getting in touch. Do you have a transcript of Professor Morton's interviews, and if so, would it be possible to mail me a copy of the interview with Maria?

Her reply came almost immediately:

Dear Caroline,

Unfortunately the written transcripts have been lost, but we still have the original cassette tapes. If you are prepared to pay for transcription, we could arrange that through the university. Alternatively, you would be welcome to listen to them here—we probably have an old cassette player you could use.

I arranged to meet her in three days' time. The university was just a few miles from Holmfield, so I could fit in a visit to Mum too.

When I texted Ben to thank him, he replied: Great news. Are you free for a drink afterward?

The concrete brutalist architecture of the university campus that must have been considered so bold in the sixties now looked weary and rain-stained. The wind howled unhindered from the Arctic Circle via the North Sea, and horizontal sleet soaked me on my short walk from the parking lot. To soften the hard edges of the place, they'd planted shrubs and trees in large concrete tubs in the center of each of the linked squares, but at this time of the year, the plants were dark and leafless, struggling to survive the drifts of litter gathered at their bases. Students, almost uniformly dressed in black, huddled in groups or hurried across the squares while small whirlwinds of paper cups and plastic bags whipped up in every corner.

I negotiated my way through miles of anonymous linoleum corridors with that nostalgic college smell of polish and stale coffee and entered the door marked Administrative Office, Department of Sociology.

"Caroline? I'm Sarah." A large smiley woman levered herself up from her chair. "The professor's teaching at the moment, but she'll be back in a bit. You've come about the Helena Hall tapes?"

We shook hands. "Thank you so much for helping me at such short notice."

"It's no trouble. Now, let me see…" She tapped a perfectly French-manicured finger on her temple. "I think they're in here." As she opened a large gray metal filing cupboard, a roll of flip chart paper fell from the top shelf, glancing off her head on the way down.

"Are you all right?" I asked.

She chuckled. "No problem. I'll leave it there for the moment, probably safer."

After further excavation, she lifted from the back of a shelf a large cardboard box labeled "Helena Hall" and set it down on a nearby desk.

"It was Maria Romano you were looking for, wasn't it?" She started to rifle through the plastic cassettes stacked inside. "Should be in there somewhere." She took them out of the box onto the desk one by one, but none appeared to be what we were looking for, and I was beginning to fear I'd had a wasted journey when she peered into the depths of the box once more and pulled out a label which had stuck to the bottom.

"Hurrah," she said. "Maria Romano. Now we just have to find the bundle it's fallen off."

In the pile on the desk, there was a set of four numbered cassettes held together by a withered elastic band. "That'll be it," she said. "Patsy said there were four. Now all we need is the cassette player."

She delved into the cupboard again with no luck, then wheeled over an office chair and began to climb precariously onto it.

"Do you think that's wise?" I said, holding firmly onto the back of the seat. Undaunted, she stood on tiptoe to peer into the upper shelves of the cupboard, shouted "Here we go!" and hauled out a rectangular black plastic box with a transparent panel in the top and a heavy flex hanging out of the back.

"This must have been the latest technology in the seventies," I said, helping her safely down from the chair. "An ancestor of the Walkman I used to love as a teenager. Does it still work, do you think?"

"We can but try. I've reserved a seminar room so you can listen in peace. There's a coffee machine if you're desperate, or the café in the square's a better bet."

As we set off along the corridor, a slim, athletic-looking woman in a figure-hugging cerise cashmere sweater and a showpiece necklace of brilliantly-colored abstract enameled shapes came toward us, breaking into a smile.

"You must be Caroline Meadows." She shook my hand with a firm grip. "Patsy Morton." I'd calculated that she would be well into her sixties, but she looked ten years younger, and only the unapologetically gray hair—gently swept into a soft bun—belied her years. She was nothing like the person I'd imagined, none of the clipped vowels, severe haircut, sensible shoes, and brisk manner of female academics I'd met in the past.

"It's very kind of you to help me, Professor Morton."

"Call me Patsy, please," she said with an appraising glance. "I see Sarah's found the tapes and my trusty old cassette player. Have you got time for a quick chat before you start?"

Her narrow office, lined from floor to ceiling with book-shelves, had just enough room for a desk and a visitor's chair covered with a beautiful handwoven throw. Sun poured in through the windows onto several dusty house plants. Beyond them, the view spread away from the concrete squares, across the valley to the townscape and the clock tower of Eastchester town hall in the distance. On the pin-board above her desk were pho-tographs: a good-looking man on the beach with a small child on his shoulders, the professor with other small children—perhaps grandchildren—all grinning uninhibitedly at the camera.

As we sat down, she looked me directly in the eye. "Forgive me for asking so directly, Ms. Meadows, but are you by any chance related to the late Professor Richard Meadows?"

My heart did several skips. "He was my father. Did you actually know him? I thought perhaps you might have done," I said. "I was going to ask, but…"

"Yes, I really *am* that old," she replied, laughing. "I was lucky enough to have been taught by him for a seminar in my second term as an undergraduate. The university was very new in those days, and everyone felt it had been fortunate to attract someone of his caliber. We were all in awe of his reputation; he had a brilliant mind and was also highly respected in the field, but he was very approachable all the same, generous and kindly toward us first years. I'm sure it was partly his influence which prompted my interest in mental health," she said.

It was heartwarming to hear that my father had been so loved and respected, but painful too. "I was just three years old when he died. I wish I'd known him properly."

"You're his very image, did you know?" she said, her voice tender now. "It gave me a bit of a jolt when I saw you."

"Apart from my mother and grandmother, I don't think I've met too many other people who knew him," I said, feeling self-conscious in the directness of her gaze.

"Is your mother still alive?"

"Oh yes, she's only seventy-three, but sadly losing her memory a bit now. She was much younger than him, of course; she was one of his students at UCL, before he came here."

"I'm not surprised. I think we were all just a bit in love with him. So handsome, still blond-haired even in his fifties, and

with extraordinary blue eyes. I think you've inherited them."
She smiled across the desk. "He made you feel as though you
were in the presence of someone quite special."

"That's lovely of you to say so," I said, ambushed by a sense
of loss and the deep ache of envy that she had been old enough
to know him, even to have been taught by him.

We both fell quiet for a moment.

"Now, tell me why you are so interested in my research," she
said, breaking the silence.

I explained about the quilt I'd inherited from my grandmother, the royal silks, and the woman we knew as Maria,
who we believed had sewn it, the woman she had interviewed
for her research. "She stitched a little verse on the back of the
quilt," I said, reciting it from memory.

"Hmm. Oversentimental, but not untypical of the time,"
she said.

"Can you remember Maria?"

She shook her head with a rueful smile. "It's all a bit hazy
now, but since you contacted us, I've been doing my best to
bring her to mind. All I can really recollect is that she was quite
a character, a tiny person with a big personality. The hospital's
medical officer tried to warn me off, told me I shouldn't believe
a word she said."

"Because she was insane?"

"That's what he told me and that's what the hospital notes
said, but by the time I met her, she didn't appear the slightest
bit insane. She'd been discharged by then and had gone to live
in London with an old friend. She had an incredibly tough life;
her story doesn't make for easy listening."

She glanced up at the clock on the wall. "I'm so sorry, I've got
a lecture to get to. Can I leave Sarah to look after you now?"

We were about to leave the room when she turned back to

her desk. "I nearly forgot to give you this." She handed me a much-worn hardback notebook.

"It's my PhD research diary," she said. "There are a couple of references to my meetings with Maria in there which might help for context. I've marked the relevant pages. But please make sure you put it back with the tapes on Sarah's desk when you leave. They're all rather precious, you understand, but being the prof's daughter, I know I can trust you."

The seminar room smelled of dusty central heating and fatty fast foods recently devoured by hungry students. I closed the door and sat down at a table marked with cup rings and felt-tip scribbles.

I flicked through Professor Morton's diary, reading through the pages that she had marked, and photographed them for later. I propped up the photograph of Granny and Maria against my coffee cup and clicked the first cassette into the slot of the ancient recording machine.

Then I took a deep breath and pressed PLAY.

My heart nearly stopped in my chest as the initial hiss of the tape gave way to a husky voice, burning with humor and intelligence. The bare seminar room and the rain-stained concrete outside disappeared as I listened, totally absorbed, each squeaky revolution unveiling layers of history that had been locked inside these cassette time capsules for more than forty years.

The individual in my photograph had seemed fleeting, impermanent, like a will-o'-the-wisp. Now this voice brought her vividly to life: bold, rebellious, and cheerful, even chirpy in spite of all she had faced. I would so loved to have known her.

Three hours, several more cups of coffee, and a stale cheese sandwich later, I loaded the fourth cassette into the slot and then, for the final time, pressed PLAY.

14.

*H*OW DOES IT FEEL, TALKING ABOUT YOUR TIME AT *the Hall after all these years?"*

Strange, dearie, very strange. Like another life, and I suppose that's what it was. Not that I minded so much, in the end, being in there. I had me friends and plenty of ciggies and the sewing and that. Enough food, most of the time. The main trouble was that no one ever believed me, so I stopped talking about me past, locked it away inside me, kind of. Whenever I did talk about it, they would say it was me voices, the old fantasy stuff.

But your history is what makes you who you are, doesn't it? And after all them drugs and treatments, I felt like a sort of nonperson. Everyone, even the staff, insisted on calling me Queenie, so it's hardly surprising that I almost forgot who I'd once been. They stole the real Maria away from me. It wasn't till I got out, around 1950, that sort of time, that I started feeling like my old self again. It's been lovely talking to you, my dear.

"And I have enjoyed meeting you too."

Gawd, just think of it. That was more than twenty years ago. *She sighs.*

Twenty years of freedom, and I've counted me blessings

every single day of it. Coming out has given my past back, and I've been trying to make up for it ever since. I was very angry for a while about the life they took from me, but it doesn't get you anywhere fuming to yourself all the time, so I just decided to put the past behind me and get on with enjoying the years I have left. But I hear the place is closing down for good now, is that right?

"So I understand. Most of the patients, like yourself, have been settled in the community."

A fierce, bronchitic chuckle.

Hah, is that what they call it? I've seen them on the streets with their cardboard and their bundles.

"Yes, I am afraid that's the choice some of them have made."

Don't have no other choice, you mean.

She lights a cigarette, and there is the deep rattle of her inhalation and a long exhalation before she starts to speak again.

Still, s'pose I got lucky, having someone to come to. Didn't have much luck in the rest of me life, so perhaps I was due some.

It wasn't easy at first, mind. I was scared of every little thing: cars, and buses, and people everywhere, like swarms of ants. Making up me mind was the hardest thing: brown bread or white, butter or margarine, jam or marmalade, tea or coffee? Just deciding what to have for breakfast was like a day's work. We never had choices in there—you ate what you got, and if it wasn't enough, or someone like Winnie nicked it off your plate, which used to happen a fair bit, you went hungry.

We went pretty hungry in the second war, I tell you; that was a miserable six years and all. Most of the male nurses went off to fight and the women into war work, so there was hardly any staff left here to look after us. They had to close some wards and pack more of us into the rooms they kept open. I think I mentioned that I'd got myself moved to one of those villas out on the edge of the estate? By then I was sensible enough not to give them any trouble. Anything for an easy time. It was nice out there, peaceful, surrounded by beautiful gardens, very civilized. Almost like normal life.

But when the war came, they closed the villas and moved us all back into the main building, all those terrible corridors echoing with the howls of crazy people. To top it off, we was stuck on the wards for most of the day because they couldn't spare the time to take us out.

As the war went on, the food got worse and worse—almost everything disappeared: there was no tinned milk or bananas, no lemons or chocolate, and there was very little butter, cheese, and meat. They were all rationed, of course. You would hear the cooks grumbling about it, as they slapped their latest concoction of brown slosh onto your plates, made out of carrots and turnips mostly, day after day.

They dug up the gardens to grow food, the men did, but their seedlings got the carrot fly and the white fly and the black fly; every kind of fly in the kingdom flew to Helena Hall, because they didn't have the know-how to deal with that sort of thing and no chemicals neither—they was all saved for dosing up the patients. The plants withered in their weedy patches, and our stomachs grew hungrier by the day.

The sewing room stayed open, thank the Lord, 'cause without it, I would have truly lost my mind again. But we was full time sewing heavy khaki serge into army uniforms, you see, doing our bit for the war effort. It was terrible fabric to sew, especially on our little machines—they weren't designed for industrial work. The needles would break and the shuttles would jam every few minutes, and our fingers and backs ached from pressing the material flat enough to flow under the foot.

I still managed to steal a few minutes each day, during the break and over lunchtimes, to work on me quilt, though. By now they trusted me with scissors and needles so I didn't have to be watched every minute, like most of the others. The two central panels—the one for the prince and the one for the baby—were finished, so I started work on designing a third.

The supervisor found me some leftovers: scraps of lavender-stripe cotton we'd been making into uniforms for the junior nurses, gray shirting for male patients, and some cream poplin shirts we'd had in from the admin side which were beyond mending. The colors blended well enough, but the fabrics was plain and dull after the brocades and intricate designs I'd been working with on the inner panels. So I decided this panel was going to have to be completely different, and I asked for some magazines to give me ideas. Have you heard of cubism, dearie?

"It was an artistic movement, wasn't it?"

Something like that. I read about it in one of them magazines, about how they were turning pictures into blocks of color—even people and landscapes—so I tried to think of a way of using my plain fabric in blocks. They was certainly easier to patchwork than curves, I can tell you.

The idea came to me as I was doodling my name: M for Maria. Also for Margaret. If I could join a row of capital letter Ms in blocks of contrasting fabrics next to each other, it might create an interesting pattern. After I'd played about with the ideas for a bit, I came up with a pattern that used the Ms and also like the zigzag of a staircase, which felt right to me, given the stairs my short legs have had to climb in all of them tall buildings I've lived in.

I was lucky, you know, because I nearly lost the lot, my life included, one terrible night in 1942. Those ruddy Germans bombed the place and made a direct hit on one of the women's ward, just along the corridor from where I was sleeping.

What they thought they were doing, bombing a place full of crazies, we'll never know. I expect it looked like a factory or a hospital, and of course the army was stationed just down the road, so perhaps they thought they was killing soldiers. Anyway, it caused mayhem, and though we pulled a few of them out alive, thirty-six patients and two nurses died that night.

"You helped to save people? They allowed you out?"

One of the bombs fell that close, the blast blew the door off our ward too. Just as well we was all cowering under our beds by this time, otherwise we'd have been thrown across the room. So once the bombs stopped and we could hear the wailing and the shouting, all the night nurses ran out to help and I went too; no one stopped me. It had blown the wall right off the end of the building, you see, and the ward with it, just knocked over like a great hand had come and swiped it. The bricks and the roof was all on the ground in a heap and bits of people sticking out, cursing and crying for help. It makes my skin crawl when I think of it, even all these years later.

It was mayhem. There was no one in charge, so I just got stuck in and started pulling lumps of bricks and mortar away from the bits of people I could see, calling to them that help was on the way. My hands was cut to shreds in a few moments, but I never noticed, not till much later, that they was bleeding all over the place. After a bit, the wardens and fire service arrived and started telling us how to dig without harming the poor blighters any further. We did pull quite a few of them free but they was mostly in a bad way, broken arms and legs and the rest, and stuck into ambulances and off to the proper hospitals for treatment. I'm not sure if many of them ever returned.

By dawn, and this was August, mind, so dawn came early

still, we got a proper view of the terrible damage, and nearly forty still missing as far as anyone could account for. We was herded back to our wards for a bit of patching up, and they had to chase a few crazies around the grounds to get them back as well. We heard later that they pulled two old dears out of the rubble twenty-four hours later, thanks to the sharp ears of a local copper who heard them whimpering.

I must have been in shock, because they sedated me and I slept for hours after that, but not even the drugs could blot out the cries or the blood and broken bodies we saw that night. They return in my nightmares, even now that I'm an old woman.

There's a long pause.

"Are you all right, Queenie?"

The sound of liquid—water?—poured into a glass and gulped down.

That's better, thank you. Shall I carry on?

"Yes, please. If you are feeling better?"

I think we're on the home stretch now, dearie, not much more to tell, because it was only a few years after the war ended that *the day* arrived. The best day of my life, dearie.

We didn't get letters, you see, not usually. So that morning after breakfast, when I was getting ready to head over to the sewing room and the matron came walking down the ward with an envelope in her hand, I took little notice until she stopped at my bed.

"Letter for you, Queenie," she said, handing it to me. "Do you need any help reading it?"

She meant well, of course, but I snapped at her all the same, flustered by the strangeness of the moment.

"I can read it for myself, thank you," I said, grabbing it and tucking it into the top of my blouse. She was desperate to know what it said, I could tell, but it was mine and I was sharing it with no one, thank you very much. My heart was hammering so loud in my chest it's a miracle I could walk, but I got myself into the toilet and locked the door.

The envelope was addressed simply to Maria Romano, c/o Helena Hall Hospital, Eastchester. Everyone in here knew me as Queenie, so though I didn't recognize the handwriting, I thought immediately that it must be from Margaret. It couldn't be anyone else. She was the only one who'd ever asked whether I minded my nickname, and when I'd told her I preferred my real name, she'd always used it from then on.

I've kept it all this time and got it out to show you. Look.
"Would you like to read it out to me?"
Okay, dear. Just need to get out me glasses. Here they are.
She clears her throat and begins to read:

Dear Maria,

I hope this finds you well. Do you remember me, your friend Nora? From The Castle, and the palace?

I promised to find you, but after you went away, they wouldn't tell me where you was, so I have been looking all these years. Then I got a letter forwarded from the palace what they must have been sitting on forever. I left there years ago and am a widow now but am blessed with a son and daughter-in-law, living close by.

From the address, I'm afraid you must be poorly. But perhaps that was just long ago and you are out now? If so, I hope they forward this on to you. I would dearly love to see you again, and learn what has become of you and the baby.

Write soonest and tell me where you are so I can come and see you.

Love Nora (née Featherstone, now Kowalski)

"What a beautiful letter. You must have been so excited to hear from her?"

I'll say, dearie. But at first it was like a dream, and I kept having to pinch myself to tell myself it was true. Nora! Alive, and coming to see me? The girl I'd always considered to be my sister, the only family I'd ever really had? The last thing I ever imagined was hearing from my childhood friend like that, after thirty years of being locked away in that place.

I thought she'd long forgotten me or perhaps given up trying to find me, busy with her own life. I even wondered whether she might have died in the Blitz. So her letter was a complete surprise, like all the Christmases and birthdays you ever had rolled into one, not that those days had ever been any great shakes for me, but you know what I mean? My heart seemed to swell till I hardly had room to breathe, my head felt as though it might explode with happiness, and I had to tuck the letter back in me blouse for fear the tears would smudge them precious words.

Then I pulled myself together and went back into the ward. As I passed the nurses' station, the matron looked up with question-mark eyebrows, and she must have known something good had happened, because by then I couldn't wipe the smile off my face, but I wasn't going to give her the satisfaction of knowing, not just yet.

I went off to the sewing room, and the day dragged by. I had to wait until teatime before I could go to the patients' sitting room where there was paper and pencils and even envelopes in the desk drawer, what we could use if we asked the supervisor. The place had got a lot more civilized by then. From what I remember, I wrote something like: *"Dear Nora, I am so happy to hear from you. Yes, I am still here and not going anywhere fast, so please come to visit as soon as you can."* And signed myself off: *"Your little sister, Maria."*

It seemed like months passed before her second letter arrived, though it was probably only a few days. It said that she was coming to visit the following Saturday, on the bus. It was only then I began to believe it and started to panic. The last Nora had seen of me was as a young thing of eighteen, round in me belly but otherwise sweet-faced and innocent. The years of madness, drug treatment, chain-smoking, and neglect had done for my looks, and I took care not to look in mirrors anymore. If I could not face myself, whatever would Nora think? She might even take one look and run away, terrified by the old witch that had once been her childhood friend. I still had four days to pull myself together and remedy the mess I was in, but I couldn't do it without the matron's help.

The old dragon come up trumps, bless her cotton socks. When she learned I was to have my first visitor for thirty years, her eyes softened and she broke out into a great gap-toothed grin.

"Well, my lovely," she said, "we'd better get you smartened up then, hadn't we?"

Our visits to the hospital hairdressers was usually just a matter of seconds for them to chop off the ends, pudding-bowl style, but this time the matron had given them the wink, and I was there well over an hour. After the cut, they daubed on some color to cover up the gray, then rollered it all over and lathered on some foul-smelling perm lotion to hold the curls in.

By the time I was done, they said I looked like Rita Hayworth.

"In her coffin, you mean," I said. "Get along with you." They laughed, but I was secretly so bloody thrilled I could hardly stop from smiling. When I got back to the ward, my friends hardly recognized me, and they didn't half tease.

"Ooo-er, look at madam," they called. "Got a fancy boy, has yer?"

"Got a few of 'em, looks of her."

"Where'd yer get the cash to pay for that then, Queenie?"

"Doin' someone a favor, I'll be bound."

But I didn't care, and I certainly wasn't telling anyone why.

The matron pulled me aside and showed me a couple of dresses and three pairs of shoes she'd found in a storeroom. There was even a new bra and a suspender belt and nylons, still a scarcity in them postwar days, and usually banned in mental hospitals because they was just right for hanging yourself.

"Get in those toilets and have a little try-on," she said. "But don't tell the others or they'll all want fancy new togs."

The curious thing was, once I'd put on the bra and nylons and the best of the two dresses—I still remember it, a little cotton shirtwaist in a flowery print—what with that and the new hairdo, I looked like a normal human being again. My figure was still there and my waist still small from the years of poor rations, and it give me a picture of the woman that I might have been, had I not been so naive as to fall for the blue eyes and soft words of a handsome boy.

So instead of being happy, I got a bit depressed, and by the time the matron came in to see how I was getting on, she found me sitting on a toilet seat blubbing me eyes out.

"It's a shock, dearie," she said. "But this could be the start of something, you know? A new kind of life for you. They've changed the rules."

Changed the rules? What did that mean?

She went on, "Depending on your friend, how she feels and how we feel about her, you could go for days out, or even spend a night out, get a feel for the world outside, you know, ready for leaving."

"Leaving here?" You'll hardly believe it, dearie, but the thought of leaving the place after all those years was bloody terrifying, 'scuse my French. So I shouted at her, "No! I don't want to leave. What about my friends?" and I started sobbing all over again. She put her arm around my shoulders then, the first time I remember a member of staff had ever showed physical affection. Margaret had given me hugs, but never anyone else.

"Don't worry, Queenie," she said. "Nothing will happen unless you want it to. Now, take off those clothes and put them in this bag—I'll keep it safe till Saturday."

Well, from that moment onward, all my waking thoughts were about Nora's visit. Would she even recognize me, I wondered, after thirty years? Would I recognize her? I knew how I had changed—even in spite of the hairdo and the clothes—but had she? Would she be afraid, as some were, dearie, that madness could be catching? What if she turned around at the last moment, before I had the chance to prove that I was not crazy?

Then I remembered the old tough, rebellious, funny Nora, whose shoulders would break into the shakes whenever she was nervous, who had stood by me all those years but stood up to me when she knew I was treading the wrong path.

She'd never take fright.

I was in such a lather waiting in the patients' sitting room that morning, I tell you, but soon enough, she arrived and we fell into each other's arms like long-lost family, and from that moment on, we chattered and laughed till we was hoarse, and all my nerves disappeared like the years we swore had surely never passed, we was so familiar to each other. She was just as before, towering over me, all gangly limbs and big hands, pointy nose and sharp features but a sweet expression under that mop of gray hair. She swore I hadn't changed one bit, though of course, our eyes were doing that usual deception; because we had aged together, we could not see what changes the passing of time had brought to us both.

While I'd been stuck in the Hall, Nora had had a very exciting life. After the first war, once she got over poor Charlie, she met a coachman called Sam Kowalski, a Pole whose parents had come to Britain to avoid the pogroms. Sam fought in the trenches and happily returned unscathed, but once they were courting, of course, she had to leave as they didn't allow couples to work together. By the time she and Sam had got themselves hitched, she was already knocked up and the second arrived a couple of years later.

Sam wasn't getting any promotions—it was deadman's shoes and they never had the courtesy to bloody die, Nora told me with that big gale of a laugh. In any case, the family had taken to using motor cars most of the time, which meant they needed fewer staff, so he got himself a new job as driver for an East End wheeler-dealer, and for a few years, they was in the pink, till the second war came along.

The wheeler-dealer's business was booming in the black market, but Sam could see it was getting dodgy and decided to quit. He was too old to fight by that time, but he signed up as a spotter and went off to the Essex coast each night to look out for bombers, except one night when the bombers spotted his station first and he never came home, leaving Nora with two boys just coming up for conscription.

To cut a long story short, one of them got himself killed in the trenches, and after the war, the other son—that's Sam junior, who you've met—came back from North Africa to marry his sweetheart, so Nora was now living on her own with her son and daughter-in-law just up the street and a grandchild on the way.

"I miss them both so much," she told me. "But I count myself blessed that little Sam came home, and I still have my eyesight so I can carry on with the needlework to supplement me war widow's pension," she said, putting away the photographs of Sam and the boys. "That's enough about me. What about you? I tried so hard to find you but no one would tell me where they'd sent you, and it was like they closed ranks."

"How *did* you trace me, in the end?" I asked, dead curious.

"The oddest thing, it was," she said, shaking her head. "I got this through the post." She reached into the handbag again, pulled out an envelope originally addressed to the palace but forwarded to her Bethnal Green address. Inside was a scrap of paper and on this, in the same careful italic handwriting as the envelope, there were just five words: "Queenie Romano, Helena Hall, Eastchester." Nothing else.

After a moment, it dawned on me: the only other people I had told about Nora were my psychiatrists and…Margaret. I'd never discovered why she had deserted me without saying good-bye, but this made me realize that she must have felt guilty and tried to make up for it by putting Nora in touch with me.

When I tried to explain this to Nora, she shook her head. "People do the strangest things," she said. "But it turned out right, didn't it? At least I'm here now. But why did she call you Queenie?"

"It's my nickname in here," I said, "because when I arrived, I was trying to tell them about where I'd come from—though of course, they never believed me. Told me it was all fantasy—no one like me could ever have worked for the queen. Someone called me Queenie to mock me, I suppose, and it kind of stuck."

"Did you tell them about the prince too?"

I shook my head. "Only at the very beginning, talking to the psychiatrists. But I soon gave it up, 'cause they only went and took it as proof that I was insane."

She paused and looked at me close in the face then, trying to judge whether to ask the question, so I decided to tell her right out.

"It was a boy," I said. "I never got the chance to hold him. I heard him cry but later they told me he was dead."

She sat beside me on the sofa and put her arms around me again.

"The bastard," she said quietly.

I'd accepted it in my head long ago, but it was harder to admit it to my best friend, so I stayed silent. Somehow, in here, I'd managed to put all that behind me, but talking to Nora reminded me of the hurt and deception, the way my life had been wasted, because of a few short hours. And because I had been foolish enough to believe what he told me: that he loved me and would protect me if anything should happen.

The fury came over me all of a sudden then. "Yes, he *was* a bastard," I hissed under my breath, not so loud as the other patients and visitors could hear it. "Tricking me with his beautiful eyes, Nora, drawing me in and making me feel something special so as he could have me with the click of his fingers. That's what he did, and I was too young and foolish to realize what was happening."

I was wringing my fingers so fiercely it made them hurt. Nora put her hands over them to calm me, and then the tears came, angry, bitter tears, shaking my shoulders till I could hardly draw breath, like a waterfall that had been shut up in some dark underground lake for years and years and the dam was now broken. I was that hysterical the nurses rushed over to us and started saying they needed to give me a pill, but Nora sent them away and suggested we go for a walk around the gardens instead. We headed out into the sunshine, where the birds were singing and the roses glowing red in their beds, the sound of a lawn mower chugging in the distance, and she told me to take deep breaths of the sweet afternoon air until the sobbing settled and I could talk again.

I told her all the things I had been through in the Hall, the narcosis and losing my speech, about Margaret and the war, the bombing and the bodies. All those horrors stored up in my brain, festering, like rotting fruit, pouring out their poisoned gases. I could tell she was pretty horrified, believe me, but went on listening without giving her own opinion. There was little she or anyone could do to right those past wrongs, not now.

"He took away my life, Nora," I said. "None of this would have happened to me if he hadn't existed and I hadn't fallen for him. I should feel angry about it, but we was like children, both of us, and even now, I do believe that for those short moments, he loved me."

It felt so good to talk to someone who understood—someone who actually believed me—and we took several turns of the gardens as I gabbled on. After a bit, it started to rain, but we both ignored it, and even though we were soon soaked, we went on walking. It was like the rain was washing away my horrors, and I began to feel there might be hope in the world after all. When we reached the front door for the fourth time, Nora turned and looked at me, and I looked back at her, with her straggly hair, the rain dripping down her face, the dark patches of damp on her clothes, and her shoes squidgy with water, and realized that I must look the same. She started that big gale of a laugh that she'd always had, and as per usual, it set me off too, and we were soon hooting so much we couldn't get any breath, so bad we had to sit down on the step to recover ourselves.

"It's like we was girls again. Like those years never passed."
She stopped laughing and looked at me, then gave me a
soggy hug.

"Perhaps that's the best way," she said. "Put it behind you
and look forward."

"What's there to look forward to?" I said, feeling miserable
again. "Stuck in here for the rest of my life, more than likely."

"Things are changing here, you told me. Let's just see what
happens, shall we?" she said mysteriously. "Listen, it's time for
me to head off, but I'll be back again soon, promise, in a few
weeks if I can. Just hold on for that, and we'll see if something
can be sorted out."

I couldn't imagine what she might be thinking, but Nora was
good as her word. A letter arrived a few days later, and after a
few weeks, she came to see me again. Those visits became my
lifeline. It felt as though we'd turned back the years. We was
like sisters again, talking a mile a minute from start to finish.
And though the sadness seemed to hang over us like thunder-
clouds when we recalled the difficult times, we always managed
to laugh them away. We'd been raised to expect nothing, and I
suppose the fact that we'd lived so long and were still alive was
probably good enough.

But there was one cloud even Nora's laughter couldn't
chase away. Inside, with few visitors, we was that cut off from
outside life, we never saw or spoke of children. For Nora, her
sons were her life, and as she showed me photographs and
described the joyful days of their childhood—the one she had
lost, and the one she was now pinning all her hopes on—my
heart seemed to hang so heavily in my chest that I could barely
breathe. As much as I tried to show interest, I could not find it
in myself to share her pleasure.

Years of treatment play havoc with the old memory cells,

believe me, but the one event I can recall like it happened yesterday was the night of his birth: the terror and pain, the clumsiness of the staff as they tried to help me, the joy of hearing his cry, the desolation when they took me from him, the suffocating blackness when they told me he was dead. I couldn't help myself; when Nora complained one day about her son's failure to remember her birthday, I blurted, "Stop being such a moaning Minnie. You should count yourself bloody lucky to have a son at all." It sounded as bitter as I felt.

For a moment, she was taken aback. "My poor love," she said, with those sorrowful eyes of hers. "I am so sorry you never had any children."

"I *did*, can't you see? I *did* have a child. But they took him away from me," I shouted, not caring that the other patients and visitors all looked up from their conversations to stare in my direction.

"I thought you said the baby died?"

"That's what they told me. But I heard him cry, Nora. I heard him cry." My voice faded into a whimper. "What if he didn't die? What if?" I scarcely dared to imagine. "What if they just took him away and gave him to someone else?"

"There'll be records," she said firmly, straightening her back. "If the baby died, they would have had to register it as a still-birth. If he lived, there will be a record of adoption. I will ask to see the records for that year—what was it, 1918?"

"Eleventh of November, 1918. How can I forget it? Armistice Day. But it brought me no peace, and that's a fact."

"Perhaps if we can find out for certain what happened, you might feel happier?" Nora said. "I'll find out, promise. Leave it to me."

♒

On her next visit, she turned up late and breathless, with a great smile splitting her face.

"Sorry to be on the drag," she said. "I was with the medical superintendent, and he was running behind." My mouth was gaping, I was that astonished. The superintendent? He was just a name, a kind of God; you never saw him and he just controlled your life from on high. Then the breath stopped in my chest when I remembered her promise.

"You've found out about...?"

The smile faded for a moment. She took off her coat and sat down beside me.

"I'm so sorry. They have checked for me, but they haven't got any records going back that far, they say, because the place where they were stored got hit by the bomb. But I haven't given up yet. In every town, there's an office called the Registrar of Births and Deaths where all these things are supposed to be recorded. I'll go there next time."

I hadn't really hoped for anything, so it wasn't much of a blow.

"It was something else I wanted to ask him," she said with a twinkle like she was about to give me a present.

"Tell me then." There have been that many setbacks in my life, I can live with just one more, I thought.

"Your psychiatrist has told them there is no reason for you to stay here any longer. You are ready for life in the community, he says, if someone will sponsor you."

"Sponsor?" Sane or not, my brain was struggling to keep up with this extraordinary turn of events. "What does that mean? Money?"

"No, you ninny, someone you can live with, who will look after you and keep an eye on you," she said, still beaming. "So? Who do you think that might be?"

I studied her face closely, wondering whether she had been drinking. She was laughing now, and her words made no sense.

"It's *me*, don't you see?" she said.

I shook my head.

"I've offered to be your sponsor. I would like you to come and live with me—not that I think you'll need much looking after once you've adjusted to life outside. We can look after each other. I've got me pension, and they say you'd be due some kind of allowance money too. Sam's offered to do up the second bedroom for you—it's small, mind, but you'll get used to it soon enough. What do you think?"

What did I think? It was like being in a dark room when someone opens a door and there's a brilliant light coming through it, enticing and wonderful, but so bright that it blinds you, dissolves your ability to think, like the bleach they used for sheets in the laundry. Through that door was an unknown world which, even with Nora by my side, felt terrifying and uncontrollable. I've heard that these days, they prepare you for leaving, with counseling and what they call "life skills," but in them postwar years when everyone was still making do and rationing was still causing problems, they was obviously only too keen to get rid of us.

Nora was waiting for me to reply. Well, I couldn't speak for happiness, but I managed to croak something like, "I can live with you? Really? I can leave here? Do you really mean it?" I didn't believe it, to be truthful.

"I really do," she said.

There's a long pause, and then the sound of someone blowing her nose…

And that's how I came back into the world. Not before time, mind, in me late fifties already I was. Better late than never, eh? Been making up for lost time ever since. Oh, we've had some good times, dearie, believe you me. Been on coach trips all over, seen the sights. We don't have much money, but it don't stop us having fun. Honest, I never knew there was so much in the world. And it's all down to my lovely Nora. Poor old Nora.

She coughs a bit and sighs.

"*You said she wasn't well. How is she now?*"

Still in the hospital. They're doing tests, but I've got a funny feeling about it.

"*I'm sorry to hear about that, Maria.*"

I think I'm done now, dearie, if you don't mind. Shall we turn that thing off?

The final tape clicks off.

PATSY MORTON RESEARCH DIARY
JULY 5, 1970

Finished interviews with Queenie/Maria and had to say good-bye for the last time. It made me quite sad because there's no reason for us ever to meet again. Still, I need to stay emotionally detached and maintain my "objective distance," as Prof would say. I also really need to finish the rest of the interviews and try to get my research findings sorted out into some kind of order to show him—getting urgent now as looks like my funding will dry up next year.

Thankfully no more complaints from Dr. Watts—he seems quite happy for me to meet the other staff and patients on my list—but he might not like my conclusions. Too bad, I have to tell it as I find it. Academic rigor and all that.

Besides, the past is past, and the place is closing. Why should he feel it necessary to defend what went on there?

Excerpt from medical notes, Patient M. R., November 1952

Miss M. R. was discharged from hospital into the supervision and care of Mrs. Nora Kowalski of Bethnal Green, London. She was visited by a community mental health visitor four weeks later and is considered to be doing well, without medication. No further visits necessary. Local mental health services have been informed.

15.

As the cassette player shuddered to a halt and fell silent for the final time, I kept my eyes closed for several minutes, reluctant to let Maria go. After listening for more than two hours, it felt as though I knew her personally, as if she were part of the family. Knowing that there was no more to hear was like a small bereavement.

After the initial excitement of hearing her voice, a profound sadness had settled on me. She was so convincing, the way she talked so powerfully credible, yet the medical notes told another story: she was suffering from delusions, a fantasist who heard voices and lived in a world of romance and intrigue. Even though she wasn't educated in a formal sense, Maria was obviously naturally bright, so I had no doubt that she would have been perfectly capable of concocting a convincing yarn. It was almost impossible to disentangle truth from fantasy.

That she had been a seamstress in service at some large house—perhaps even Buckingham Palace—seemed credible enough. At least that might explain how she'd got hold of the royal silks. But her claim to have been seduced by the Prince of Wales sounded so much like the romantic delusion of a young, impressionable girl. From what I'd read, he had a penchant for high society ladies, so why would he have bothered to seduce a servant girl?

On the other hand, why would she claim that the prince had seduced her? So that the child would be adopted as a royal heir? Surely she could have seen that this would have been a serious miscalculation, understood the potential consequences?

So I might have found my Maria, but she was still a mystery.

Just as the professor had warned, the tapes had not made for easy listening. My hands had moved instinctively to cup my own belly as she described the birth of her baby, spoke of her love and the pain of her loss: "It's a love so total it fills you up, drenching your whole body like a wet sponge, so there's no room for feeling anything else." The words were so heartfelt, and yet nowhere in the medical notes was there a single mention of any pregnancy or a baby. Was all of that just a fantasy too? Perhaps most of the story was true, or just delicately embroidered, like Maria's elegant stitching?

But wherever the truth lay, I loved her descriptions of how she had made the quilt and how she had designed the individual frames. Each concentric section had been created to represent or commemorate individuals she had known: her lover—whoever he was—the lost baby, and the hospital visitor who befriended her and helped bring back her speech. Her history was held in the fabrics she'd used, the designs, and the appliquéd figures. It was the patchwork of a life—the metaphor pleased me—and now I understood the meaning of that little verse. She'd stitched the quilt for a baby and had added those lines just in case the child should one day turn up to claim it.

Coming to a greater understanding of all this, discovering how precious it was, how important to her, I now felt its loss even more, like a sharp ache in my chest, each time I thought of it. Recovering the quilt became suddenly much more vital, and more urgent.

It was well after five and the offices were now deserted, so I left a thank-you note with the tapes and the notebook on Sarah's desk and walked in a daze through the bleak university squares back to the distant, windswept parking lot with Maria's voice still running through my head.

In the car, I rang Jo. It went to voice mail and I remembered that she and Mark were still away in Morocco. My head was bursting with questions, and I really needed someone to talk to. Ben's reply came back almost at once. **No problem. I'm at 24 Burton Close, CL3 2RX, about 10 mins drive from uni.**

"It's just a temporary stopping place," he said, welcoming me inside. "All I could afford after my marriage ended. It's got a small spare bedroom for Thomas, and it's close to his school."

He certainly wasn't showing any signs of putting down roots: the single downstairs living-dining area was sparsely furnished with chain-store basics and barely a decorative item in sight: no side lights, just a bare bulb hanging from a central cord, no photos, no cushions or ornaments of any kind, except for two Tate Modern prints tacked to the wall: a brilliant color swirl of Jackson Pollock and a Californian-blue Hockney swimming pool.

"Like your choice," I said, meaning it.

"I should get around to giving them proper frames, but I never seem to have the time. You must think I'm living like a student, just sticking up posters on the wall." He laughed with that deep rumble that had made me feel so safe. "Anyway, what brings you to Eastchester? You look like the cat that's got the cream."

"I've been to see your Professor Morton. The one who wrote the book. And I've found my quilt-maker."

"In person?" he laughed. "The oldest woman in the world, and still quilting?"

"That's what it feels a bit like, weirdly. I've been listening to her voice for the past couple of hours."

"Result! Come in and tell me everything. Wine?"

"Just one glass then," I said.

Over slices of reheated day-old pizza washed down with several glasses of a surprisingly good Pinot, I described everything I could remember of Maria's account, what Patsy had written in her diary, and the medical records that she had transcribed. It all sounded even wackier in the retelling, but he listened without interrupting, his expression sympathetic but not fixed, and didn't even raise his eyebrows when I mentioned the palace and the prince.

"What's your gut feeling?" he asked, when I finally stopped.

"My head's still reeling. She was so convincing, but her psychiatrists and the excerpts from her medical records give another picture."

"Isn't that what they say about fantasists? They're very convincing liars."

I shook my head, as if it would help the pieces fall into place. "But none of this really matters anymore, because the quilt's still gone."

"Did you get in touch with those shelters yet?"

"I've emailed and sent my sketch, but no replies so far."

Ben steepled his hands in that characteristic pose, pressing the tips of his fingers to his lips as he deliberated. The gesture was so unselfconscious, so *human*. I caught myself rubbing a fingertip to my own lower lip and experiencing, for a moment, an alarmingly strong desire to pull those fingers away and kiss him. I gave myself a mental shake. Listening to those tapes all afternoon must have left me a bit deranged.

He leaned forward to open his laptop, interrupting my reverie.

"Let's check a few facts to see how much of Maria's story stands up. For a start, we can see if the Prince of Wales' dates fit," he said, tapping away.

We soon discovered that Edward VIII was born in June 1894, so he would have been a few years older than Maria. The same website outlined his naval training and short stint at Oxford, all of which she had mentioned, as well as his notoriety as a womanizer until meeting Wallis Simpson and embarking on the famous affair which led eventually to his abdication from the throne.

"I suppose there's no way of checking whether someone called Maria Romano really worked at Buckingham Palace?"

He shook his head. "Very unlikely. Palace records are strictly confidential."

"What about whether she ever had a baby? I can't believe she would have spoken with such sadness if her pregnancy was all just a fantasy. Can we check at the registry office?"

"Good plan. I can pop down on Monday, if you like?"

"That'd be great, to confirm it either way." A few weeks ago, I'd have hesitated, fearing he might still be after a newspaper story. Now I could see that he was as curious about the mystery as I was and just as keen to discover the truth. "It would prove her point about making the quilt for the lost child and why she stitched that verse into it. I can't think why else she would have done that."

"What was the name of her friend again?" he asked.

"Margaret?"

"No, the one who rescued her."

"Nora Kowalski? Why?"

"It might be worth checking the register of voters for Bethnal Green. It's not a very common name."

I paused for a long moment, frowning as I tried to remember what Maria had said about Nora's son and grandson. Ben glanced at me curiously, frowning a little. Then he sighed loudly and shook his head, abruptly slapped down the lid of the laptop, and rested his hands on the lid, palms upward.

"What's the problem?" I said, laughing at his petulant expression. It was seriously endearing.

"How long is it going to take you to get it?" he burst out suddenly. "I am not doing this for the bloody newspaper. I am doing it because I like you. Isn't that enough? Or am I getting too involved? Would you rather I just backed off?"

"No, it's not that at all." I nearly laughed again but stopped myself at the last minute. He'd got completely the wrong end of the stick. "It's just that…"

"You *still* don't trust me."

"No, Ben. It's the very opposite," I managed to gabble before allowing instinct to take over. I leaned forward, put my hand to the back of his head, and pulled his face toward mine. I caught a look of surprise in his eyes, but he didn't resist.

In the morning, I panicked. What could I have been thinking? This man, who I barely knew, was dozing peacefully beside me with a childlike smile on his face. Still, the sex hadn't been bad at all, I remembered hazily, considering he'd apologized several times for being out of practice.

We ate a bachelor's breakfast of white sliced toast, cheap jam, and instant coffee, making slightly stilted conversation while skirting around the fact that we'd ended up in bed together. I started to clear the table, taking the dishes to the sink.

"Do you have to leave?" He hugged me from behind.

"I have to go sometime," I said, enjoying the comforting warmth of his body in spite of myself. "We've both got lives to get on with, my mother to visit, your son to see, football to watch, whatever." In the window, I could see our reflections, his large frame dwarfing my own, hair falling forward as he bent down to rest his cheek on the top of my head.

"Before you go, let me take you to see what's left of Helena Hall?" he asked. "It won't take too long, and I think you'll find it interesting. It's just down the road from here."

After ten minutes walking, we emerged abruptly from the soulless maze of newly built houses into an area of greenery: unkempt parkland studded with mature pines, oaks, and spreading copper beeches that had obviously once been planted as part of a large estate.

Passing between high redbrick gate posts and the ruins of what must have been the gatekeeper's lodge, we followed the unmarked tarmac road as it wound between shrubberies of laurel and rhododendron, past several handsome Edwardian houses set in their own gardens and one particularly impressive building that, Ben said, had been the medical superintendent's residence. No wonder Maria had been impressed with the fact that Nora had talked to him, the person she referred to as "like a God."

Although the houses were obviously still inhabited and reasonably well maintained, their surroundings were shabby with neglect. A small wooden hut with peeling white paint must have been a cricket pavilion, and the swath of overgrown grassland in front once a perfectly manicured pitch. Nearby, broken-down chain-link fences surrounded ancient tennis courts, with the remains of their nets hanging limply between rotting posts like ancient cobwebs, reminding me of the "airing courts" in which Maria had felt like a caged animal. Each turn of the road revealed another relic of what had once been a thriving community, now abandoned to nature.

As we turned the corner, our route was abruptly blocked by an enormous, shiny metal fence, three meters high and topped with ferocious-looking spikes, reaching out on either side as far as the eye could see. In front of us was a gate plastered with fierce instructions: DANGER, NO ENTRY; WARNING, 24 HOUR CCTV IN OPERATION; KEEP OUT.

"I think they've made their point," I said.

"Kids were getting in and setting fires," Ben explained. "Wait till you see this."

Pushing through the undergrowth, we emerged into a clearing where it was possible to see, through the metal uprights of the fence, an expanse of grass that must have been a wide lawn and a weedy gravel driveway leading to an enormous building. It really was a mansion, in redbrick with white-painted pillars around a high doorway at the top of grand entrance steps. Above the entrance loomed a tall, square clock tower.

"That's the front entrance to the hospital," Ben said.

"It's just how Maria described it! I can see why she thought she'd arrived at a stately home. It must have been beautiful, once."

Stretching away on either side were long three-story build-ings of the same red brick, with rows of sash windows on each floor. "Those were the wards?"

Ben nodded. Every window was bounded by close-packed upright metal bars. The thought that Maria and my beloved Granny had once been incarcerated behind those bars made me shiver.

He put his arm around my shoulder. "Doesn't seem quite so idyllic from here, does it?"

"Poor things," I whispered. "Locked away in all this beautiful parkland, and all because they didn't conform."

"I'm sure most of them were genuinely ill and needed to be protected from harming themselves or others. But I'm glad it's now closed, and all the brutal treatments with it."

"What's going to happen to the place?"

"They're still wrangling over planning agreements, but it'll probably become yet another estate of little boxes like Burton Close."

"And after a while, no one will remember what happened here."

"There was a real community of people who worked here, and they've spent the last couple of decades getting all nostalgic about it and chewing my ear off to help them campaign to stop it being demolished," Ben said. "But I think knocking it down is probably for the best. It will close that chapter for good."

We stood there a few moments longer, in the cold silence of the woods. No birds sang, no leaves rustled, and I couldn't even hear the sound of traffic from the distant A12. Despite the grand architecture and beautiful grounds, I couldn't help seeing it as the prison in which Maria had spent the best decades of her life.

"Let's go, Ben." I took his arm. "This place is depressing me."

∽

Back at Burton Close, he made sandwiches and more coffee while I checked my phone.

"Ohmigod…" I whooped, punching the air and dancing around the kitchen. "It's a text from Justin, the designer." I read it out loud: Please call asap. Have a buyer interested in your designs. Justin.

"I told you they were something special," Ben said, grinning broadly and catching me mid-jig for a hug. "I've got a good eye for these things."

But initial euphoria was turning to panic. "What if I get a commission from this? How am I going to get them made up?"

"You'll need a bloody good upholsterer who can interpret what you want," he said. "Do you know any?"

"I thought I might do it myself." My training was at least fifteen years ago, and I hadn't attempted anything since.

"Where would you work though?"

Good question. The flat was entirely unsuitable. I hadn't thought this one through carefully enough. "I might have to rent a workshop."

"What about using your mum's place? The garage would make the perfect workshop. All it needs is a few more windows and some heating."

"It's no good. You know I've got to sell it. How else am I going to pay for Mum's care home?"

"You could sell the flat instead," he said mildly, as if this was the most obvious thing in the world.

"Are you crazy? That's not going to happen! All my friends are in London, my contacts, my job…" I checked myself. "Well, you know what I mean. I need to find out what Justin wants first. It might come to nothing, in the end."

"It was just a thought." He made a mock-chastened face, sweet and rather sexy and, for a moment, I was tempted all over again.

"I really have to go, to visit Mum before it gets too late," I said, giving him a hug. "Thanks for everything."

✍

Perhaps getting together with Ben was meant to be, a sign of good things to come because, after that, my day turned out better and better.

Mum told me straight out that she liked "this hotel" and had already talked to the matron about extending her stay. As I left Holmfield, I found myself skipping across the parking lot with a huge beam on my face, as though a boulder had been lifted from my shoulders. I would worry about the cost later. The matron had given me details of a financial adviser who could suggest ways of releasing capital from the cottage.

Then when I got home and called Justin, it turned out that not one but two significant clients were interested in my designs. "How soon can you get me some sample pieces?" he asked. "Nothing too elaborate, say a chair and a footstool?"

"No problem," I said, silently shouting *Yes!* and punching the air with excitement. "Can you give me till the end of the month?"

I'd have to work day and night to achieve it, but I couldn't let this big break slip through my fingers. Life seemed suddenly so full of possibilities: I'd found my quilt-maker, had some great sex, got Mum happily settled, *and* got two commissions that might just kick-start my fledgling company.

The following day, still in a jubilant mood, I scoured two flea markets and, in my enthusiasm, spent a great deal more than I should have on a dilapidated spoon-back Victorian armchair with a mess of straps, horsehair, and cotton wadding bulging below its seat. I also bought a footstool that was sufficiently similar in design so that, when both pieces were re-upholstered in the same fabrics, they would look like a match. Both needed so much work I would never recover my costs, but they would be my "showpiece" items and, I hoped, an investment for the future.

As I lugged them up the three flights of stairs, risking the wrath of the traffic wardens gathering around my illegally parked car, I began to see that Ben's suggestion of using the garage at Rowan Cottage made a lot of sense. Stripping down old upholstery is a messy, dusty business for which my flat was completely unsuitable. Besides, to do the job properly, I would need to invest in specialist tools, power staplers, glue guns, and the rest.

So I spent a fruitless few hours telephoning every professional upholsterer in North London, but none were able even to start such a project until the end of February, and the quotes they suggested were completely over the top for my projected budget. Reluctantly, I concluded that there was nothing for it. I would have to do the work myself, and this time around, the flat would have to double as a workshop.

In the spare bedroom, I pushed the bed aside and covered the furniture and carpet with old sheets. With everything now covered and protected, I set to stripping the old upholstery and padding. It was satisfying to work with my hands once more, rediscovering my practical skills, seeing tangible results. I put on my favorite tracks and sang along to them loudly and unselfconsciously.

When my fingers became blistered from pulling out tacks, I made a start on the upholstery scheme, working with swatches of fabrics, paper, and paint, trying to create stunning, unique patchwork designs that would wow Justin's clients. At college, I'd received my best marks for drawing. My skills were rusty but I knew they would improve with practice, and in future, I would need to learn computer-aided design. For now, I relished the process of sketching and applying paint to paper.

Next, I hauled out my long-neglected sewing machine and set to work on a few test-samples, creating collages of fabrics and bindings. It was exhilarating to see the creations that I'd had in my imagination and had then sketched onto paper now taking physical shape.

In the middle of the week, Ben texted, "Good luck with the designs xx." The double x was new, but being apart for a few days had left me uncertain about what I really felt for him. We'd become comfortable together and seemed to enjoy each other's company, that was true. But he was so different from anyone I'd imagined myself ending up with.

Then he rang. "You *are* real then, not just a figment of my lurid imagination?"

"Sorry, Ben, I've been manic with this upholstery project."

"How's it going?"

"Slowly, messily."

"I've been to the register office, like you asked," he said, after an awkward pause. "I'm sorry to say that there's no trace of any baby born at Helena Hall with the name of Romano. Nor any babies at all registered around 1918, the time you said she was admitted. None born, none registered as having died. So we have to wonder whether the baby was also a fantasy."

"I don't suppose the hospital could have disposed of it without anyone knowing?"

"That would have been illegal, even back then, so unlikely but not impossible," he said. "But there's good news on the other front. The Register of Voters in Bethnal Green records only three Kowalskis, and they're all living at the same address."

My heart leaped. This had to be Nora's family. "Wow. What are their names?"

"Just a sec." A flick of notebook pages. "Samuel, Andrew, and Tracey."

It was a moment before the obvious dawned. "Father and son? Nora's son and grandson, perhaps, and the grandson's wife? I'll phone them this evening." My thoughts were sprinting ahead, and I was already imagining the conversation we might have about the woman their grandmother had rescued from a mental hospital. Maria was constantly in my head, especially when working on the patchwork designs, and I often found myself asking, "How would she have done this? Would she have put that color against this one?" These people were the closest she had to family, so surely they would be able to confirm some of her story and what had happened to her?

"I've checked, but can't find a number. You could write. Or just knock on their door."

"Are you crazy? This is London. People don't open their doors to strangers."

"They can only turn you away, and if they do, you could write instead. But in my experience, if people haven't got anything to hide, they are usually quite generous. They might just invite you in. You never know."

"I'm not sure…" I dithered.

"Would you like me to come with you? It could be less threatening if we turn up on their doorstep together, and safer for you in case they turn out to be ax-murderers." He laughed. It seemed unlikely, but he had a point. "I could come on Saturday."

"What about Tom's football?"

"I'm free from dad duties this weekend," Ben said. "He's off on a school trip. What about visiting your mum?"

"Not a problem. I can go on Monday. I'm my own boss now." I repeated the words in my head: *my own boss*. I could do what I liked, to hell with being cautious. "Come on Friday evening," I said quickly, before I could change my mind. "I'll cook. It'll make a nice change from pulling out tacks."

"Perfect."

It had become clear that the chair's upholstery was in a terminal state and would need to be stripped back to its wooden frame before completely rebuilding. By Thursday, it was a skeleton, cleaned and stripped of old tacks and staples, but my spare room looked as though a cyclone had hit it, with wadding, horsehair, and webbing scattered all over the floor. Years ago, at college, I'd completed an evening class in upholstery and we had tackled something similar, but then we were working in pairs, in a fully equipped workshop, with an experienced tutor helping at every stage. This was an altogether more daunting task.

I wrote a list of the basic kit that I would need:

- Workmate bench
- scissors
- chisels (x 2)
- mallet + magnetic hammer
- staple gun
- tack lifter
- webbing stretcher

– regulator
– materials: webbing, horsehair, cotton wadding and
  hessian, cording + trimmings

This lot would cost well over a thousand pounds, I figured, on top of what I'd paid for the chair and stool, and this first commission would never make a profit. But I tried to reassure myself that all new businesses have to operate at a loss to start with, and there must be a value in my designs or why would Justin and his clients have been so interested in them?

On Friday morning, I examined myself in the mirror and decided that I needed to invest in myself, as well as in the business. First, a trip to the hairdresser's for highlights to conceal the ugly stripe at my parting and a cut which shaped without shortening too much. I watched happily as she feathered the ends, softening my face and taking years off me. Then it was off to the beauticians for a manicure to sort out my work-roughened hands and to get my eyebrows shaped and lashes and brows tinted.

I spent a blissfully domestic afternoon cooking a nut roast for me and a lamb shank for Ben—he'd told me this was his favorite meal. It was so long since I'd cooked anything significant, and I'd forgotten how much I enjoyed it. Even so, for a vegetarian, handling hunks of raw meat is a sign of true friendship. I hoped he would appreciate it.

"Mmm, that smells delicious. I'm starving." He stood back to appraise me. "Like the new look."

"Thank you." He'd made an effort too. The leather jacket and stonewashed jeans had gone, replaced with black trousers and a fitted V-neck sweater in deep purple that instantly made him appear slimmer, less bulky. Who advised him on this new style? His ex? More likely a friend or work colleague. Whoever it was had done a good job.

"Food's nearly ready. Why don't you pour yourself a glass of this while I light the candles?" I handed him the bottle of Burgundy that had been warming on the mantelpiece and I'd already started.

At that very moment, my phone rang.

"Miss Meadows?"

"Speaking. Who's this, please?"

"My name is Arun. I'm the manager of the King's Cross night shelter. You emailed us about your stolen quilt? I think we may have found it."

"It's the night shelter," I squeaked with excitement.

"Have they found it?" Ben mouthed.

"Sounds like it."

"Are you there, Miss Meadows?"

"Sorry it's just…I am almost speechless," I gabbled. "Thank you so much! When can I come and collect it? Do I need to bring anything to exchange it with?"

"It's not quite so simple, I'm afraid," the man said. "Let me explain. We had a meeting of our volunteers this morning, and I mentioned your friend's request. One of them remembered talking to one of our regulars, a man called Dennis, about his bedroll. It was unusual, she says, because it was made of patchwork."

Surely there couldn't be too many tramps in central London with patchwork quilts in their bedrolls? "Is he there now?"

"Sorry, I should have explained. They only come for the night and have to leave in the morning. But you can speak to our volunteer if you like. Just a sec." He shouted away from the phone, his voice reverberating in what sounded like a large room. "Leylah? Can you come and talk to Miss Meadows about Dennis's quilt?"

A tentative voice with a strong Jamaican twang: "Hello, can I help you?"

"I hear you recognized the quilt. Thank you so much."

"I didn't see much of it. When I offered to get it laundered, he told me to bugger off." Her smoky chuckle reminded me of Maria's.

"What about colors?"

"Well, there was a lot of blue," she said, "with flowers. And a design like a sunrise. Hard to see, the thing's pretty grubby."

My heart danced, remembering the grandmother's fan. "That sounds like the one. Thank you so much. By the way, if he does give it to you, please don't wash it, because it's very delicate and might damage the fabrics."

"No problem."

She handed the phone back to Arun. "It sounds like my quilt," I said. "I wonder where he found it?"

There was a hushed conversation at the other end, before he came back on the line. "He's adamant that he didn't steal it—he found it in a pile of garbage."

"Would he agree to part with it, do you think? Perhaps I could offer something to replace it: a new blanket, a winter coat perhaps?"

"We can certainly ask him when he comes back," Arun said.

"Is he there every evening?" My imagination was fast-forwarding to the happy moment of exchange: the tramp delightedly trying on his new coat, me returning home with my precious quilt. The vision was instantly dashed.

"He's not one of our regulars, I'm afraid. He often disappears for weeks, or even months. But as soon as we see him, we'll get in touch."

"It's so frustrating," I wailed to Ben after ringing off. "For a moment, it felt as though I was almost close enough to grasp it, but now it's gone again."

"Dennis will turn up again, somewhere," he said calmly. "If not at King's Cross, then somewhere else."

All we could do was wait.

16.

O VER BREAKFAST NEXT DAY (CROISSANTS AND REAL coffee, of course), we chatted easily and planned our trip to the East End. The meal had been a success, and our previous awkwardness seemed to have evaporated. As Ben bent his head over his phone to check the route, the back of his neck looked so vulnerable my fingers itched to stroke it. Or bury my head in it. Or even take him straight back to bed.

But first, we had a mission to achieve.

Bethnal Green is in the throes of a patchy process of gentrification. Trash bins litter its narrow residential streets, where Audis jostle with ancient Astras and neglected motorbikes. Among the DIY replacement doors and windows, some frontages have been restored to Edwardian glory, with glimmering Farrow and Ball paintwork and brass fittings. Many of the tiny front gardens are just dumping grounds, while others have been landscaped with York stone pathways, box hedges, and other tasteful adornments.

The Kowalskis' house, a three-story, bay-windowed Edwardian terrace, was somewhere between the two extremes. It had a comfortable, lived-in look, by no means gentrified but in a reasonable state of repair. The paintwork was fresh, and although they were now dead and frosted, the window boxes had once been bright with geraniums. Unlike many of its neighbors, the house had not been converted into flats, and there was a single button for the bell, which sounded hollowly inside the house. After a short pause, the gaunt face of a middle-aged woman peered through the lace curtains.

I waved in what I hoped was a friendly and nonthreatening gesture. The face disappeared and we heard a shout: "Andy! Are you expecting anyone?" There was another pause, then the sound of footsteps on the stairs, and the door was opened by a tall, bony man in his fifties with a wild crest of wavy gray hair and an overnight growth of stubble.

"Yes?" he said suspiciously, his frame blocking the doorway.

"I'm sorry to trouble you. Are you Mr. Kowalski?"

"Who wants to know?" he said with a strong Cockney inflection.

"My name is Caroline Meadows and this is my friend Ben. I think our grandmothers may have had a friend in common. Was your granny's name Nora? Nora Kowalski?"

"Possibly." His eyes narrowed with mistrust.

"And I think she was friends with a woman called Maria Romano?"

The fierce expression cracked into a snag-toothed grin. "Maria, the fruitcake? Your granny was her friend?" He swiveled his head and shouted into the house, "Trace? People here knew Nora and Maria." The person we had seen at the window, another slender, wiry fifty-something, appeared beside him in the doorway wearing a flowery apron, wiping her hands on a tea towel.

I explained again that my granny had known Maria, who we believed was also a friend of Nora's. "I'm trying to find out a bit more about her. Is there any chance we could talk?"

"Sorry, loves, we'd invite you in but right now we're in a bit of a pickle with Andy's old dad," she said. "He's very lame, you see, and I'm trying to get him sorted."

"Perhaps we could come back," Ben said, "at a more convenient time."

They both hesitated, and then the woman nudged his arm. "You go, Andy. Take them down the Queens. I'll get Sam sorted and follow you down."

"You sure, Trace?"

"Off you go," she said. "Have one for me."

From the way he told it, Andy Kowalski, grandson of Nora, East Ender and jack of all trades, spent his life ducking and diving, making a bob or two here and there while his wife Tracey "brings in the reg'lars" as a cleaner at the nearby Royal London Hospital. He confirmed that his grandmother was Nora Kowalski, née Featherstone. He had barely known his grandfather, Samuel Kowalski, son of a Polish refugee, who died long before Nora. Andy's father, who he confusingly referred to as old Sam, Sam junior, or sometimes just Sammy, was the only survivor of Nora's two sons, the other having died in the war. After his wife died, Andy and his wife Trace had moved in to look after him.

Yes, it was hard having the old boy around all the time, he said, fussing about his food and what powder he wanted his clothes washed in, but what could you do? He couldn't go on living on his own, what with his legs gone and the rest.

I nodded sympathetically, sipped my glass of wine, and tried to banish guilty thoughts of Mum. These good people had thought it perfectly natural to move in with their widowed father, perhaps because they could afford no alternative, and they seemed to be managing just fine.

"So what was it you wanted to know then?" he asked.

I explained about Helena Hall, the tapes, and what Maria had said about having worked with Nora at Buckingham Palace. "Did Nora ever tell you any of this?"

"We all knew Maria was a bit of a nutter, to be honest," he said. "But she wasn't lying about Buckingham Palace."

"She really did work there?" I gasped, catching Ben's eye across the table. He was grinning from ear to ear.

Andy hesitated, taken aback by my reaction. "Leastwise, far as we know. Nan was tight-lipped about it, of course; they was sworn to secrecy, I 'spect. But we knew in the family that she and my grandpa both worked there, long ago. Maria was there for a while too," he went on. "They was seamstresses, I seem to remember. She was always good with a needle."

"That's incredible," I whispered. "In the hospital, they said she was making it all up." His words felt like a gift. If only Maria could have been here to celebrate with us—she'd have loved it.

"Did they ever talk about the Prince of Wales?"

"Our Charlie? What was she up to with him, then?"

"No, Charlie's great-uncle, the one who married Mrs. Simpson and resigned from the throne, back in the thirties. He would have been about the same age as Maria and your Nan. Maria said she knew him...you know, erm, personally."

He shook his head. "Nah, don't recall any talk of that, but we can ask Dad when he gets here. Not that he remembers much these days. Nan used to say she was quite a looker when she was young, that Maria, but I can't see her catching a prince."

"What do you remember about Maria?" Ben prompted.

"I was too young to know her properly, like," Andy went on, getting into his stride. "We was just kids when she left. Mum and Dad said they never knew what to make of the woman, to be honest. They was already married when she arrived and Nan—Nora, that is—told him she was just a friend, come to stay 'cause she had nowhere else to go. Besides, old Nora was that lonely after her hubby died, and she said it was nice to have company, doing their needlework and that."

"Do you remember Maria sewing patchwork? My granny left me a quilt she made."

His eyes lit up, bright as a child's. "Bloody hell, that's something I *do* remember. I was only a kid but I loved them lovely little ducks and flowers," he mused, "and the dragon, I remember that, with the flames coming out its mouth. I used to tell her it was a dinosaur. Nan said they had worked on one of the sections together, the one with the flowery patterns, because they used to love them flowers when they was girls. You still got it, then?"

"Sort of," I improvised. "We lent it to someone but hope to get it back soon."

"Think of that, after all those years." Andy took a deep drink. "Still, there was nothing for it once Nora died."

"Nothing for what, exactly?"

"They had to give Gran's flat back to the council, and Maria wasn't on the tenancy so she had to leave."

"What happened to her? This is what I'd really like to find out, how Maria came to live with my grandmother."

"To be honest, I never did discover," Andy said, frowning.

"Would your father remember, do you think?" Ben pressed.

"I doubt it. His memory's that bad. He can't remember the time of day, mostly. But he do talk about the old days, so you might get something out of him. He's deaf, though, won't wear his hearing aid, so you have to shout. Let's see if Trace has got him out of bed yet." He drained his glass, pushed back the chair, and we all got to our feet.

Just then the door opened and in came Tracey, backward, struggling to maneuver a wheelchair containing a frail old boy with a mop of white hair. Ben went to help her over the step as we cleared a space at the table. The old man looked around, bewildered, as she parked the wheelchair next to me and firmly put on the brakes.

"This is Andy's father, Sam," she said. "I'm Tracey."

Ben shook the old man's clawlike hand. "What can I get you to drink, sir?"

"Lager and lime for me, a pint of mild for Sam, thank you very much," Tracey answered for him.

Andy put his face close to his father's ear. "This lady wants to know about that Maria woman who lived with Gran in the old days. Do you remember her?"

The old boy turned his head slowly in my direction and peered at me with milky gray eyes. "You're Maria?" he asked in a quavery voice.

"No, Dad. She wants to find out about Maria," Andy said more loudly.

Old Sam shook his head. "Don't shout, boy. Maria, you say?"

"Who lived with Nora, your mum?"

There was a pause as Ben returned with the drinks and the old boy took several noisy gulps. "What was you talking about?" he muttered to his son after a moment.

"MARIA," Andy bellowed. "Woman who used to work with Gran and Grandad. At Buckingham Palace?"

"Oh, Maria," Sam said, his face brightening with recognition. "Strange old bat. Worked with Mum at the palace, didn't she?"

"THIS LADY WANTS TO KNOW IF SHE HAD A THING WITH THE PRINCE OF WALES?" There's no such thing as a discreet conversation with a deaf person. The barman glanced at us curiously, and across the table, Ben appeared to be inspecting something of vital importance on the floor, shoulders shaking as he tried to stifle his laughter.

Old Sam appeared to be even more confused than ever. "Didn't hear nothing about a prince," he grumbled.

"They was both seamstresses for the queen," Tracey chipped in. "We've still got some of Nora's work, at home."

"Did you ever see Maria working on a quilt?" I said loudly, close to old Sam's ear.

He shook his head.

"A QUILT," I shouted again, trying to ignore the earthquake now convulsing Ben's shoulders. "A bed cover, you know?"

"They was always sewing something," he muttered. "They kept each other company, you know."

Tracey piped up again. "She was a kindly soul, that Maria. Looked after Nora once she got ill and nursed her as well as she could before she was taken into the hospital for the last time. She was a great help in them final days."

"What happened after Nora died?" Ben asked.

"It were a shame really, after all she done for us, but she said she got a friend up Essex somewhere," Tracey said. "Something about a son."

"A son?" I nearly fell off my chair. "Go on."

"When Nora was poorly, in them last days, Maria got a letter," Tracey went on.

"What happened next?" I asked.

"This friend offered her a place to stay," Andy went on. "It was a relief, to be honest. There was precious little space in our house already, with Mum and Dad and us three kids getting big by then."

"Did you know who she went to live with?"

"WHO WAS IT MARIA WENT TO LIVE WITH, DAD?"

The old boy shook his head. "Long time ago. Name's gone."

"Could it have been someone by the name of Jean, Jean Meadows?"

"Not that I know of."

"DID YOU SEE MARIA AGAIN, AFTER SHE LEFT?" Andy shouted.

"No, never saw hide nor hair of her," old Sam said, more cheerfully now. "Good riddance too. She never would stop talking." He drained his glass with a noisy gulp. "Now," he said, looking up hopefully, "who's for another drink?"

In a jubilant mood, I suggested dinner at the Italian around the corner from my flat.

"Here's to the fabulous Kowalskis," Ben said, clinking his glass to mine.

"You make them sound like a circus act," I laughed.

"What about this son then?" Ben asked. "That Tracey mentioned? She said Maria had found him."

"If it was the baby she gave birth to in the hospital in 1918, by now he'd be…" I did a quick calculation, "…ninety-four. Jeez, he could still be alive!"

"The bastard son of the Prince of Wales?"

"Alive and living in Essex? Do you really think so? I wonder if we could trace him?"

"If he was adopted, he won't be a Romano," Ben said, tucking into his spaghetti.

"But Tracey suggested that Maria had found him, and if so, how?"

"Chances are she checked the local authority's records."

"Could we check them too?"

"They're not likely to tell us anything, since you're not related," he said.

"The only thing we know for sure is that she ended up living with Granny. I could go and look through those photo albums again, see if they offer any clues."

By the end of dinner, we had agreed that Ben would make initial inquiries with social services and local adoption charities and would put a small item in the *Eastchester Star*'s weekly "Looking Back" feature, to ask whether anyone knew a man adopted around 1918 who might have been related to a Maria Romano. It was a very long shot. I would check the family photo albums and quiz Mum once more to see if she remembered anything about Maria having a son or how Maria came to meet Granny. She was our last link, but I didn't hold out much hope.

Early on Monday morning, I was woken by a phone call.

"Miss Meadows? This is Gill Lewis, deputy matron at Holmfield."

"What's happened?" I panicked, confused by being roused from deep sleep. "Is Mum okay?"

"Nothing too serious," she said, "but we just wanted to let you know that your mother took a bit of a tumble last night. She was quite distressed, but there doesn't seem to be anything broken. She settled okay, but this morning, she seems a little more muddled than usual, so we're getting the doctor in to check her over."

"I'll come right away. Be there in an hour or so."

As I sped down the A12, anxiety stirred up the now-familiar argument in my head. Was Holmfield the right place for Mum? Now that I wasn't in a nine-to-five job, surely I should be looking after her myself, just as the Kowalski family cared for old Sam?

I went at once to see the deputy matron, who told me more about the fall—apparently it was in the dining room, after supper-time. The doctor had already checked Mum over and found her bruised but nothing broken.

"You'll find her a little more confused though," she cautioned. "It's not uncommon in dementia patients if they take a bit of a knock or have a shock. It'll probably ease after a few days."

I'd expected Mum to be in bed, but I was led to the conservatory where, to my surprise, she was up and dressed, sitting in a chair by the window. From a distance, she looked healthier than I'd seen for a long time, her cheeks rosy, her hair neatly held back in an elegant roll, her eyes bright and alert. But when we came into her line of view, she did not break into her usual welcoming smile; her face remained blank and strangely unwrinkled, giving her a curiously youthful look.

Only when I sat down and took her hand did she turn to me, with a little crease of concern creeping between her eyebrows.

"Mum?" I whispered. "It's me, Caroline."

The frown deepened and she blinked rapidly, as if trying to clear the haze of confusion.

"Your daughter, Caroline." If Mum didn't even recognize me, this was the beginning of the end. It had happened so terrifyingly quickly. Her memory loss continued its merciless march, and the fall had made it so much worse. Now she'd even forgotten who I was.

"Ah, Caroline," she whispered like a sigh, her brow smoothing. Somewhere inside her head, synapses were making links, but not in the right order. "My dearest grand-daughter," she added.

"I'm your *daughter*," I said gently, "Jean's granddaughter."

Her eyes flickered away, across the room. "Is Jean here?" she said with more urgency.

"No, she's not here." I stroked her hand to bring her focus back to me. "Granny Jean died years ago."

Mum slumped back in her chair, shoulders drooping and hands limp, and closed her eyes. "Oh dear," she sighed. "They're all dying off now."

"Shall I get a cup of tea and some biscuits?"

"Yes please, dear," she whispered without opening her eyes, as if the business of trying to figure out who I was had drained all her energy. "I had a bit of a fall, did they tell you?"

"Yes, Mum. But the doctor says you are all right now."

"All right now," she repeated, like a child.

When I returned with the tray, Mum's face was alert again. "Thank you, dear," she said. "You girls are so good to me.'

"I'm Caroline." I poured the tea and gave her an extra spoonful of sugar. "Your daughter. I don't work here. I've come to visit you."

After a moment's pause, she said, "Caroline?"

At last, she recognized me. "Yes, Mum. Your daughter, Caroline. Have a cup of tea."

She took the cup and saucer with a surprisingly steady hand and took a sip. "Delicious," she murmured. "Dearest Caroline. It is so nice to see you. Now, what were we talking about?"

"I've got some exciting news, Mum. Remember that old quilt we found in the loft, Jean's quilt? I've been finding out more about the person who sewed it. Just as you thought, it was made by Maria, the woman who came to live with Granny."

She looked at me blankly. "Pass me a biscuit, dear, would you please?"

I pressed on. "Do you remember Maria?" She shook her head.

"Jean's quilt," she parroted vaguely, munching on her biscuit. "Someone called Maria?"

I was about to give up and change the subject when it came out, that shocking non sequitur, "Has Jean told you…?" She stopped midsentence and reached over for her cup of tea.

"Told me what, Mum?" I stuttered, passing the cup. Whatever could it be that Granny had wanted to tell me?

"Said she wanted you to know, when we were all gone."

A chill started in my scalp and traveled down my spine. What kind of dark place was Mum in, that she was summoning messages from the grave?

"What was it she wanted me to know?" I asked, struggling to keep my voice level.

"Before she died, dear," Mum said mildly, taking another biscuit. "Long time ago now."

I relaxed a little; her sense of time had corrected itself, and we were back on normal territory at least. "Was it something important? Something you ought to tell me?" I probed.

"About Richard," Mum said, a faraway look in her eyes. "My darling Richard. He's waiting for me, you know?"

"I'm sure he is, Mum," I soothed, trying to envisage how she imagined him. Sitting on a cloud, perhaps, or in a paradise garden?

"Back home. He'll have my supper ready when I get back."

I tried to enter her world, follow her train of thought. "And what will he tell you about Jean's secret, Mum? The thing she wanted me to know?"

She turned her sweet face toward me, putting a finger to pursed lips. "Shhh," she said conspiratorially. "Arthur's not supposed to know."

I shivered again, despite the stifling heat of the room. "What is Grandpa not supposed to know, Mum?"

She turned to gaze into the distance out of the window, her

expression frighteningly blank. The effect was strange: as the wrinkles relaxed and smoothed out, her face became almost youthful again.

"What are we not supposed to know?" I repeated, moving my face into her line of vision. "You can share it with me, you know. I promise not to tell him." My stomach was churning uneasily. Was this just the ramblings of a demented old woman? Or had Granny really wanted something concealed from my grandfather?

Just then, an old man in a wheelchair parked a few yards from us let out a loud groan, like an animal in pain. "Yaaaaahhh," he shouted and again. "Yaaaaaaaaaah. Help me." His face was screwed up in agony.

I leaped to my feet and went to his side. "What is it?" But he just closed his eyes and roared again.

A young assistant ran toward us, talking urgently into her pager, and within moments, three nurses were by his side. I backed away, relieved to entrust the poor old soul into their care, and returned to Mum. But in all the noise and commotion, she had fallen asleep. I sat quietly beside her for ten minutes, but when she continued to doze, I went to see the deputy matron.

"She's sleeping now," I said. "Shall I leave her in the chair?"

"That's probably for the best. Sleep's a good healer. Don't worry, Miss Meadows. Give us a ring in the morning and I'm sure she'll be feeling a lot better by then."

With my head full of conflicting emotions—curiosity and anxiety, relief and guilt—I retraced my steps back along the corridor to the entrance hall, negotiating a couple of people pushing walkers en route. On the hall table was a display of newspapers and magazines, and my eye was caught by a copy of the *Eastchester Star*.

The teaser headline below the paper's garish red masthead read: "PALACE TIGHT-LIPPED ON HELENA HALL CLAIM. Turn to page 5."

No! It couldn't be. I grabbed the paper and opened it with shaking hands. The piece wasn't exactly prominent, and there was no byline but, as my eyes skimmed over the words, it confirmed my worst fears:

> ROYAL officials today refused to comment on claims that a former Buckingham Palace servant was held involuntarily at Helena Hall Mental Hospital for several decades before being released into the community in the 1950s.
>
> Retired Eastchester nurse Mrs. Pearl Bacon, 86, who identified the patient only by her nickname of "Queenie," says that the woman claimed to have worked for the royal family, but psychiatrists had always dismissed the claims as fantasies. After she was released into the community, her story was eventually proved to be true, Mrs. Bacon says.
>
> "Queenie" went to live with a friend who told staff that both of them had indeed worked at Buckingham Palace. Mrs. Bacon declined to speculate about why the patient had originally been sectioned under the Mental Health Act. "It was all long before my time," she said.
>
> The revelation echoes the recently revealed plight of two royal cousins, Nerissa and Katherine Bowes-Lyon, who were incarcerated in a mental

institution for the whole of their lives because they had learning disabilities.

Eastchester Mental Health Trust said that they did not discuss individual cases because of patient confidentiality, and Buckingham Palace said it was not their policy to comment to the media.

The words skittered in front of my eyes as I struggled to make sense of them. Why would Pearl have told her story to the newspaper? Now, after all these years?

There was only one person who could possibly have written the article.

I sat down heavily on one of the chairs, sick and dizzy at the enormity of this betrayal. What I had learned to love about Ben lately was his openness and apparent honesty. Surely he couldn't have been planning this all along? Getting to know me because he wanted to dig out the story behind the quilt? Had he wangled his way into my confidence—into my bed too—all for a pathetic little page-five story based on ancient hearsay about people who were long dead?

An unpleasant vision reared before my eyes: Ben's large form perched on that hard chair in Pearl's little forties parlor, notebook in hand, smiling in that sweet, confidential way of his, inveigling the vulnerable old woman to divulge the information he needed to confirm what the Kowalskis had told us. And she had finally given in, confirming the facts that she had concealed—or perhaps conveniently forgotten—on our first visit.

I shuddered, feeling dirty and used, and punched the shortcut key for Ben's number, but it went to voice mail. I left an angry message, threw down the newspaper, and ran out to the car. As I went to call him again, a text message was waiting in my inbox.

Please ring asap need to tell you something important. Ben x

I'd fucking tell *him* something, I swore to myself, starting the car and revving the engine unnecessarily. Not over the phone either. I would go to his office and bawl him out, publicly and humiliatingly, in front of his colleagues. Driving off, too fast and part-blinded with a red mist of fury, I rehearsed a speech which included words like "underhand" and "perfidious treachery" as well as plenty of imaginative expletives. The message tone beeped again and again till I grabbed my phone and turned it off.

By now it was rush hour, and as the procession of cars on the A12 slowed to walking pace, I cursed again and again, turning on the local BBC radio station in hopes of discovering whether it was an accident or just what they infuriatingly refer to as "sheer weight of traffic." The presenter wittered on until I heard the news jingle and a new voice reading the bulletin which mostly seemed to consist of stories about corrupt local councilors and "nimby" planning controversies.

"And finally," she wrapped up in that time-honored way, "royal officials have refused to comment on claims that a former Buckingham Palace servant was held involuntarily for decades at the now-closed Helena Hall Mental Hospital in Eastchester. Although doctors always claimed the woman was a fantasist, a former nurse has now come forward to confirm that the claims were true."

A familiar, quavery voice came over the airwaves, Pearl's: "We don't know how she ended up in there in the first place. It was all long before my time, you know. But when she come to be released, the friend she went to live with said her stories were all true, poor old dear. They had both worked at the palace, long ago."

The newsreader's voice cut back in again: "The story follows recent revelations about two royal cousins with learning disabilities who were incarcerated for the whole of their lives. Neither Eastchester Mental Health Trust nor Buckingham Palace officials were prepared to comment."

"Shit, shit, shit!" I slammed off the radio and whacked my palm against the steering wheel until it smarted. Of course, local news organizations all suckled off each other, repeating stories with only minor variations until they were wrung dry or…my head went hot at the thought…they made the national tabloids. Please God, this wasn't a strong enough story for the nationals? Surely not, with only the claims of an elderly lady to substantiate it?

Furious thoughts rampaged through my brain as the traffic crawled slowly forward, and I cursed Ben, his wretched newspaper, and the parasitical way that news spreads throughout the world, until finally, I reached the Eastchester exit.

On the way into the town, I must have passed at least six newsagents, and each time my fury grew as I read their billboards proclaiming:

ROYAL RUMPUS
OVER HELENA HALL

There is no public parking outside the offices of the *Eastchester Star*, so I dumped the car in a loading bay and ran inside. Ahead of me at reception, a very large elderly man dithered about which photograph to order. "Do you think she would like this one…? Or perhaps that one is better…? Which one is best, do you think?"

With the anger still boiling inside me like a pressure cooker, it was impossible to wait quietly. After a few moments, the receptionist, unable to ignore my frequent sharp sighs, peered around the old boy's considerable bulk and said she would be with me shortly.

"I need to speak to Ben Sweetman," I barked. "It's urgent."

"Just give me one moment, please," she replied with well-trained composure. "I think he may be in a meeting."

"I don't care about his bloody meeting," I snapped. "My car is in a loading bay and I need to speak to him. Now."

The smile evaporated and her face pinched with annoyance. "Who may I say is waiting for him?"

"Tell him it's the woman he's just betrayed. He'll know who that is." Had I been in the mood, I might have found it quite comical.

The old man turned and glanced at me curiously. "I think I'll come back another time, dear," he said quietly, giving her a sympathetic smile before wobbling his way out of the door.

I loomed over the poor girl as she dialed and spoke nervously into the phone. "Someone in reception for Ben Sweetman. Can you get him out of his meeting, please? I think it's urgent." The person at the other end apparently sensed her anxiety and asked whether any help was needed. "No, I can handle it, I think," she replied uncertainly. "Thanks, though. But send him down soon as you can, please."

I was about to apologize for being so rude when the double doors burst open and Ben was there, jacket off, a shirt button undone and hair awry.

When he saw me, his cheeks flushed. With guilt, I assumed. "Caroline? I've been trying to get in touch with you. Your phone's turned off."

I grabbed a copy of the newspaper from the display and jabbed it at him, like a bayonet.

"What the hell do you think you're doing, writing such crap, betraying me and the Kowalskis and everyone else, worming your way into my life and then just using me...for this?" I flapped the newspaper in his face. Behind her desk, the receptionist stood up, ready to dash for help to deal with this crazy woman.

"I wanted to explain..." he said, properly red in the face now but standing firm and unflinching.

"No explanation needed, thank you, Ben," I snapped, cutting him off. "This speaks for itself. You're nothing but a small-town hack, exploiting people for stupid little stories that no one cares about which might, just might, sell a couple of extra newspapers."

The blush disappeared in an instant and his face went gray as newsprint. "You've misunderstood. It wasn't like that..."

In a blind fury now, I shouted over him. "Don't waste your breath, Ben. I'm never going to believe a word you say. And I don't want any more to do with you, ever."

For a millisecond, I entertained the idea of hitting him around the head with the newspaper, but instead threw it on the floor at his feet and stormed out into the street. A traffic warden was leaning over my windscreen, attaching a plastic envelope.

"Oh, please, no," I pleaded. "I was unloading."

"Sorry, miss," he said. "You've got no sign in your window, and I can't rescind a notice once it's written. It's regulations."

"Sod your bloody regulations." I ripped the notice off the windscreen and threw it into the gutter before letting myself into the car and slumping into the driver's seat.

The warden knocked on the window, three times, waving the plastic envelope until I was forced to open it. "I think you ought to take this, miss," he said. "Nonpayment is only going to cost you more. Besides, you wouldn't want me reporting you for abuse, would you now?" He pushed the envelope onto the passenger seat, and as he stood back, Ben stepped forward, leaning his head through the window like a penitent in the confession box.

"Caroline, please. Just give me a minute to explain."

I pressed hard on the window button, and he pulled away just before it sliced through his neck. I started the car, crunched the gears, and pulled away so violently that it spun the wheels and, I truly hoped, would run over his foot, or at the very least leave him choking in a pall of exhaust fumes.

By the time I got back to London, my anger had cooled into queasy bitterness, fueled by a deep sense of humiliation.

I poured a supersized glass of wine and slumped onto the sofa, close to tears. Beyond my fury lay a feeling of emptiness, of desolation. How could I have been so stupid to trust someone so implicitly? It was only a pathetic little local story, not even important enough to make the front page. It would probably disappear without a trace, but that wasn't the point. The point was Ben's betrayal of our friendship. We hadn't known each other long, but I'd grown to trust him.

We'd spent a great weekend together, and just yesterday evening when the time had come for him to head home to Eastchester, we'd been reluctant to part. I'd liked him, a lot. I fancied him, a lot. I had even begun to entertain the notion that we might be on the brink of something serious, that I might be falling a little bit in love with him.

How could I have gotten it all so wrong?

I poured another glass, but my head was still jangling with angry thoughts. To calm down, I went out for some fresh air.

A chilly wind whipped up a vortex of discarded plastic bags, and the park opposite the house, usually so lively with dogs and children during the daytime, was deserted and creepy in the gloomy orange light of the streetlamps.

I turned back up the stairs, poured myself a third large glass of wine, turned on the television, and started watching a mindless reality show. When the doorbell rang, I ignored it. It rang again, and then continuously.

"Okay, okay, you can stop now," I shouted into the intercom. "Who is it? If you're a cold caller or religious fanatic, you can sod off."

"It's me." A distant, crackly voice. Ben? At my front door? I could scarcely believe my ears—the nerve of the man. Had he driven all this way, well over an hour, to explain away his betrayal in an attempt to wheedle his way back into my affections?

"Will you stop bloody stalking me?" I shouted. "Just go away, will you?"

"If you won't come with me, I'll go on my own."

"You can go where you effing like," I said, failing to understand, in my fury, what he was saying. "And don't bother coming back."

"Okay. If Dennis is prepared to give up the quilt, I'll come back later."

"What the hell are you talking about?" I yelled, livid now.

"Arun phoned. From the night shelter. Hasn't he got hold of you yet? He said your phone kept going to voice mail, so he called me instead. Dennis is there, right now! He'll disappear again tomorrow morning, hence Arun was so keen to track you down. You still wouldn't answer your phone, so I just got in the car and drove."

I let go of the intercom button, leaned my forehead against the cool plaster of the wall, and took several deep breaths, trying to make sense of this latest twist. My phone is never turned off, ever. And yet tonight, of all nights, it was. And Ben—who had so bitterly betrayed me—had now driven all the way from Eastchester to tell me about Dennis. It didn't make any sense.

The bell rang again, even more insistently than before.

I pushed the buzzer. "Oh for God's sake, come in, will you?"

As I opened the door, he was already there, pale, disheveled, and exhausted-looking.

"If you're just after another pathetic story for the newspaper…" I started.

"Are you going to the night shelter or shall I?" He turned to leave. "My car's on a yellow line. I can just as easily turn around and go home again."

"Hang on a second. You said Dennis is at the shelter?"

"That's what I've driven all this ruddy way to tell you," Ben said wearily, leaning on the door jamb. "That's why Arun was trying to get hold of you."

I was about to retort that I would go on my own, thank you very much, when I remembered the three large glasses of wine that I'd downed.

"Can you give me a lift?" I asked tentatively.

He tipped his head a fraction.

"Just let me grab my stuff, and I'll be with you."

As Ben navigated the tortuous route to Tottenham Court Road, I had little choice but to listen to his explanation, what he'd been trying to tell me before, as he put it more mildly than I deserved, I flew off the handle.

His story was that, over the weekend, Pearl Bacon and her daughter Julie had attended the funeral of her old friend, the former Helena Hall matron. At the wake, they found themselves reminiscing with the woman's son, and Pearl had mentioned the conversation that we'd had with her about Queenie, just a few weeks ago.

"It was the royal connection that stuck in the son's memory," Ben said, slowing down to let an ambulance go by. "The matron had apparently let slip that Maria's story about working at the palace turned out to be true, after everyone had thought for years she was a liar."

It seems that, this very morning, Julie—who works at the newspaper in advertising sales—had been innocently gossiping about this to a friend when she was overheard by the news editor. He immediately quizzed her, and not understanding the implications, Julie recounted the tale. The editor sent a junior reporter to visit Pearl, getting verbatim quotes and making calls to the health trust and the palace.

"I was on the afternoon shift," Ben went on, "and by the time I got into the office at midday, the story had already been set on page five. I really did try to stop it. In fact, I made a bloody nuisance of myself with the subs until someone called the news editor and he went ballistic, warning me to lay off. So it went to press; there was nothing I could do about it. I knew you'd hit the roof once you found out, so that's when I texted you. The news editor was giving me an ear bashing for interfering with his editorial decision when you arrived at the office."

There was a long silence as he negotiated a complex junction.

"Caroline?" He glanced at me sideways, his face lit by the moving orange stripes of passing streetlights.

"I'm still listening." My head was fuzzy from the wine, but even so, I couldn't imagine how he could have concocted such a complicated story just to cover his tracks. "Did you know that the local radio station ran the story too? Even interviewed Pearl?"

"Oh Christ, poor old lady. But it doesn't surprise me. That's the way news goes, I'm afraid. Once it's out, nothing can stop it. I'll have to go and see her, apologize that she's been bothered like that. Tell her to refuse any other approaches."

Neither of us spoke for several moments, until he said, "Look, I've said all I can to explain, haven't left anything out. It's a bloody mess, and I'm so sorry, but that's what happened. Do you believe me?"

"I'm not sure," I admitted. Relinquishing anger never comes easily to me, and acknowledging that I had made such an embarrassment of myself at the newspaper offices, plus having been extremely insulting to him in front of the receptionist, was even harder.

"We have a choice," he said, with a new resolve in his voice. "Either you believe what I've told you and accept my sincerest apologies, so we can move on. Or you don't, in which case I will drop you at the night shelter and be on my way. Our paths need never cross again, if that's the way you want it."

"That's not what I meant. I *want* to believe you. Of course I do. But it was such a coincidence, that story coming out two days after we met the Kowalskis and it was properly confirmed that it wasn't all in Maria's imagination."

"I know," he said, more patiently now. "But what else can I do to convince you?"

I took a couple of deep breaths, trying to clear my head of the day's emotions and dramas to put things into perspective. Ben was here, he had apologized, he had given a reasonable explanation, and all I had to do was to get over it and accept that it wasn't his fault. I still felt hurt and confused, but he deserved a second chance, not least for driving all the way to London to tell me about Dennis returning to the night shelter.

"You can help me get that quilt back," I said. "And then we can talk properly. See where we go from there."

"It's a deal," he said.

17.

I SHAPED UP PRETTY QUICKLY WHEN WE ARRIVED AT the night shelter and found ourselves having to press through a ragged gaggle of men and women huddling against the bitter cold in the doorway. A neat, balding man who'd have looked more at home in a library answered the bell and ushered us in quickly to prevent the others from following us in through the door.

"Hello, I'm Arun," he said, shaking hands. "Glad you could make it. Dennis is still here, taking a bath." In the bleak concrete hallway, the mingled smells of gravy, cabbage, and stale cigarette smoke were almost overpowering.

"Haven't you got room for the people outside?" Ben asked.

"It's not that," Arun said. "We don't allow alcohol or drugs. They know the rules, but they try it on every time."

"What happens to them?" I asked, remembering the two men I'd approached in the street on my first search for the quilt, just a few weeks before. It seemed an age ago—so much had happened since then.

"Some will finish their drinks and then we'll let them in," he said cheerfully. "The others will have to sleep rough, I'm afraid."

He led us through to the canteen, a large, brightly lit room with a stainless steel kitchen hatch and about fifteen men and women sitting on benches at trestle tables, heads hunched over platefuls of meat, vegetables, and gravy, greedily shoveling it in as though they hadn't eaten for weeks. Volunteers in green overalls moved among them, offering more food and drink or sitting alongside, conversing quietly. The walls were covered with posters warning of the perils of sharing needles, the importance of medical checkups, the dangers of alcohol poisoning, and listing other sources of help available.

"We sober them up with dinner and then we offer baths and a change of clothing if they want it before they go off to the dormitories," Arun said. I was getting used to the smell, but the hunger and sadness were heartbreaking.

He caught my glance. "You get used to it soon enough. They're fascinating characters, all sorts, and we often have a laugh with them. Some get to be old friends—albeit unreliable ones. The best reward is when we never see them again. It usually means they've managed to find fixed accommodation. I see you've brought a peace offering." He pointed to my rucksack. "Let's see if we can find Dennis."

We threaded our way between the tables and through a door at the other side of the room, then along another corridor until we arrived at a sitting area where five or six men and women smoked on ancient sofas and chairs, transfixed by the television flickering in the corner. Some were still in street clothes, others in dressing gowns, their hair still wet from the shower.

Curtained cubicles were ranged along one wall, a rack of square lockers along another. Arun led us toward a gnarled-looking old man with a straggly gray beard, snoring deeply on one of the sofas. He was wrapped in a red toweling dressing gown; his massive feet with discolored, knobbly toes and yellowing toenails stuck out into the center of the room.

Arun shook Dennis gently by the shoulder, trying to rouse him. The old boy opened his eyes and started to curse loudly and incoherently, mistaking him for a thief. Eventually he quieted down and gazed around belligerently.

"I think Leylah's been talking to you about your bedding?" Arun said, sitting down and gesturing for us to do the same.

"Nuttin' wrong wi' it," Dennis slurred through jagged teeth.

"It's getting pretty cold out there. We'd like to give you something a bit warmer." Arun gestured to my rucksack. I took out the fluffy woolen blanket and the once-expensive camel coat that I'd found in a charity shop.

"Take a look at these." Arun put a fingertip to his lips, warning us to say nothing. Dennis took the blanket, fingering its thickness, lifted it to his nose, and sniffed it. He dropped it on the floor and picked up the coat, examining it carefully inside and out, checking the pockets and hems and reading the label, for all the world like a discerning customer in a menswear shop. Then, in a sudden movement, he jumped to his feet, throwing off the dressing gown and exposing his surprisingly white naked body to the room before pulling his arms through the coat sleeves and carefully buttoning it up all the way down the front.

All faces had turned away from the television screen to admire the fashion show. Dennis looked up with a broad smile. "Wha'd'ya think, lads?" he said, strutting around the carpet, setting his shoulders and angling his head like a model, to the great amusement of his audience. I could see what Arun meant about interesting characters.

"Fits yer good, mate," shouted one, and the others clapped.

"I'll take 'em," Dennis said simply, and I sighed with relief. I'd been holding my breath, waiting for this moment.

"Right," Arun said. "Shall I keep these safe for the morning? And you can let me have your old stuff to get washed."

Dennis went to one of the lockers and pulled out a roll of rags so discolored it took a moment or two to recognize the quilt.

He handed it to Arun, who passed it to me. It had been rolled inside-out, and I flipped a corner to see the inner fabric. There, under a layer of mud and other unidentifiable stains, was the unmistakable sunrise pattern.

"Is this it?" he asked.

I nodded, suddenly overcome with emotion. "Thank you so much, Dennis," I started, as Arun ushered us quickly away.

"Before he changes his mind," he whispered.

In my elated state, I'd been chattering away about Arun and Dennis, failing to notice that Ben said almost nothing on the way back to the flat.

Then, as we pulled up, he said, "I'm on the early shift tomorrow and it's past eleven, so I'd better be heading home."

"Won't you come in for coffee or a quick bite to eat? To celebrate?" I asked, trying not to plead. "You haven't given me a chance to thank you for helping me get the quilt back, and at the very least I owe you an apology for flying off the handle earlier."

"I appreciate the gesture, but not tonight, I'm afraid." His voice was clipped and curt. "I'll give you a call."

Bugger. Just as we were beginning to like each other, I'd gone and messed it up. I leaned over to give him a kiss, which he accepted, but he didn't return it or hug me back.

"You were a star tonight. I didn't deserve it, especially after the things I said to you. I jumped to the wrong conclusions and I really am sorry. Please believe me," I said.

"It's okay. I think we both just need a little time." He started the engine. "Good luck with the quilt."

I covered the dining room table with an old sheet and carefully pulled the quilt out of its black garbage bag, untied the string, and gingerly unrolled it across the table, releasing a pungent odor of mold and stale urine.

The quilt was in a terrible state, the colors faded, with stripes of mud and other stains, and worse, there were several rips along the lines of Maria's delicate stitching. Specialist repair was definitely going to be needed. I'd tried to visualize it so many times, attempting to re-create it in sketches and paintings, and in my mind's eye, the design had assumed a heightened intensity, the colors more vibrant, the patterns more electrifying. The grubby rags in front of me seemed to mock those loving re-creations.

I rolled it up again and put it back into the bag to contain the smell. Exhausted, feeling slightly hungover and close to tears, I texted Jo: Hope you had a great holiday? Can't wait to hear all about it but also really need your help re quilt. Please call when you're back. xx

I woke in the early hours with a headache and a raging thirst, and as I went to the kitchen for a drink of water, a shaft of streetlight fell through a gap in the living room curtain, silhouetting what looked for a moment like a figure crouching on the table. I was about to cry out when I realized it was the bulky mass of the quilt in its black bag, where I'd left it.

"Get a grip, you silly cow," I berated myself, pouring the water and slugging down a couple of aspirin. I snuggled back under the duvet, but sleep was chased away by visions of Dennis in his camel coat, the laughter of his fellow sheltermates, the smell of the quilt, and the despair I'd felt when I unrolled it.

Then I began to worry about Ben. Would he forgive me for how I'd reacted? Would I ever see him again?

There was nothing for it. I put on my dressing gown and made a cup of tea, then took the quilt out of its bag and carefully unrolled it across the table once more. The smell was less pungent now, just sour and sad. I took out a large soft paintbrush and began to stroke the hairs gently across a stained area at the edge of the quilt, trying to lift the worst of the dirt away without rubbing too hard on the fabric. After a few moments, I could already see the difference. Perhaps the damage was repairable, and all was not lost.

As I worked, in the early morning silence of my flat, I began to hear Maria's voice in my head again, that rough, smoky, East End twang, describing how she'd started the quilt in the lonely hours after Nora had spurned her. How she had begun to embroider the intricate lover's knot on that silk from the trousseau of her beloved Princess May. Poor lovelorn Maria. I got the strangest feeling that the seamstress was close by, just at my shoulder, watching and listening—a weird kind of presence, conjured up in my imagination, that made me shiver.

The border around the central panel, a row of elongated hexagons or what Miss S-D had called "lozenges," pieced from small scraps of plain and patterned silks, was muddy and ripped in places. I brushed each piece delicately for fear of creating even worse staining or more damage. There were several rips in the fabric and along the stitching that would certainly require professional attention.

The next panel, with its little appliquéd figures that had so intrigued me and Andy Kowalski as children, seemed to have survived without too much damage. I recalled Maria's words, "*His name and mine are concealed in the figures,*" and realized that this was not simply a random collection of images. The duck, apple, violin, the curious triangular leaf, like ivy perhaps, and that fiery dragon spelled DAVID. And below, the mouse, an oak leaf and acorn, a rabbit, another kind of purple flower—a lily of some kind, ah yes, it must be an iris—and the anchor spelled MARIA. The names of mother and child embroidered into a sad little memorial.

Surely this was even further proof that Maria was telling the truth? Why would she create a quilt panel for an imaginary baby? I checked the corner of the lining and the little cross-stitched verse. More threads were missing, but it was still legible. I was now convinced that Maria had dedicated the panel to her own child, the baby so brutally taken from her, and even all those years later when she completed it, she wanted to make sure that everyone would understand, even after her death, by these few sentimental words. A wave of melancholy swept over me for this poor misunderstood woman.

Now that I'd heard Maria telling her own story, I saw her designs and use of colors through new eyes. If the central panels were dedicated to her lover and the baby, might the outer ones also have additional meanings hidden within their patterns?

The third panel was dull by comparison to the inner ones: lilac and dark gray cottons were carefully arranged in linear patterns of lines and angles, like a staircase or a series of blocks, creating an almost three-dimensional effect. The shapes held a zigzag pattern on their outer edges, with straight lines reaching in toward the center.

It seemed unlikely that such a regular, geometric pattern could hold any message. But then I saw that she had sewn a row of tiny chain stitches half an inch from the seam edges of each fabric shape, and recalled her description. These were rows of capital M letters, for Maria or, perhaps, for the visitor Margaret who had left her so suddenly and without explanation. She'd been important to Maria, more than just a passing visitor. Who was she, and could she still be alive?

The two outermost panels, which had been at the edges of Dennis's bed roll, were by far the grubbiest. The triangles of fine lawn cottons, in delicate floral and other traditional patterns, were joined together and cleverly juxtaposed into light and dark sections so that a larger, bolder pattern emerged.

The cottons reminded me of a blouse that my mother used to wear—the fabric so soft and delicate that she was immensely proud of it. Her voice came into my head: "The finest Liberty lawn," she'd say, "the best cotton in the world." Then I realized, yes! These cottons were Liberty prints, designs produced for the famous shop still going strong in Regent Street. How could I have missed this obvious clue? This was so clearly a tribute to the greatest gift that Nora could have given to her friend: her freedom. How joyful she must have been as she worked with Nora on this panel in their shared flat. And in gratitude, Maria helped to nurse Nora in her final illness.

It all became brilliantly clear now. Each of the frames had been created in tribute to or memory of an individual. The central panel was for her lover, the appliqué figures for her baby, the zigzag Ms for Margaret, and the Liberty prints for Nora. But what about the outermost border?

As I dabbed the muddy stains on the grandmother's fan designs, I wondered when, and for whom, Maria might have sewn them. Was it when Nora became a grandmother? Or even, I thought with a little thrill, was it intended for my own Granny Jean? Perhaps that's why, as Mum said, the quilt meant such a lot to her?

Suddenly, I felt utterly exhausted, the troubled night and the dramatic events of the past few days catching up with me. It was time to give myself a break and perhaps wait for Jo's return before doing any more work on the quilt.

As I hung it over the back of the sofa to air and dry out, something unusual caught my eye. Along the line of elongated hexagons surrounding the inner panel, one of the rips gaped wide open, exposing the inside of the patchwork. Beneath it appeared to be another layer of white fabric—or was it paper?

I took up my paintbrush again and, with its blunt end, tentatively eased open the ripped seam. Sure enough, there did appear to be a small scrap of paper, sewn inside the fabric. There were more small rips further along the border. I eased these open too, but could see nothing behind them. I was looking for scissors to start unpicking the seams to see what else I could find when my phone beeped.

Brilliant holiday, thanks. So nice to get some sun. But can't wait to see you—are you free tomorrow evening? xox

"What is that disgusting smell?" Jo wrinkled her nose, freckled and peeling from a week in the sunshine.

"It's the quilt. It's been on the road for the last few weeks keeping a homeless man warm. It's a long story."

"And what's *that* all about?" She peered through the open door of the spare room where the skeleton of the chair stood, neglected and unfinished, on top of a table. "My God, is this the start of your world-beating interior design company? *How* exciting!"

"It's a sample for Justin to show to his clients, but I've got a bit stuck. Turned out to be a much larger and scarier project than I thought. Christ, I'm so glad you're back. There's so much to tell you."

I described my meeting with Justin and showed her my designs.

"They're amazing, you know," she bubbled enthusiastically, examining my sketches and samples. "Completely original, especially with that fabulous retro thing going on. Wherever did you get these great sixties fabrics?"

"Found them in Mum's loft, hidden in a suitcase; they'd probably been there for years. I think they could be original Warner & Sons designs. Couldn't believe my luck."

"Look, I know a good upholsterer in South London if that helps," she said. "But it'll cost, you know?"

"But worth the investment this time around, don't you think? In the long run, I'll have to set up a proper workshop, of course."

"What about your Mum's place?" she asked. "That's got a garage, I seem to remember."

"I've got to sell it, to pay her nursing home fees. Anyway, I couldn't travel there every day."

"You could if you sold this place—you'd get a fortune for it."

"Strangely enough, that's what Ben suggested," I said before I could stop myself.

She was on it like a heat-seeking missile. "Ben?"

"Sweetman. You know, the Eastchester journalist?"

"Oh yes, *that* Ben?" She gave me a sideways look. "And how *is* Ben, then?"

"I'm not sure," I mumbled. "I think I've blown it."

"How?"

"Long story. I've apologized, but he's gone to ground."

"Do you care?"

"I'm not really sure…" I stuttered. "I think so. Oh God, Jo, I don't know."

"I've got time." She settled herself on the sofa, patting the seat beside her. "Come on, tell all. I want to know everything about Ben, *and* all the other things that have been happening. Every detail. That's the price of my expert opinion on your stinky quilt."

"Do you mind if I pour myself a glass? What about you?"

She blushed, avoiding my glance.

"Is there something *you're* not telling *me*?"

She nodded coyly.

"Ohmigod, Jo. You're pregnant?" I hugged her. "That's amazing news! When's it due?"

"I'm only ten weeks along; it's early days. I'm sorry. I didn't want to tell you right away. It must be hard, after…"

"Oh, don't worry about me. I'm fine. Really," I said. "I've been so bloody busy I've hardly given it a thought. But I am *so* excited for you. It's amazing—happened so quickly! When's it due? Boy or girl? What does Mark say?"

"First scan next week." She allowed herself to smile. "Mark's really chuffed but pretending not to be, of course, and underneath I think he's terrified. Keeps worrying about having to sell his motorbike and clear all his albums out of the spare room."

As I poured myself a glass of wine and put the kettle on for Jo's herbal tea, she chattered on about how she hadn't suffered much morning sickness but felt completely exhausted all the time, about the names they'd already been discussing, and the terrifying responsibility of bringing another human being into the world.

"Enough of this baby talk. I want to hear all about Ben," she said.

I tried to summarize the crazy events of the past ten days: Pearl's realization that Queenie was indeed Maria, and how I'd listened to the tapes, then stayed at Ben's house that night and wondered whether I regretted it, the newspaper article and our argument, our visit to the night shelter and the meeting with Dennis.

"And I suppose this paragon of virtue is astonishingly handsome and filthy rich?"

"Not rich at all, and not even very handsome, to be honest, but sweet-looking and sort of cuddly. He's the sort of person who needs time to grow on you. Tall, lots of hair. Hazel eyes, the longest eyelashes you've ever seen."

"Sounds perfect."

"Oh, and he likes Howard Hodgkin."

"Better and better. But you haven't heard from him since your quarrel?"

I shook my head. "Two whole days. I wish he'd text or something, if only to say he's forgiven me."

"Give him time; he'll come around," she said. "How could he possibly resist the gorgeous, talented Caroline Meadows? And if not, you should just text him again. But give it a bit longer; don't let him think you're desperate."

She was right. Perhaps it just needed time to heal.

"Tell me about these people in Bethnal Green," she said, wisely changing the subject. I described how we had traced the Kowalskis and their confirmation that Maria and Nora actually had both worked at the palace.

"You know what this all means? It solves the mystery of where she got the May Silks. Do you suppose she stole them?"

"I don't think she was a thief. On the tape, she talked about finding a bundle of scraps that her predecessor had left in a cupboard and using them for the first panel of the quilt. But I don't think she ever knew how precious they were."

"All the same, it's brilliant to confirm where she got hold of them. I love it when history proves you right," she smirked.

"I can't wait to tell Annabel. She'll probably try to claim all the glory for herself, but she'll know it was me who first noticed them."

⸎

Jo sighed a lot as we unraveled the quilt across the table. "Jeez, this is a mess. It's certainly going to need professional cleaning and repair."

"Don't I know it? But take a look at this." I showed her the rip in the edge of the hexagon, where I'd seen the paper inside.

She took out her magnifying glass and gently lifted the edge of the stitching. "You're right. There is something odd in there," she said. "It looks like a template that's been left inside for some reason. It's unusual to find that in a finished quilt."

"What can we do to find out?"

"We'd be in danger of ripping the fabric even more if we try to look from this side. What we need to do is take off this lining and unpick whatever's been used for the wadding so that we can get to the back of this section." She rummaged in her handbag and pulled out a pair of the finest scissors I'd ever seen. "I'll use these. Have you got a pair of unpicking scissors so that we can tackle it from both sides?"

"We're going to do this *now*?" I was astonished. "Wouldn't it be a bit risky?"

"Trust me, I'm a professional," she laughed. "It'll have to be done some time, and if you took it to a studio for repairs, they would remove it anyway to fix mending mesh on the reverse. They'd put the lining back afterward. Besides, I'm mighty curious about this template paper, aren't you?"

"Seems a bit drastic. And won't it damage the cross-stitching, the poem on the lining?"

She examined it. "It's not sewn through, so no problem."

"Then let's go for it," I replied, suddenly certain. "It might be royal silk, but we're not exactly endangering the crown jewels."

I set up two reading lamps for extra light, and we joked about feeling like students again, working on our final projects together, as we started at opposite sides of the table, working along the edges of the quilt, carefully unpicking the sheet lining from the edges of the patchwork. It came away quite easily but revealed a more daunting task beneath. Maria had used a light woolen blanket as wadding between the quilt and the inner lining, and this was quilted to the patchwork with the finest of running stitches along the seams of each concentric frame and its borders. It must have taken her hours, and unpicking it was slow and painstaking. Her stitching was so meticulous that slipping a scissor blade beneath each tiny little loop required a steady hand to avoid piercing or pulling the delicate fabric.

As we worked, I described in more detail my meeting with the professor and that extraordinary day of listening to Maria's tapes. As I talked, snipping and releasing the stitches the seamstress had made with her own hand, I began to experience again the curious sensation that she was close by, listening to us, watching us to make sure we treated her cherished creation, the work of almost her whole lifetime, with respect.

We made more drinks and started back at our task, snipping and parting the woolen blanket from the quilt beneath as we chatted about Jo's holiday, and she described her hilarious but rather terrifying camel trek. I told her about our encounter with Dennis and the way he'd stripped off his Father Christmas dressing gown in front of the assembled company without a moment's hesitation. We discussed my struggles with the chair and footstool and what I should do to get them completed in time.

After an hour or so, we'd reached the border of elongated hexagons—which Jo called "lozenges"—surrounding the inner square, where I'd found the template.

"Come and look at this," she whispered.

"What is it?" I hurried to her side of the table.

"Just a sec, I'll clear it properly," she said, as I peered impatiently over her shoulder.

Three more snips, and the blanket pulled away. Beneath it was the back of a lozenge with the hem of the fabric tacked carefully around a piece of yellowing paper. Jo delicately lifted the hem until we could just make out what appeared to be old-fashioned copperplate handwriting in faded blue ink.

"She's used the paper for a template. See if it's the same on your side." Her voice was squeaky with excitement. "This is extraordinary. I saw something like this in a book some years ago, about a quilt that was unfinished. But the way these papers are tacked looks as though they've been left in deliberately."

I took up the scissors again, with unsteady fingers, and unpicked a few further stitches to reveal the lozenge shapes on my side of the square. Just as on the other side, the fabric had been folded over the paper templates and fixed with wide, even tacking stitches and extra back stitches to secure the folds. Beneath the folds, I could see more scraps of paper, with more handwriting. It was like excavating long-buried treasure.

"I've got more words here, but I can't really see them because of the tacking," I said.

"It won't do any harm to snip the tacking," Jo said. "Look, like this."

I watched, in awe of her dexterity, as she carefully released the stitches and delicately folded back the wide hem of the fabric to reveal the full width of the paper template below. It was just possible to make out the words "*My dear…*"

"It's a letter," we chorused.

"Oh…my…God," I whispered. "Is it from her lover? The prince? Just imagine…"

"We'll soon find out."

Because the paper had been cut up into shapes, the words and sentences were chopped up too, and frustratingly, some of the templates were blank. As we snipped away the tacking stitches on each side of the square, we shouted the words and syllables they revealed:

"*…and that the…*"

"*…se arrangem…*"

"*…my contro…*"

"*…is war is mo…*"

"*…nce, May 1915…*"

"Nineteen fifteen. It must be the Great War. And that word's probably France. You know what this is?" Jo looked across the quilt at me, grinning from ear to ear. "It's a letter from the front," we said, almost in unison.

"Bloody hell," I said, trying to control my excitement as I snipped around the next hexagon.

"*…that I go to…*" Jo read.

"*…eep every night dr….*"

"*Keep s….*"

"It *is* to Maria," I shouted, reading out the next one. "Listen, it says, '*…eet smile…aria.*'"

Then Jo yelped, "It's a *love* letter to Maria. Come and look at this."

The ink was smudged and stained, but the words were clear to see: "*…afe. I love yo…*"

The four little syllables stunned us into silence. Finally I managed to gasp, "My God, do you realize, Jo, if this letter really is from the Prince of Wales, it proves that her story was true? She said the prince wrote to her, but I never imagined for one second that she would hide his letter inside the quilt."

"Steady on. We haven't got any proof yet of *who* it's from."

"There must be other clues. Let's take all the pieces out so we see what the letter really says."

She hesitated. "I'd be reluctant to do that right now. This is like an archaeological excavation, and we need to be careful not to destroy any evidence by mistake."

I sat down again, struggling to curb my impatience. At last she said, "I've got an idea. We can avoid taking them out by photographing each template. Then we can assemble all the photographs on the screen and figure out what the letter says that way. What do you think?"

It was a brilliant plan. A couple of hours later, after revealing all of the templates with writing on them—twenty in all—and carefully photographing each one, we transferred the photos to my laptop and moved them around the screen like an old-fashioned computer game. When we finally got them into what seemed like the right order, they read:

…*nce, May 1915…My dear…to think…you witho…know yo… and that the…se arrangeme…beyond…my contro…his war is mo… rrible, and I may…ot retur…for ma…nths…But I wa…ou to know, a…aria,…that I go to…eep every night dr…aming of your swe…et smile…and…of you…Keep s…afe. I love yo…*

"But no signature," I said. "How frustrating. Do you think we've missed anything?"

Jo shook her head. "Only blank templates, none with writing on."

"It's a beautiful letter," I said, reading the screen again, trying to elicit more clues. "A very educated hand, wouldn't you say, hardly written by your average soldier?"

"Even so, you can't assume it was written by a prince," Jo said, stretching her shoulders with hands behind her neck. "Besides, he wasn't allowed to go and fight, was he?"

"He did go to France, just not to the front line." I sighed. "Oh, I don't know. She's such a mystery, this woman. We know she worked at Buckingham Palace. In my heart, I'm sure the story about the baby is also true. Why would they have locked her away unless there was a secret they wanted to protect?"

Jo leaned back in her chair. "You know, what we've discovered this evening is extraordinary. Even if the letter is not from the Prince of Wales, it's still a remarkable document. And what with those silks…" she tailed off.

"What is it?"

"It's even more important to get this thing properly cleaned and conserved and to verify that these silks really are what we think they are. I know just the person. She's a conservator and silk specialist. Used to work at the Warner Archive, and I seem to remember she wrote a thesis about the May Silks a while back."

"Sounds perfect. Is she in London?"

"Tucked away in some village in Essex, I think. I can look her up."

18.

———

ELLIE BEVAN'S ENTHUSIASM CAME BUBBLING DOWN the telephone.

"Wow. Double wow. If Annabel and Jo think they're May Silks, they are probably right," she said in a singsong Welsh accent. "That's extraordinary. If you can bring your quilt to me, I can certainly try to verify them for you and at the same time see what we can do to clean and conserve it."

"When would be convenient?"

"Next week?" I could hear the pages of a diary being flipped. "Ah, I have a couple of hours free tomorrow morning, if that's not too soon?"

"Perfect." Her workshop wasn't far from Holmfield, so I could see Mum afterward and then go on to the cottage to finish sorting out the boxes.

There was still no news from Ben, and by now, after a few days of thinking about him and missing him, I was quite certain that I wanted to see him. Something felt unfinished: I needed to apologize properly and, hopefully, start again.

I texted: I'll be at the cottage this evening—are you free? I can promise log fire and a good bottle of wine! C x

∽

Ellie Bevan's workshop was tucked away on the edge of an

insignificant Essex town in a small industrial estate, a bleak place which appeared to be only part occupied, judging by the boarded-up windows. Her premises were unidentified—a deliberate policy to avoid drawing attention to the valuable fabrics she housed. As instructed, I parked in the bay beside the funeral home and telephoned her. Soon afterward, a short, dark-haired, blue jean–clad woman in her middle years opened the door, welcoming me with a cheery smile.

The workshop, with its white walls, ceiling, and floor and brilliant overhead lights, had the intense, hushed atmosphere of an operating room. An enormous table dominated the center of the room, covered with three long sections of faded pink damask on which two young women conservators were working, wielding their delicate instruments with surgical precision. Ellie explained that they were rearranging the threads of the light-damaged silk in readiness for attaching a fine net backing to hold the delicate tissue in place. Much of her work was for public organizations like English Heritage and the National Trust, she told me, but they did get the occasional private customer.

She led me through to a room next door with another large table. "Now, let's see what you've got," she said, pushing aside rolls of textile and piles of paper.

As we unfolded it out across the table, the quilt felt flimsy and fragile without its sheet backing and heavy wadding. Despite my attempts at cleaning, it still looked grubby and faded, but Ellie's expert eyes were not deceived.

"Well, that's in a mess, but I can see it's a very fine piece of work," she said approvingly, standing back and surveying it.

"It's the silks in the center panels that Jo and Annabel were so excited about."

"Let's make a start then." She put on white gloves and

trained her magnifying glass on the cream damask, exclaiming to herself: "Mmm...my goodness...how wonderful...quite extraordinary." After a few moments, she said, "They were quite right, you know, this really does look like one of the May Silks."

She wandered over to an untidy desk in the corner of the room, returning with a handful of loose sheets of paper and a small booklet. "This is the brochure for a Warner Archive exhibition back in the nineteen eighties that I helped prepare," she said, handing it to me. "Unfortunately, the photos in the brochure are all in black and white, so to revive my memory, I also checked online and printed these off."

As she laid one of the photographs onto the quilt beside the central panel, I recognized it at once. "There it is! The very same pattern." It was a perfect match to the silk with its rose, shamrock, and thistle design and the garland of ribbons.

"I think that's pretty convincing, don't you?"

She opened the booklet at the front page and read out loud: "*In 1891, the Duchess of Teck announced that for the wedding of her daughter, Princess May, the dresses of the bride and bridesmaids would be of British silks, which were duly commissioned from the Silver Studio and woven by Warner Brothers. Sadly, the bridegroom, the Duke of Clarence, died only six weeks before the wedding. However, Princess May later became engaged to George, the duke's younger brother, and it was decided to use the so-called 'May Silks' for their marriage on July 6, 1893, instead. Her wedding dress was made from the finest white silk and silver thread with a rose, shamrock, and thistle design, including May blossoms and true lover's knots.*"

"What a tragic story," I said. "But a triumph of royal pragmatism."

She pointed to the triangular sections at each corner of the central panel. "This one is a different fabric. I haven't got a photograph, but I'm pretty sure it's another May Silk." She read again from the booklet: *"Other designs by Arthur Silver, many of which featured a lily-of-the-valley design, were woven for use in the wedding trousseau."*

She gave an appreciative sigh. "The fact that you have *two* designs here makes it even more likely. This has made my day! It's certainly a first for me in thirty years of textile conservation."

"Does it need further authentication?" I asked. "Miss Smythe-Dalziel talked about the need to study the weave structure and strand testing."

"She's right, of course. And we can certainly do that for you. I'd also like to trace the designs and match them against the whole repeat of the pattern, which is about this long"—she held her hands about a meter apart—"but I can tell immediately from what I can see from the weave, the pattern, and the fact that it's obviously silk with silver threads, a bit tarnished now, of course, but obviously silver, and those three things are enough to convince me." She seemed transfixed, barely able to take her eyes from the fabric.

After a few long moments, she turned to me: "Now, let me make you a coffee or tea and you can tell me where you found this extraordinary piece."

As the kettle boiled in a small side kitchen, I tried to explain, in as few words as possible. "I inherited it from my granny, but she was given it by someone called Maria who, we now know, worked as a seamstress at Buckingham Palace. She was later locked up in a mental asylum—Helena Hall, you've probably heard of it—and she was only released in the late fifties."

Ellie looked doubtful. "The May silks were woven long before, in the 1890s. When did this woman work at the palace?"

"She joined the staff when she was about fourteen, which would have been around 1910," I said, making a quick calculation.

"Shortly after that, the chief needlewoman went off sick and Maria was promoted. She talked about finding the fabrics in a basket in the needlework room, so they could have been collected and hidden away by her predecessor, some years before."

She raised an eyebrow. "How do you know all this?"

"We discovered that Maria was interviewed by a sociology student at the University of Essex for a research project in the seventies, and I was lucky enough to have an afternoon listening to the tapes. She pretty much poured out her whole life story, but no one believed her. The hospital records have her as a delusional fantasist."

"How extraordinary. Was she really insane, do you think?"

"On the tapes, she sounds completely sane. And we traced the grandson of the friend who looked after her when she was released from the hospital, and he confirmed that at least part of the story was true. Maria and his grandmother both worked at Buckingham Palace together. But there are some parts of her story that we haven't been able to prove yet."

"Such as?" she prompted, raising an eyebrow.

"Maria claimed she was locked up because she'd got pregnant with the Prince of Wales' child. I know that really does sound like the fantasy of a madwoman, but take a look at this."

We flipped the quilt over, and I lifted the hemmed fabric at the back of one of the hexagons. "We found twenty of these, and rather than lift them out, we took photographs." I gave her the printout of the "letter" that we had created. "We think it was sent from France during the First World War and was deliberately sewn into the quilt, to hide it."

Ellie read it carefully. "Phew. I suppose you're wondering whether it's from the prince?"

I nodded.

"Shame there's no signature."

"I know. It's so tantalizing. We think she might have removed it on purpose, to conceal his identity."

"You photographed *all* of the templates?" Ellie asked.

"All those with writing on."

"And the ones without?"

What an odd question. "No, we didn't bother with the blank ones."

Ellie went to her desk again, and from a drawer, she took a flat-ended smooth metal blade and a small flashlight. Examining each hexagon in turn, she carefully lifted the hems with the metal blade to reveal the template beneath and then placed her magnifying frame over the paper and shone her light onto it from different angles. Five minutes passed, then seven, then ten, as she worked her way all around the border as I waited, wondering what she could be searching for.

Suddenly she shouted so loudly that it made me jump: "Eureka! Look at this."

She took a couple of very long, fine pins to fasten the fabric back so we could more easily examine the template beneath. At first, all I could see was a blank piece of cream paper, but then, as she swiveled the beam from different angles, it became clear what she had discovered: an embossed mark, so flattened by wear and damp that it had become almost invisible, until highlighted by the bright, precise ray.

"It's a crest," she said simply.

"The Prince of Wales' feathers! Oh my God, Maria was telling the truth. It *is* a love letter from the Prince of Wales. However did you know what to look for?"

"It's an old trick I use for examining the three-dimensional weave of a fabric. That can reveal secrets, and for some reason, I wondered whether it might do the same for paper. Call it a sixth sense," she said, laughing.

As the full implication hit me, I felt light-headed and had to sit on the stool again, repeating the lines of the verse in my head: *I stitched my love into this quilt, sewn it neatly, proud and true.* Maria had, literally, sewn his letter into the quilt so that she could keep his love close to her forever.

More than that: *absolutely everything* she had told Patsy Morton, the story that the psychiatrists and nurses dismissed as delusions, was all correct. Hidden in the quilt was the complete vindication of a woman who had been disbelieved and dismissed as a fantasist for most of her life. She had been locked away to avoid a royal scandal and the staff bribed to keep silent. Anyone else who heard the story thought it so ridiculous that they simply could not believe it.

Yet she was telling the truth all along.

"You were right to leave the templates *in situ,*" Ellie was saying, interrupting my thoughts. "This letter makes the quilt even more historically interesting and potentially valuable. Any conservation plan will need to take this into consideration."

Gathering my senses, I managed to explain that right now, I couldn't afford anything too expensive.

"So, how would you like to proceed?" she asked. "How's about I work out some estimates and we can then agree on the level of work you want me to undertake?"

"Sounds perfect." She could not start on it for several months though and suggested that I look after the quilt until then. This suited me. Having only just got it back in my possession, I was reluctant to let it go again so soon. Besides, discovering the prince's crest on the template had made it feel even more precious, and I was dying to show it to Jo.

We folded the quilt carefully back into its case, and I bid Ellie farewell and left with my head reeling from the latest revelations. As I drove away in the direction of Holmfield,

I found myself thinking about Maria, determined to make it up to her. If I had the quilt restored and displayed, future generations would have no choice but to hear and believe her story.

Then the sad realization struck me: as far as we knew, she had no heirs; there were no future generations to hear her story. We had failed to find any mention of any Romano through the adoption agencies, and no one had responded to Ben's newspaper plea. Even if he were alive, Maria's son would be a very old man by now, and in any case, he'd disappeared without a trace.

Arriving at Holmfield, I was overjoyed to find that Mum recognized me immediately. She had obviously recovered fully from the shock of her fall, and we spent a happy hour or two chatting away in a series of non sequiturs. I asked if she knew whether Maria had had a son, but she couldn't remember who Maria was. I had to accept that the trail had gone cold.

As I left, seeing the newspapers on the hall table at Holmfield was an unpleasant reminder of my embarrassing behavior toward Ben. He still hadn't texted back, and my hand had hovered over the phone many times, on the point of calling him. But I'd managed to curb my impatience, telling myself that it was best to let him decide in his own time whether he felt our relationship was important enough to forgive me. If all else failed, I would send him a handwritten "sorry" card. Somehow words on paper seem to mean much more than emails and texts.

Back at the cottage, I laid a fire and went up to my old bedroom to tackle the rest of the boxes from the loft. But I had all evening ahead of me, and there was still no news from Ben, so I started opening and sorting through them, then resealing and assigning them to separate piles, old clothes, crockery, books, and the old ice skates for "charity," old shoes, linen, and carpet remnants marked "trash." The wallpaper and broken chairs would do for lighting fires. I sorted through a suitcase of toys and games—setting aside only a threadbare and once much-loved fluffy rabbit to keep—and marked it for charity.

Finally, I opened a heavy box which appeared to contain my father's academic papers, dating back to the sixties. Would they be of any interest to Patsy Morton or her department? I wondered.

Downstairs again, I lit the fire, opened a bottle of wine, and settled down on the hearthrug to sort through the papers. Most seemed to be typed notes, essays, and dry academic treatises that I returned to the box for taking to the university next time I was passing. Among them were also some personal letters and notes in my father's handwriting, which I set aside on a separate pile for reading later.

At the bottom of the box was an A4 envelope. Without thinking, I ripped it open and pulled out an old red accounts book with a well-worn cardboard cover—probably my father's household finances, or perhaps something to do with budgeting for his department at the university. I was about to replace it in the box when I noticed a yellowing label on the front: FOR MY DEAREST RICHARD.

I flicked through the pages, slowly coming to understand, with butterflies in my stomach, that every sheet, from cover to cover, was filled with Granny Jean's neat, careful handwriting. At the beginning, on the first page, were four lines set out like a poem.

EASTCHESTER, JUNE 1970

The days of our years are threescore years and ten;
and if by reason of strength they be fourscore years,
yet is their strength labor and sorrow;
for it is soon cut off, and we fly away.
  Psalm 90

My dearest Richard,

Yesterday was my 70th birthday picnic, and as Arthur and I sat in the sunshine with you and Eleanor, watching our precious new granddaughter sleeping contentedly in her pram, the realization came to me. I may indeed "fly away" before long, but before I go, there is something that you have to know, which must not fly with me, and which you may wish to pass on to your daughter if and when you see fit.

It pains me greatly that we cannot have this conversation in person, but your father forbids it, and I must respect his wishes. He gave so much to help save our country in the Great War and is a wonderfully loving and supportive husband and father. This is the one thing he is utterly adamant about, so I cannot deny him. You must never let him know that I have told you.

But I happen to believe that children have a right to know about their origins, and especially as they are discovering so much about genetics these days, so I cannot go to my grave at peace without telling you the truth. I pray it is not too much of a shock and that you will forgive us both for withholding this information from you until now.

Before I go any further, I want to reiterate, once and for all, that you are everything we could ever have wanted in a son. We love you more than you can ever imagine, and you have made us very proud with your career, your lovely young wife, and beautiful baby.

Forgive me for the length of this missive, but I think it needs to be told carefully, so that you understand.

To begin at the beginning. Your father and I fell in love at first sight. He was the most handsome, funny, and kind man I had ever met. There was and never will be anyone else for me, and I am confident that the same applies to him. None of us knew what horrors the war would bring, and when it came, he signed up keen to protect his country, and even though we had only known each other for a few months, I supported him. We married in October 1914, just a few weeks before he left for France.

Your father fought bravely before being seriously wounded and was sent home. At the time, we praised God that he was returned to us alive when so many were not, but the more serious consequences of his injury only became apparent once he was discharged from the hospital. There is no pleasant way to tell this, but to put it bluntly, my dearest Richard, he was no longer able to participate fully in the intimate side of our married life.

At first, he told me it would soon come back, and I endeavored to be the most loving and attractive wife in the world in hopes that all would return to normal. He struggled so much to satisfy me, but nothing seemed to help. After a year passed, he ordered me to divorce him and find instead, as he put it, a "whole" man. I managed to persuade him that I had never felt the slightest doubt that I wanted to spend the rest of my life with him, and that doing without the physical side of marriage was a sacrifice I was quite prepared to make.

But what I did <u>not</u> expect was that, no matter what your rational mind tells you, a woman's desire to bear children can become utterly overwhelming. It began to affect my whole life, invading my thoughts night and day, and became an obsession, almost a mania, that I could not control. I would cross the road to avoid other people's prams and stopped going to our local park because I could not bear to hear the children's happy voices. When my two closest girlfriends had babies, I could no longer bear to spend time with them, seeing their lives so happy and fulfilled. The envy in my heart made me spiteful and mean, and our friendships withered.

At night, I dreamed about holding a warm, sweet-smelling bundle in my arms and would weep silently into my pillow when I woke to find it wasn't true. Arthur knew what was happening, but he would not talk about it. When I suggested, tentatively, that we might consider adoption, he became angrier than I had ever seen him before and shouted at me: "I may be only half a man but if you think I'm going to admit that to some bleeding-heart social worker, you've got another thing coming. If you can't bear the thought of spending the future with me, then you can pack your bags."

He grabbed his coat and left without a further word, returning after several hours slurring his words and bumping into the furniture. He was more intoxicated than I had ever witnessed before and had never been much of a drinker, so I chided myself even more for driving him to such extremes. I never dared raise the subject again, but it began to affect our marriage. We started to argue, and each time, he clammed up further.

One day when I could bear it no longer, I went home to my mother. But she went on asking when they were going to hear "the patter of little feet," and I missed Arthur so much that after one night, I went back again. He just hugged me and said, "Welcome home," and never said a further word about it.

It was not long after this that Arthur began attending what he called his "meetings," and though he was very secretive about it, I discovered that a friend had told him that he would never progress through the police ranks unless he joined the Masons. A few weeks after I returned from Mother's, Arthur returned from one of these meetings and said he had heard of a baby that was going to be put up for adoption. I didn't question what had taken place to change his mind but asked him, "Don't we have to be vetted first?"

He just said, "Don't you worry, love, it is all arranged. But you mustn't say a word to anyone."

It was a few days later, on Armistice Day, he turned up with a little wriggling bundle wrapped in a hospital blanket. A newborn baby, wrinkled like an old man. As he passed you into my arms, I fell instantly in love. There is no other way of putting it. You were perfect, with plenty of blond hair and your black eyes—they had not yet turned blue—gazing intently back into mine, as if trying to puzzle out who I was.

"Where did you get him?" I asked, with my heart banging in my chest so hard I could barely breathe, but Arthur just shook his head and put his finger to his lips.

"But if you haven't signed anything, he's not ours to have." The panic was threatening to stifle me. "It's stealing. For goodness' sake, Arthur, you could be risking your job. Take him back," I shouted, trying to push the little bundle back into his arms.

In the hullabaloo, you started to howl, and I was weeping too, seared with a terrible pain because I knew you were not really mine and could be taken away at any moment.

"Sit down and I'll make us both a nice cup of tea," he ordered, and that is what I did, rocking you in my arms and giving you the tip of my little finger to suck on until you stopped crying and your eyes closed with weariness. Arthur came back with tea and talked in that same calm voice, lulling me into accepting that everything would be all right and that we could, in fact, keep you as our own. He produced some baby clothes, diapers, and pins, as well as two glass bottles with rubber nipples and a packet of baby milk powder.

He would not tell me where you had come from, but he promised that it was all above board. May God forgive me, but in that moment, because I so wanted to believe him, I stopped protesting and did not ask any more. If we needed to explain, he told me, we would say that you were the son of a relative who had died—as so many did in those terrible years of war—and who had entrusted us with your care. I agreed to the deceit. Even after holding you in my arms for that short time, the thought of losing you was too great an agony to contemplate.

We talked about what we would name you, and the next day—November 12, 1918—Arthur returned with a birth certificate for Richard James—after his father and mine. We have celebrated that date, your birthday, with such joy ever since.

Please do not judge us too harshly, my son. As you hold your new baby daughter, I can see in your eyes that you have already discovered that the love for a child is one of the most powerful emotions any human will experience. Your father did what he could to make sure that I was happy and so that our marriage would survive. I was too weak-willed to reject the blessing I had dreamed of, so I went along with the lie. It seemed a small price to pay for the extraordinary joy of loving you.

When you were about fourteen, Arthur was promoted again, to become a detective with the Eastchester force, so we had to move house. I was unpacking clothes into our wardrobe when I came across a small black suitcase. I knew what it was; he had already shown me: it contained his Masonic regalia and must always be kept locked, he said, and never opened by anyone outside the Order.

As I picked it up, the latch flipped open of its own accord—for some reason it had not been properly closed—and this felt like an invitation to look inside. In my heart, I understood it was a wrong thing to do, but the secrecy surrounding his Masonic activities made me so very curious. I lifted out the gold badge and a medal on ribbons and what looked like a blue silk collar and a square bag, heavily embroidered with symbols and letters in gold and red. Underneath were some papers which I tried to read, but they were full of long religious-sounding words that meant little to me, written in an archaic kind of script that was so difficult to decipher that I quickly gave up.

I was about to put everything back when I noticed the small buff envelope. It had already been opened, slit carefully with a paper knife as Arthur always does, and looked like an invoice. Curious to check how much he might be paying to the Masons, I pulled out the single sheet of thick, cream bond and unfolded it.

My dear Brother, it said. *Regarding our discussion the other evening, please come to Helena Hall this evening at 9 p.m. for receipt of said item. At the security gate, ask for me and the guards will direct you to my office.*

Roger.

Well, I thought nothing of it—this was probably just a simple message between friends. I put away the papers and replaced everything as I had found them, shut the case as best I could, and put it back into the cupboard.

As you know, for it was your childhood home, we lived in a small cul-de-sac, and the children could play on the green in front of our houses without danger of traffic. We gave you a bicycle, and you stayed out there every evening with the other children until it grew dark.

One evening, I went to call you in and met a woman also waiting for her children, who smiled in a friendly way, and we got chatting. Her name was Mary and she told me that she was a nurse. She was very excited because that very day she had been accepted for a new job. "At Helena Hall, you know, the mental institution? It's just up the road." Helena Hall. The mystery was solved—Arthur's Masonic colleague worked at a hospital.

Mary and I became great friends, and she liked to drop in after her shifts and gossip about what was happening at work. One day, in a lowered voice, she told me about the latest scandal. "Apparently Lord B was having an affair and Lady B found out about it and threatened to go to the press. So he took her to the doctor and bribed him to certify her."

I was shocked. "She's locked up in a mental hospital even though she's completely sane?"

Mary nodded. "In a private villa, mind. That's how he buys off his conscience. And she's not the only one."

"The only woman locked up because her husband is having an affair?"

"Because someone wants them out of the way. There's a couple of younger women who claim to have been locked up because they inconveniently got pregnant out of wedlock and their families don't want anyone to know."

"What do you mean, 'claim'?"

"That's what they say, but of course there's no proof, because they are supposed to be insane, after all, hearing voices and inventing fantasies. And in any case, there are no babies to show for it."

My heart turned over. "But what if they are telling the truth? Where did the babies go?" I managed to whisper through the lump blocking my throat.

"Just slipped away, I expect. Given up for adoption or something," she said, looking at her watch. "Goodness, is that the time? Peter will be home for his supper any moment, and I haven't even peeled the potatoes. Love to Arthur, see you later."

Her words rang in my head: *Just slipped away. Given up for adoption.* What if—my mouth went dry at the prospect—you were one of those babies from Helena Hall? Was that what the letter to Arthur was all about? Had the birth mother of my child been imprisoned in a secure ward through no fault of her own except that she was unfortunate enough to get pregnant? I became transfixed by the thought that you might have been the child of some poor girl who was still mourning the loss of her son, fourteen years on. I was horrified and desperate to have my suspicions proved unfounded but couldn't tackle Arthur, because he would either deny it or just refuse to talk to me.

One day, Mary told me the hospital had opened a new sewing room to give patients a craft. "They need volunteers to help," she said. "You'd be perfect."

The idea was alarming, but at least I would get to see inside the place and perhaps be able to discover for myself whether these rumors about women being locked up for "inconvenient" pregnancies had any basis in fact. In any case, Mary's stories about the place had intrigued me, and now that you were at school, I really needed some activity to occupy the long days and my active mind.

"I'll have to ask Arthur," I said tentatively.

"Oh, don't!" she blurted out, and then tried to recover herself. "I mean, don't ask him right away. Give it a day or so and if you really enjoy it, then ask him. Say it's about helping the community or something..." I got her drift. Your father's first reaction would be to say no, and then where would I be?

Since I could get there and back while you were at school and he was at work, no one would ever know. I decided to give it a try.

On my first day, I was welcomed at the entrance by a woman in a smart dark blue uniform who introduced herself as matron of the female side and said she needed to go through a few questions before we went to the sewing room. When she asked my name, I panicked. What if Arthur should find out from his Masonic colleague that his wife had volunteered without asking him? He'd blow a gasket. So I said the first name that came into my head—that of our queen's second child, Margaret. On the wall above her head was a notice board with a list of all the ward names and their telephone extension numbers.

"Langham," I blurted, choosing a name at random. "Margaret Langham." Then I gabbled out a false address, and to my relief, there were no more questions.

The needlework room was just as you would imagine any normal production room: a long rectangle, well lit with windows all along one wall and electric lightbulbs hanging over each of the tables—about eleven of them in rows from the front to the back of the room. Along the front were ten treadle sewing machines and at the back was the cutting table.

In no time at all, I was sitting with a group of women doing handsewing—repair work, mostly, and hemming. My job was to help if needed, look after the scissors, and count the needles and pins at the start and end of each session. Their skill and the variety of work was impressive: while the handsewers were darning and repairing, the machinists efficiently ran up new staff uniforms and patient clothing.

Although the women were generally calm and seemed fairly sane to me, they all appeared old before their time, pallid and unhealthy, their hair straggly and unkempt, their clothes ill-fitting. And when I tried to engage them in conversation, they replied in monosyllables, looked away, or worse, looked back at me with heavy-lidded, uncomprehending eyes. The supervisor explained that most of them were on drug therapy to control their moods and delusions. But once in a while, I would get a shy smile, which was reward enough. The three hours whizzed by, and I found myself looking forward to the next week, when I would return.

One of the patients interested me more than the others, perhaps because she was closer to me in age. She was tiny, quite childlike in stature, and must have been pretty once upon a time, with her dark curls and almost black eyes. Though she never uttered a word, her eyes were always bright and interested. If she wanted to say something, she would write on scraps of paper in a sprawling, uneducated hand. Her name, the others said, was Queenie.

"Dumb," the supervisor said bluntly. "Used to be able to talk. In fact we couldn't shut her up. But after the narcosis therapy, she stopped. Sometimes they do that, just to annoy us."

One day, as we were hemming dresses for patients, she seemed to be mouthing a word. It sounded like "quilt," and she smiled when I repeated it. Perhaps she wants to do some patchwork, I thought, so I went to town to buy a bag of scraps from the drapers. She didn't show them much interest, and the following week, she wrote: "*quilt what got lost.*"

I made dozens of inquiries and even braved going to see the matron, all to no avail. Eventually, I wrote to the superintendent. To cut a very long story short, we eventually found her scrap of quilting in an old bag which had been hidden in a basement since she had arrived there.

She set to work with a will to complete the enterprise she'd started so long ago. As she sewed, little by little, she found more words, and as her speech returned, she became much more friendly, laughing and gossiping with me and the others as she worked. Watching her confidence grow, I could hardly imagine why she should ever have found herself in such a place.

One day, she told me that she was going to sew this panel of quilt for her baby, proudly showing me the design which included a row of figures: a duck, an apple, a violin, ivy leaves, and a dragon, which spelled the word D.A.V.I.D.

"His name," she said. I asked where David was now, imagining that he was being cared for by her family outside.

"He died," she said. "The night he was born."

I said how sorry I was and thought not much more about it until a few months later when the quilt was starting to take shape, and she had finished the appliqué figures that spelled out the name of her baby and had started embroidering figures along the sides of the panel.

"What do these mean?" I asked, all unawares.

"My baby's birthday," she said, and my blood ran cold. For now I could see clearly that the figures I had taken to be an abstract design were in fact four numbers: 11.11. On the other side was another number one and a nine, and she had begun to embroider a number one beside that—she was writing the date on which you had been born: 11.11.1918.

My head began to spin with the thought that her baby might, just conceivably, be the same child as my own lovely boy. But I told myself not to be silly, to think rationally. Her baby had died. In any case, the medical staff all agreed that she was a fantasist, so almost everything she said should be treated with suspicion. I'd developed a loyalty to the place and particularly to this woman. I had built up a friendship with her. She seemed to trust me, and I enjoyed her company.

So, the following week, I pressed her again to talk about her child, feeling sure that she would tell me again that he had died, so that I need no longer feel the ache of guilt each time I talked to her.

"That's such a lovely way of remembering him," I said, as she appliquéd a new row of figures, starting with a mouse, which spelled out her real name: Maria.

She stopped sewing and looked me straight in the eye.

"I don't tell many this, but I likes you, Margaret." She lowered her voice to a whisper. "They said he died, but I'm sure I heard him cry."

That was the moment, my dearest boy, when my agony began. The moment I became convinced you were that baby and terrified that you might be taken from me. Imagine the horror: a woman wrongfully incarcerated by some heartless man, had her baby stolen, and still grieving fourteen years later.

I am ashamed to admit that I ran away that day, never to return. I could not face her again. I concocted a weak excuse for the hospital, although my friendship with Mary cooled from then onward—I think she knew that I was lying, though she never knew why.

My initial terror of being found out, of losing you, slowly eased, and in its place came the guilt, its insidious acid etching my mind with its poisons. I rarely slept, but when I did, I would wake a few hours later feeling strangely at ease with life until, a few seconds later, my conscience would ambush me all over again with that ferocious clawing at my heart, like an enraged animal. I imagined it might be the same for that poor woman as she woke each morning, remembering all over again her loss.

Whenever I touched you, stroked your hair, or held your hand, I felt like weeping. The love for you that had once been complete and unconditional was now unlawful, even immoral, because you had been stolen from another woman. You were no longer mine to keep.

Over and over and over in my mind, I replayed the conversation. Had I imagined everything? Had I jumped to ridiculous conclusions? Each time, my conviction grew that you were indeed her son. But you had none of her looks: she was small, olive-skinned, and dark-haired; your hair was blond and your skin was creamy, becoming golden each year in summertime. She was tiny; you were average-sized for your age and still growing. So where did you get these looks?

It pains me to admit that we will probably never know, my dearest boy, who your father is, or was. How could I ever find out without raising suspicions or revealing your identity? I could tell no one and thus could seek no help. I was jittery in my skin, withdrawn and prone to crying at the slightest thing, unable to concentrate even on the simplest everyday tasks such as following a recipe or a knitting pattern. Though usually careful with my skin care and makeup, I began to neglect myself.

Looking back, I can now see with dreadful, painful clarity how remote I became toward the people I loved most: you and your father. And this made me feel even more guilty. Arthur, my poor kindly husband, could never understand why his wife, formerly so loving and attentive, had withdrawn from him, almost overnight.

You were growing up, of course, heading away from us toward your adult life, busy with your friends and your studies—you were always a naturally bright boy. Each time you returned with a good school report, I would recall Queenie's sharp, intelligent mind, despite the fact that she appeared to have had little or no schooling.

Over the weeks and months, I began to lose touch with reality. One day, as Arthur tells it, he returned from work to find the doctor by my bedside. You had come home from school to find me in bed, weeping uncontrollably, and called the doctor's office. My heart was beating a mile a minute, I was trembling all over, and my limbs were so heavy I could barely move, even to go to the bathroom. The doctor called it an "episode of nervous exhaustion," but I now know that it was a breakdown.

The nightmare continued: they sedated me and admitted me to Helena Hall. What terrible irony: my guilt had rendered me insane. The perfect punishment for my sins.

I was not put into the same ward as Maria, thank goodness, although for a few terrifying days, I became convinced that she was by my bedside, demanding to know why I had stolen her child. They drugged me heavily for several weeks and then slowly began to reduce the dose, but the world around me remained muffled, as if a blanket of cotton wool had been thrown over it.

After a while, they discharged me, with pills to take every day. These made me feel disjointed, out of touch with reality; colors appeared faded, sounds were monotonous, food tasteless and unappetizing. But they also dulled the pain of guilt. It seemed a fair deal: I had stolen a life, and now my life had been stolen from me. Like a pact with the devil.

All that changed with the advent of the Second World War, dearest boy. When you joined the navy, every waking moment was a living hell of anxiety. When the war ended, the relief of having you home safely seemed so much more important than my previous concerns, and life returned to normal. You found your niche in the academic world and married your beautiful Eleanor.

With your new job, you have now moved closer to us, which is a great solace in our fading years, and your lovely daughter Caroline has arrived, a granddaughter for me and surely the most wonderful gift I could ever have hoped for.

We have to make the most of what life offers us, for better or worse. You could not have been a better son, and we have both loved you with all our hearts. Please do not utter a word to your father that I have told you all of this. And above all, please forgive me.

Your loving mother, Jean.

19.

B Y PAGE THREE, MY EYES WERE ALREADY SWIMMING, and I had no choice but to stop reading and fetch a roll of paper towels to prevent the tears cascading onto the pages and smudging my grandmother's careful handwriting.

Finally, after reading those final, tender words, I slumped back into the sofa with my eyes closed, exhausted by the emotional roller coaster I'd been through. It was the way Granny had described the sorrow of her childlessness—"invading my thoughts night and day"—that first started me weeping. To my eyes, she'd always been such a strong, positive person, and to read of her suffering in silence, out of simple loyalty to her husband, was almost too hard to bear. Then, as she told of her meeting with Maria, I began to anticipate, instinctively, what she was going to say but could scarcely bear to read on. The implications were just too much to take in.

Everything I'd discovered over the past few weeks now added up: Granny Jean was the "Margaret" that Maria had talked about on the tapes. She had run away because the coincidence was just too great: my father's birthday had always been celebrated on November 12, but he had actually arrived in her arms the day before, November 11, 1918, Armistice Day, the day that Maria gave birth to her baby boy.

What must it have been like for my grandmother, knowing only too well the sorrow of childlessness, finding herself face to face with the woman whose child she had quite unwittingly, and at first unwillingly, taken as her own? And then enduring the pain of guilt and shame, living with it every minute of every day for most of her life, a terrible burden she had been unable to share with another soul? What a bitter irony that she too had ended up in the same hospital, having had a nervous breakdown.

I could still hear Maria's voice describing the day she arrived at Helena Hall and the child she nearly died giving birth to with only the aid of inexperienced and probably uncaring nurses. I began to ache all over again for her too, for the baby snatched from her, for the lie she was told. And all the while, she knew, in her heart of hearts, that she had heard his cry and that he might, just possibly, still be alive. I could understand why this had sent her crazy.

The labyrinth of sorrow and guilt that had bound these two strangers' lives together was almost impossible to comprehend.

In the deluge of emotions the notebook had triggered, the most extraordinary consequence of this tangled web had, at first, passed me by. Now, it slammed me in the stomach with a sickening whack: the realization that if (a) my own father was very probably, no, almost certainly, Maria's baby, and (b) the crest on the letter really did prove Maria's claim that she'd had an affair with the prince, and (c) her child really had been his, then (d) my father was the bastard son of the Prince of Wales!

For God's sake, that was just mad, stupid, plain ridiculous. Me, a lifelong republican who doesn't care a jot for the royal family, who didn't even watch Diana's wedding on television or turn out to see the queen when she came to Eastchester to open a new school?

The idea of a royal grandfather—especially a man who had been a disgraceful philanderer in his youth and a Nazi sympathizer in middle age—was distasteful enough, but further alarming visions swam into my head: of the story leaking out, of being hounded by the press and snapped by photographers as I went to the supermarket, followed of course by palace denials, setting me up to look like an attention-seeking idiot.

No. I would never let it happen. In that moment, I vowed that this was the one proven part of Maria's story that I'd tell no one. Not Mum, not Ben, not any friend, boyfriend, or even any future husband and family I might have.

Only Ellie Bevan knew about the crest on the template. I would call her tomorrow and request her professional confidentiality. Granny's letter and notebook made no mention of the Prince of Wales, and though Patsy Morton had of course heard the tapes, she had no reason to believe Maria's story. Mum probably hadn't known in the first place, and it seemed unlikely that she would tell anyone, not now. I might whisper it to Jo one day, out of friendship and loyalty, but she would entirely understand why no one else should ever know.

I determined that the secret would remain hidden in the quilt, just as it had already been for nearly a century.

I poured another glass of wine and tried to rationalize my emotions. From the moment I had pulled the quilt out of its suitcase, just a few weeks ago, and read that verse sewn into its lining, I'd known that there was something special about it. Now I understood.

I took out the photograph. There was Granny, still sitting on her sofa, with Maria behind her, her shoulder turned as if she was just leaving, or perhaps arriving. But there was something familiar about it that I hadn't noticed before. The pattern of Maria's dress—was it one of the cottons she'd used in the patchwork? I fetched the quilt from the trunk of the car and spread it carefully across Mum's dining table, scanning the patches, comparing them to the dress in the photograph.

None matched. So where could I have seen this fabric before? Then I had a brainwave, went to the bookshelf, pulled out the album, and turned to the back page where I'd found the photograph. There was the other snap of me, sitting on Granny's knee. Her face is out of the picture, but she is holding a book in which I appear to be totally absorbed.

Except that Granny is wearing Maria's dress.

It took a second to click: the knee on which I was sitting was not Granny's—it was Maria's. She was holding me on her knee and reading to me. I peeled back the transparent film and lifted the photo from the page. Then I turned it over: on it was penciled, "*Maria meets Caroline, February 1972.*"

As the memory flooded back, with almost painful clarity, the breath seemed to leave my body. That time I had stayed at Granny's house, the night she told me about the quilt, she had mentioned an "important person" coming to tea the following day. She must have been referring to Maria, my *blood* grandmother, the woman for whom her greatest luxury was a bottle of *eau de cologne*. I could almost smell the lavender-scented perfume all over again.

It was probably our very first meeting.

Tears pricked the back of my eyes once more as I imagined how Maria must have felt that day. She hadn't found the boy she believed to be her son, but at least she discovered that he'd lived a happy life, had been much loved and cherished, become a successful academic, married, and had a daughter. Tragically she never got to meet him but at least now, through the generosity of the woman who once befriended her, she was reunited with her granddaughter.

From the moment I'd heard her voice on the tapes, I had felt an unexplained affinity for her. Was it simply the timbre of her voice that I recognized, or her wicked chuckle, perhaps passed down through my genes? Certainly I admired her fierce determination to make the most of her life, to fight on undaunted, so like my grandmother, like my mother—and, I hoped, like me.

After almost a whole lifetime, Maria had completed her quilt, decorating its outermost border with "grandmother's fan" designs that, I now realized, were probably intended for me, her grandchild. And then, through Granny, she had bequeathed it to me, with her life's history and memories of the people she had loved sewn into its patchwork.

That my beloved Granny Jean was not my blood grandmother made not one iota of difference to me—she would always be the most important in my family memories and my sense of identity. Rather than losing a grandmother, it felt as though I had simply gained another one.

And after all those years of hardship, there was a happy ending, of sorts. Maria had found the comfort of her friendship with Nora and, in her last few years, contact with her granddaughter. She had come home at last.

"Coming home." The words resonated in my head. Being here, in this cottage, always felt like coming home for me. So why was I resisting it?

It made perfect financial sense: selling the flat would enable me to pay off Russell and release start-up capital to support my new venture, such as equipping the garage as an upholstery workshop. It would pay for Mum to stay at Holmfield if she wanted to, or for caregivers to look after her at home instead, should she prefer.

As I contemplated these possibilities, I could feel a heady sense of certainty returning, and my mind began to buzz with optimism once more. In the past few weeks, my life had changed so much that I barely recognized my former self: that aspirational, high-earning, eighteen-hour-a-day wage slave. Those values now appeared trivial and irrelevant, and even my visual sensibilities seemed to have been through a radical rethink. The clean, minimalist colors of my flat that I'd once loved so much had started to feel cold and characterless of late, especially in contrast to the brilliance of the fabrics for the new upholstery designs I'd been working on.

I pictured the skeletons of the chair and stool in my flat and the mess of webbing and wadding I'd left behind. The solution was now obvious. No matter the cost, I would employ a professional upholsterer to complete the work on the chair and footstool. If Justin's clients were, as I hoped, to fall instantly in love with them, the workmanship must be of the highest possible standard. My reputation as an up-and-coming designer depended on it.

Of course, much needed to be done to turn this neglected cottage, with its chaotic, clashing colors and designs, sagging shelves, and drafty windows, into somewhere that would really feel like my own home. There were obvious priorities, new central heating for a start, and over time, I would redecorate the place inside and out.

But instead of being daunting, the idea excited me: as well as the garage/workshop, I could even use the rooms as a showcase for my interior designs. There would be no cream carpets or soft leather sofas. It would be a warm, inviting family home. The phrase felt so right.

And the quilt, when it was restored, would take pride of place—always there to remind me of my two remarkable grandmothers.

Just then, my phone beeped. The text read: See you in ten. Ben x.

READING GROUP GUIDE

1. *The Forgotten Seamstress* was inspired by a single piece of beautiful historic fabric. Is there anything in your life that could inspire you to write a story or poem or paint a picture?

2. The two main characters in *The Forgotten Seamstress* were born more than sixty years apart. What does the novel tell you about how the class system in Britain changed in that time? Can you identify any parallels in the social history of the United States?

3. Maria was locked away because she threatened the rules of a rigid society. Have we become more tolerant and humane today, or are there still certain social improprieties that attract similar punishment? How do you think our views will have changed a hundred years from now?

4. What does Maria's story tell us about progress in the treatment of mental illness over the past century? Is the present-day use of "care in the community" really best for some patients?

5. Maria is a very "unreliable narrator." To what extent did you believe her story, or were you, like Caroline and Professor Morton, doubtful of her fantastical claims?

6. At the start of the novel, Caroline has been laid off and is newly single and desperate for a new direction. How does the quilt help her to find her new path in life?

7. How does the novel hint at the contrasts between urban and suburban/rural life in present-day Britain? How do these differ between the UK and the United States?

8. Caroline feels agonizingly guilty about putting her mother into a residential home and compares her actions with how the Kowalski family cares for "old Sam" at home. If you found yourself in Caroline's circumstances, what would you do?

9. Should Caroline have told her ex-boyfriend about her pregnancy and her decision to have an abortion? What were his rights in this issue versus her rights? By not telling him, was she just being selfish or guilty of a more serious moral deception?

10. Discuss how you might respond if your beloved husband returned, like Arthur, from war and you discovered that he was unable to participate in a full sex life.

11. Caroline's grandmother is so desperate for motherhood that she accepts a baby even though she knows that there may be something untoward about the baby's arrival. What does the novel tell us about the psychological corrosiveness of guilt?

12. Caroline loved her Granny Jean and feels a very special bond with her. What are the differences between a mother-daughter relationship and a grandmother-granddaughter relationship?

13. Adopted children meeting blood relatives for the first time often report that they immediately recognize them as "family." What does the novel tell us about blood-bond affinities?

14. Had Caroline, as an adult, been able to meet Maria, what do you think she might have said to her?

15. The novel touches on the issue of homelessness. Apart from providing single-night hostels (called "night shelters" in the UK), what else needs to be done to reduce the problem of homelessness? Should society intervene? Or should homeless people be responsible for sorting out their own problems?

16. Two forms of first-person narrative are used in the novel. Discuss the differences and what effect they have on the reader.

17. Why do you think the author decided to use the device of telling Maria's story through recorded cassette tapes?

18. If you met Maria as a young woman, what would you tell her about what life would eventually teach her?

19. What would your reaction be if you discovered that you had "royal blood"? Who would you tell? What do you think would happen if the news reached the royal family?

20. Will Caroline and Ben eventually get together?

A CONVERSATION
WITH THE AUTHOR

What was your inspiration for writing *The Forgotten Seamstress*?

I come from a silk-weaving family and have always been fascinated by fabrics. One day I was visiting the famous Warner Textile Archive, in Braintree, Essex, when I saw a case of "May Silks"—beautiful cream and white damasks and brocades, some with interwoven gold and silver threads, handwoven for the trousseau of Princess May (1867–1953), also known as Mary of Teck, for her wedding to the heir to the British throne, the Duke of Clarence.

Sadly, the duke died just six weeks before the wedding, and with typical royal pragmatism, it was decided that she should instead marry his younger brother George, who later became King George V. Another design from the May silks was chosen for her wedding dress.

More than a century later, these silks still glimmered and shimmered in their case, and I became fascinated by the way that the designs, featuring roses, thistles, and shamrocks with May blossoms and lover's knots, had been interpreted into the weave of the fabrics. They are truly unique and have never been woven before or since.

Are you a quilter yourself?

I'm afraid not: I once made a very small patchwork cushion cover out of simple hexagons, but beyond that I have absolutely no experience quilting. However I have always been captivated by the way that quilters manage to juxtapose and manipulate fabrics into such extraordinary and unexpected effects.

A few years ago, I went to the Victoria and Albert Museum's Quilt Show, of seventy quilts dating from 1700 to the present day, and this fascination was revived. Most of all, I was reminded of the many different ways in which quilts tell stories and decided that I would write a novel one day in which a quilt would become a "main character."

As I set out to write *The Forgotten Seamstress*, I was incredibly fortunate to be introduced to the internationally acknowledged patchwork quilter, teacher, and author Lynne Edwards, who in 2008 was given a prestigious national award for her services to arts and crafts. With typical enthusiasm, Lynne completely embraced the project. We met several times and, over bottles of wine and lots of laughter, "devised" the quilt that Maria made, taking into account the influences and sources of inspiration that she would have had at different times of her life and the sort of fabrics she might have had at her disposal.

By the time we had finished, I had, in my mind's eye, a very clear view of what the quilt would look like. We very much hope that someone, someday, will be inspired by the pattern Lynne has very generously devised (available for free at www.liztrenow.com) and create "Maria's quilt." If you do, please let us know!

Setting the story in a mental asylum creates quite a contrast to the royal theme. What inspired you to do that?

I love novels with a great sense of place, and having set my first book in the house where I grew up, I was determined to find somewhere just as evocative and atmospheric for this one.

When the Severalls Mental Asylum, on the edge of my hometown of Colchester, first opened its doors to patients in 1913, it was considered to be a state-of-the-art institution that would become a center of expertise in the very latest treatments for mental illness. It was built on a vast scale like the estate of a country mansion, with gardens and sports facilities and a range of other houses for staff, with the ideal that patients could be safely contained and soothed in these beautiful surroundings.

Of course, with hindsight, we now understand that the treatments used were sometimes inhumane, even brutal, and patients often became institutionalized by the strict routines. Occasionally its use was also sometimes abused, and tales of people being locked up for little more than social breaches (such as unmarried pregnancy) once used to abound.

In the seventies, when patients began to be discharged into "care in the community" (now itself discredited), some of the buildings and wards were used by other hospital departments, for example clinical treatments and minor surgery. This is how, as a teenager, I became an inpatient at the hospital, having a benign cyst removed from my arm. It was only two days, but that experience of the place has never left me: the scale of it, both impressive and oppressive, the locked doors and bars, doctors riding bicycles down the miles-long corridors, and the people—mental patients—sometimes behaving or reacting quite oddly as they walked or worked in the gardens.

A collection of old photographs is available on the website www.severallshospital.co.uk, and although most of the buildings are now closed (pending redevelopment), it is still possible to walk in the grounds among the pine trees. The atmosphere of the place remains as strong as ever.

Where did you get the idea of using old recorded cassette tapes of Maria to tell her story?

Because the two characters could not have met as adults, there had to be a way for Caroline to learn about Maria's life story. While researching the history of Severalls Hospital, I came across a wonderful book by the sociologist and author Diana Gittins called *Madness in Its Place* (Routledge 1998), in which she quoted from her recordings with staff and patients. These firsthand accounts really brought the place and the people to life, and in one of those light-bulb moments, I realized that this was exactly what I needed to do with Maria.

So I created a character—Professor Patsy Morton—who had undertaken a research project not unlike that of Diana Gittins's, although a couple of decades earlier. This was the perfect way of allowing Caroline—and the reader—to hear Maria's story firsthand. Although we never actually meet her in the book, the tapes help us to feel that we know her.

Your main character, Maria, is a very "unreliable narrator." Did you find her difficult to write?

Maria was not difficult to write at all—she just flowed onto the page! The tricky bit was managing the reactions of the other characters, especially Caroline, to the fantastical things that they learned about her. Because I knew the outcome of Maria's story, I had to imagine what it would be like to know nothing about her except for the small clues that we gathered along the way, so that I could establish how much (or how little) Caroline should believe (or not believe) about Maria's story.

People always say that the second book, or music album, can be trickier than the first. Did you experience this with *The Forgotten Seamstress?* And how?

My first novel, *The Last Telegram*, was based on real-life characters, events, and places from my family history and childhood, and by the time I'd finished writing it, I feared that a lifetime of memories and experience had been "used up." What would I turn to next? My husband wisely counseled me to write "something completely different" and not to try to re-create the atmosphere of the first one, which is what I set out to do.

As I wrote, *The Last Telegram* was published and received almost unqualified five-star reviews. Each time someone told me how much they loved it, I would start to panic again, wondering whether *The Forgotten Seamstress* would ever match up.

About halfway through, I watched a television documentary in which the crime writer Ian Rankin talked about the process of writing *Standing in Another Man's Grave* (now out in paperback). He talked about how, with each novel, he experiences what he describes as "the fear," a point at which he thinks he's writing complete rubbish that will never get published, and even if it did, that reviewers would criticize and readers hate. He talked about having to work your way through it and hold faith that it will come right in time.

It was so reassuring to hear that even Britain's number one bestselling crime novelist should suffer such crises of confidence that I came back to my manuscript with renewed determination. After a major restructuring and quite a lot of rewriting, I found my rhythm again, and now believe it is just as good as the first (although very different).

I hope you think so too.

READ ON FOR AN EXCERPT OF
THE LAST TELEGRAM
BY LIZ TRENOW

AVAILABLE NOW FROM
SOURCEBOOKS LANDMARK

The History of Silk owes much to the fairer sex. The Chinese Empress Hsi Ling is credited with its first discovery, in 2640 BC. It is said that a cocoon fell from the mulberry tree, under which she was sitting, into her cup of tea. As she sought to remove the cocoon its sticky threads started to unravel and cling to her fingers. Upon examining the thread more closely she immediately saw its potential and dedicated her life thereafter to the cultivation of the silkworm and production of silk for weaving and embroidery.

—*The History of Silk* by Harold Verner

P ERHAPS BECAUSE DEATH LEAVES SO LITTLE TO SAY, FUNERAL guests seem to take refuge in platitudes. "He had a good innings…Splendid send-off…Very moving service…Such beautiful flowers…You are so wonderfully brave, Lily."

It's not bravery: my squared shoulders, head held high, that careful expression of modesty and gratitude. Not bravery, just determination to survive today and, as soon as possible, get on with what remains of my life. The body in the expensive coffin, lined with Verners' silk and decorated with lilies and now deep in the ground, is not the man I've loved and shared my life with for the past fifty-five years.

It is not the man who helped to put me back together after

the shattering events of the war, who held my hand and steadied my heart with his wise counsel. The man who took me as his own and became a loving father and grandfather. The joy of our lives together helped us both to bury the terrors of the past. No, that person disappeared months ago, when the illness took its final hold. His death was a blessed release and I have already done my grieving. Or at least, that's what I keep telling myself.

After the service the house fills with people wanting to "pay their final respects." But I long for them to go, and eventually they drift away, leaving behind the detritus of a remembered life along with the half-drunk glasses, the discarded morsels of food.

Around me, my son and his family are washing up, vacuuming, emptying the bins. In the harsh kitchen light I notice a shimmer of gray in Simon's hair (the rest of it is dark, like his father's) and realize with a jolt that he must be well into middle age. His wife Louise, once so slight, is rather rounder than before. No wonder, after two babies. They deserve to live in this house, I think, to have more room for their growing family. But today is not the right time to talk about moving.

I go to sit in the drawing room as they have bidden me, and watch for the first time the slide show that they have created for the guests at the wake. I am mesmerized as the TV screen flicks through familiar photographs, charting his life from sepia babyhood through monochrome middle years and into a Technicolor old age, each image occupying the screen for just a few brief seconds before blurring into the next.

At first I turn away, finding it annoying, even insulting. What a travesty, I think, a long, loving life bottled into a slide show. But as the carousel goes back to the beginning and the photographs start to repeat themselves, my relief that he is gone and will suffer no more is replaced, for the first time since his death, by a dawning realization of my own loss.

It's no wonder I loved him so; such a good-looking man, active and energetic. A man of unlimited selflessness, of many smiles and little guile. Who loved every part of me, infinitely. What a lucky woman. I find myself smiling back, with tears in my eyes.

My granddaughter brings a pot of tea. At seventeen, Emily is the oldest of her generation of Verners, a clever, sensitive girl growing up faster than I can bear. I see in her so much of myself at that age: not exactly pretty in the conventional way—her nose is slightly too long—but striking, with smooth cheeks and a creamy complexion that flushes at the slightest hint of discomfiture. Her hair, the color of black coffee, grows thick and straight, and her dark inquisitive eyes shimmer with mischief or chill with disapproval. She has that determined Verner jawline that says "don't mess with me." She's tall and lanky, all arms and legs, rarely out of the patched jeans and charity-shop jumpers that seem to be all the rage with her generation these days. Unsophisticated but self-confident, exhaustingly energetic—and always fun. Had my own daughter lived, I sometimes think, she would have been like Emily.

At this afternoon's wake the streak of crimson she's emblazoned into the flick of her fringe was like an exotic bird darting among the dark suits and dresses. Soon she will fly, as they all do, these independent young women. But for now she indulges me with her company and conversation, and I cherish every moment.

She hands me a cup of weak tea with no milk, just how I like it, and then plonks herself down on the footstool next to me. We watch the slide show together for a few moments, and she says, "I miss Grandpa, you know. Such an amazing man. He was so full of ideas and enthusiasm—I loved the way he supported everything we did, even the crazy things." She's right, I think to myself.

"He always used to ask me about stuff," she goes on. "He was always interested in what I was doing with myself. Not many grown-ups do that. A great listener."

As usual my smart girl goes straight to the heart of it. It's something I'm probably guilty of, not listening enough. "You can talk to me, now that he's gone," I say, a bit too quickly. "Tell me what's new."

"You really want to know?"

"Yes, I really do," I say. Her legs, in heart-patterned black tights, seem to stretch for yards beyond her miniskirt, and my heart swells with love for her, the way she gives me her undivided attention for these moments of proper talking time.

"Have I told you I'm going to India?" she says.

"My goodness, how wonderful," I say. "How long for?"

"Only a month," she says airily.

I'm achingly envious of her youth, her energy, her freedom. I wanted to travel too at her age, but war got in the way. My thoughts start to wander until I remember my commitment to listening. "What are you going to do there?"

"We're going to an orphanage. In December, with a group from college. To dig the foundations for a cowshed," she says triumphantly. I'm puzzled, and distracted by the idea of elegant Emily wielding a shovel in the heat, her slender hands calloused and dirty, hair dulled by dust.

"Why does an orphanage need a cowshed?"

"So they can give the children fresh milk. It doesn't get delivered to the doorstep like yours does, Gran," she says reprovingly. "We're raising money to buy the cows."

"How much do you need?"

"About two thousand. Didn't I tell you? I'm doing a sponsored parachute jump." The thought of my precious Emily hanging from a parachute harness makes me feel giddy, as if capsized by some great gust of wind. "Don't worry, it's perfectly safe," she says. "It's with a professional jump company, all above board. I'll show you."

She returns with her handbag, an impractical affair covered in sequins, extracts a brochure, and gives it to me. I pretend to read it, but the photographs of cheerful children preparing for their jumps seem to mock me and make me even more fearful. She takes the leaflet back. "You should know all about parachutes, Gran. You used to make them, Dad said."

"Well," I start tentatively, "weaving parachute silk was our contribution to the war effort. It kept us going when lots of other mills closed." I can picture the weaving shed as if from above, each loom with its wide white spread, shuttles clacking back and forth, the rolls of woven silk growing almost imperceptibly thicker with each turn of the weighted cloth beam.

"But why did they use silk?"

"It's strong and light, packs into a small bag, and unwraps quickly because it's so slippery." My voice is steadying now and I can hear that old edge of pride. Silk seems still to be threaded through my veins. Even now I can smell its musty, nutty aroma, see the lustrous intensity of its colors—emerald, aquamarine, gold, crimson, purple—and recite the exotic names like a mantra: *brigandine, bombazine, brocatelle, douppion, organzine, pongee, schappe.*

She studies the leaflet again, peering through the long fringe that flops into her eyes. "It says here the parachutes we're going to use are of high-quality one-point-nine-ounce ripstop nylon. Why didn't they use nylon in those days? Wouldn't it have been cheaper?"

"They hadn't really invented nylon by then, not good enough for parachutes. You have to get it just right for parachutes," I say and then, with a shiver, those pitiless words slip into my head after all these years. *Get it wrong and you've got dead pilots.*

She rubs my arm gently with her fingertips to smooth down the little hairs, looking at me anxiously. "Are you cold, Gran?"

"No, my lovely, it's just the memories." I send up a silent prayer that she will never know the dreary fear of war, when all normal life is suspended, when the impossible becomes ordinary, when every decision seems to be a matter of life or death, when good-byes are often for good.

It tends to take the shine off you.

A little later Emily's brother appears and loiters in his adolescent way, then comes and sits by me and holds my hand in silence. I am touched to the core. Then her father comes in, looking weary. His filial duties complete, he hovers solicitously. "Is there any more we can do, Mum?" I shake my head and mumble my gratitude for the nth time today.

"We'll probably be off in a few minutes. Sure you'll be all right?" he says. "We can stay a little longer if you like."

Finally they are persuaded to go. Though I love their company, I long for peace, to stop being the brave widow, to release my rictus smile. I make a fresh pot of tea, and there on the kitchen table is the leaflet Emily has left, presumably to prompt my sponsorship. I hide it under the newspaper and pour the tea, but my trembling hands cause a minor storm in the teacup. I decant the tea into a mug and carry it with two hands to my favorite chair.

In the drawing room, I am relieved to find that the slide show has been turned off, the TV screen returned to its innocuous blackness. From the wide bay window looking westward across the water meadows is an expanse of greenery and sky that always helps me to think more clearly.

The Chestnuts is a fine, double-bayed Edwardian villa, built of mellow Suffolk bricks that look gray in the rain but in sunlight take on the color of golden honey. Not grand, just comfortable and well-proportioned, reflecting how my parents saw themselves, their place in the world. They built it on a piece of spare land next to the silk mill during a particularly prosperous period just after the Great War. "It's silk umbrellas, satin facings, and black mourning crepe we have to thank for this place," my father, always the merchant, would cheerfully and unselfconsciously inform visitors.

Stained-glass door panels throw kaleidoscope patterns of light into generous hallways, and the drawing room is sufficiently spacious to accommodate Mother's baby grand as well as three chintz sofas clustered companionably around a handsome marble fireplace.

To the mill side of the house, when I was a child, was a walled kitchen garden, lush with aromatic fruit bushes and deep green salads. On the other side, an ancient orchard provided an autumn abundance of apples and pears, so much treasured during the long years of rationing, and a grass tennis court in which worm casts ensured such an unpredictable bounce of the ball that our games could never be too competitive. The parade of horse chestnut trees along its lower edge still bloom each May with ostentatious candelabra of flowers.

At the back of the house is the conservatory, restored after the doodlebug disaster but now much in need of repair. From the terrace, brick steps lead to a lawn that rolls out toward the water meadows. Through these meadows, yellow with cowslips in spring and buttercups in summer, meanders the river, lined with gnarled willows that appeared to my childhood eyes like processions of crook-backed witches. It is Constable country.

"Will you look at this view?" my mother would exclaim, stopping on the landing with a basket of laundry, resting it on the generous windowsill and stretching her back. "People pay hundreds of guineas for paintings of this, but we see it from our windows every day. Never forget, little Lily, how lucky you are to live here."

No, Mother, I have never forgotten.

I close my eyes and take a deep breath.

The room smells of old whiskey and wood smoke and reverberates with long-ago conversations. Family secrets lurk in the skirting boards. This is where I grew up. I've never lived anywhere else, and after nearly eighty years it will be a wrench to leave. The place is full of memories: of my childhood, of him, of loving and losing.

As I walk ever more falteringly through the hallways, echoes of my life—mundane and strange, joyful and dreadful—are like shadows, always there, following my footsteps. Now that he is gone, I am determined to make a new start. No more guilt and heart-searching. No more "what-ifs." I need to make the most of the few more years that may be granted to me.

ABOUT THE AUTHOR

Photo by David Islip

LIZ TRENOW IS A FORMER journalist who spent fifteen years on regional and national newspapers and on BBC radio and television news before turning her hand to fiction. *The Forgotten Seamstress* is her second novel. She lives in East Anglia with her artist husband, and they have two grown-up daughters. Find out more at www.liztrenow.com and join her on Twitter @LizTrenow.